# THE
# DISCOVERY
# TRILOGY

## LUCY DANIELS

*Illustrated by*
*Trevor Parkin*

Hodder
Children's
Books

a division of Hodder Headline Limited

# THE
# DISCOVERY

This edition of *The Discovery*, *The Gift* and *The Promise*
first published in 2002.

ISBN 0 340 85240 2

10 9 8 7 6 5 4 3 2 1

*The Discovery*

**Special thanks to Ingrid Hoare**

Text copyright © 2000 Working Partners Limited
Created by Ben M. Baglio, London W6 0QT
Illustrations copyright © 2000 Sheila Ratcliffe
Jess the Border Collie is a trademark of Working Partners Limited

First published in Great Britain in 2000
by Hodder Children's Books

The right of Lucy Daniels to be identified as the author of this work
has been asserted by her in accordance with the Copyright, Designs
and Patents Act 1988.

A Catalogue record for this book is available from the British Library

Typeset by Avon Dataset Ltd, Bidford-on-Avon, Warks

Printed and bound in Great Britain by
The Guernsey Press Co. Ltd, Vale, Guernsey, Channel Islands

Hodder Children's Books
a division of Hodder Headline Limited
338 Euston Road
London NW1 3BH

# 1

Jenny Miles took a deep gulp of sea air. It filled her lungs and made her feel wide awake. From up here on the cliff path, she had a bird's-eye view of the curving, craggy cliffs that gave Cliffbay its name, and the choppy blue water below.

The path was windswept and wild, yet bathed in soft spring sunshine. Jenny gave a little sigh of contentment. Nothing to do but enjoy these last few days of the Easter holidays with her friends, Carrie and Fiona, and Jess – her beloved Border collie.

'Wait for me!'

Jenny stopped and looked back down the path. Carrie Turner, her best friend, was lagging behind. 'Come on, sleepyhead,' Jenny called. 'Catch up with us.'

'Shall I give you a little push?' Fiona McLay teased, turning round and smiling at Carrie.

'You're walking too fast,' Carrie puffed.

'Are you OK, Carrie?' asked Jenny, as Carrie caught her up and slipped an arm through her own. Carrie had been ill recently and this was the first day she'd been out with her friends.

'I'm fine.' Carrie smiled. But she was breathing hard. 'Where's Jess?'

Jenny looked around. She spotted the white tip of the collie's plumy tail waving from a clump of undergrowth and pointed.

'He's found some enticing smell, I bet,' she laughed. 'A mouse, or something.'

'Good old Jess!' Fiona grinned.

'Is it nice to have Mrs Grace back?' Carrie asked, falling into step with Jenny and Fiona.

Ellen Grace was the housekeeper at Windy Hill, the sheep farm where Jenny lived with her father, Fraser Miles. Mrs Grace had come to look after the Mileses almost two years ago, after the death of Jenny's mother, Sheena Miles. Now, she was part of the family.

'Hmm, it's great. I had a huge, cooked breakfast this morning,' Jenny replied dreamily, patting her tummy. 'What a treat.'

'Did she have a nice time in Canada?' Fiona asked.

'She had a lovely time with her sister,' Jenny said. 'But she missed us.'

'I bet she didn't!' Carrie teased.

Jenny giggled.

'Let's start back home,' Fiona suggested. 'I'm hungry.'

'Right,' Jenny agreed. 'Jess has had enough of a walk, now.' She shouted his name and Jess's sleek white nose popped up from the grass. He put his head to one side, then, as Jenny called again, he streaked towards her, his pink tongue lolling happily. Jess could run like the wind.

'Hello, boy,' Jenny said, smiling, as the collie came up at a rush. She reached out to stroke Jess's soft head. The Border collie gazed up at her fondly. 'Come on,' said Jenny. 'Time to go home.'

It was some time before Jenny realised that Jess was not at her side. 'Jess!' Jenny exclaimed, looking around. He wasn't following, either. 'Where have you got to?' she called.

The others stopped and looked back. Jenny called again, louder this time. Fiona and Carrie shouted too. But there was no sign of him.

'It's not like Jess not to come when he's called,' Jenny said with a frown.

'Where could he be?' Fiona looked worried.

Fiona loved Jess, probably as much as Jenny did. When Fiona had become ill following a terrifying fire at Windy Hill, Jenny had let her have Jess for a while, as a companion. The fire, which had almost destroyed the farmhouse, had been Fiona's fault and the shame and guilt of what she had done had kept her off school for weeks. Jess had helped Fiona to recover, and she had been friends with Jenny ever since.

'Jess!' she yelled.

Above the sound of the wind, a faint barking could be heard. 'It's coming from down on the beach!' Jenny said. She ran towards the cliff edge and looked over.

'Can you see him?' Carrie asked, grabbing onto Jenny's T-shirt and leaning over, dangerously close to the edge. Her red hair rose round her face on the wind. But before Jenny could reply, a bark came from further down the cliff path.

'Oh . . . look!' Fiona said, sounding relieved. '*There* he is! Here he comes! He couldn't have heard us calling him. Here, Jess!' She clapped her hands.

Jenny turned to look. A Border collie was trotting briskly towards them. But Jenny could tell immediately that it wasn't Jess.

'No,' she said, disappointed. 'That's not Jess. It's some other dog.' Even from a distance, she knew every inch of the collie she'd had since he was born. And this dog wasn't running the way Jess ran either.

'It's definitely a Border collie, though,' Carrie said, coming back to the path.

The dog came up. Its ears were up and its tail held straight and still. 'Hello . . .' Jenny spoke soothingly. 'Where did you come from?'

The dog's tail began to wag hesitantly. Jenny put out her hand, level with the collie's nose. She sniffed at it, then wagged her tail harder. Carrie and Fiona reached out to pet the dog too.

'She's mine,' came a voice. 'She won't hurt you.' A dark-haired boy of about their age was walking towards them. He had his hands in the pockets of his khaki shorts and the dog's lead slung round his shoulders.

'She's great. What's her name?' Carrie asked.

'Orla,' the boy answered. 'And mine's David. David Fergusson.'

'Are you on holiday?' Jenny asked him. She hadn't

seen this boy around before.

'No, we moved here just recently, to a house in Cliffbay.' David aimed a kick at a pebble and it sailed smoothly off the edge of the cliff and down to the stony shore below.

At that moment, the sound of Jess's faint barking reached them again. 'Did you hear that?' said Jenny. 'That's *my* Border collie. His name is Jess. He must have gone down the path onto the beach.'

'We've called and called,' Fiona explained. 'But he won't come back.'

'Jess usually does as he's told,' Carrie added.

'It might be that he can't find the way back up,' David suggested. 'There's only one way down. My dad and I discovered that last week.'

'It won't be that,' Jenny reasoned. 'Jess knows the beach and the cliffs really well. Something else is keeping him down there, I'm sure of it.'

Jenny went over near to the edge of the cliff and peered over again. 'Jess!' she shouted. 'Here, boy. Come on!' She yelled into the noise of the wind gusting around the rock face and wondered if Jess could hear her.

Orla stood beside her. Her ears pricked up in interest at all the shouting.

'I'll go with you down to the beach, if you like,' David said, behind her.

'Yes, it looks like we'll have to go and fetch him,' Jenny decided. She looked at Fiona, who had goosebumps all over her arms. Carrie was sitting cross-legged on the grassy verge to the path. Her chin was propped in the palm of her hand. She looked tired. Jenny felt a bit concerned, Carrie was usually so energetic and determined.

'Do you two want to go back home?' Jenny asked. 'I'll go down with . . . David,' she added, rather shyly.

Fiona looked at Carrie. 'Up to you,' she shrugged.

'No, of course we'll come.' Carrie stood up, smiling. 'Jess might need our help. Come on.'

They fell into single file, David leading the way back along the path. A fine mist had begun rolling in off the sea. Jenny's face felt moist.

'The tide's coming in,' David said over his shoulder.

Jenny felt a prickle of fear for Jess. It was so unlike him not to come when called. He had obeyed Jenny faithfully since he was a puppy. Something must be keeping him from returning to her.

Jess had been the runt of a litter produced by Nell, one of Fraser's sheepdogs. He had been born with a twisted leg and Jenny's dad had felt it kinder to put the puppy to sleep. But Jenny had pleaded with him not to. At eight weeks, an operation had put right Jess's damaged leg and since then he had led an active and happy life. Jenny adored him and had always felt protective about him.

'D'you live in Cliffbay?' David asked Jenny, interrupting her thoughts.

'No, Graston. My dad's a sheep farmer,' she told him. 'I expect you'll be going to our school – Greybridge Senior?'

'Yes,' David called back. 'What's it like?'

'It's OK,' Jenny laughed. 'We all go there. You'll survive!'

'But only if you're *lucky*,' Carrie said, then she cackled horribly, like a witch.

David laughed. 'I'm not sure if I will!' he said.

'Here's the path,' Jenny said. She stopped where a narrow opening sloped away steeply to the beach. Overgrown with gorse, its entrance was almost invisible.

'Is it safe to go down?' Fiona asked.

'We'll have to be careful,' Jenny said. 'It's probably a bit slippery.' Jenny hesitated for a moment. She looked at Carrie and then went over to her and spoke quietly. 'You're not completely better yet, are you? You don't have to come down with us, you know. You could wait up here.'

'I'm OK,' Carrie said brightly. She made a face at Jenny. 'Stop fussing, will you! I want to go with you. Honestly.'

'OK, if you're sure,' Jenny said. She turned back to David and Fiona, in time to see Orla begin the climb down to the beach. She was as sure-footed as a mountain goat, stepping sideways daintily, her sharp claws keeping a grip on the gravel path. David followed her.

'Jess!' called Jenny, as she went. 'Here Jess!' But Jess still didn't appear.

The winding path *was* slippery and Jenny found the best way to keep her balance was to walk with her hands outstretched, ready to grab onto the long grasses and wild flowering plants that grew among the rock.

David was ahead of her, helpfully calling out the places it was best to avoid stepping. 'Watch out – loose stone,' he warned.

Carrie had her hands round Fiona's waist. They inched forward together, slowly. 'I'd be better going down on my bottom,' Carrie announced cheerfully. 'Only I'm wearing these white shorts and Mum would murder me!'

'We can't see from up here, but there's a little sandy cove set back into the rock,' Jenny said, as they got nearer to the beach. 'He might be under the cliff, over towards the left.'

'Yes,' David agreed. 'I discovered that with my dad last week.'

'You know loads about Cliffbay already,' Fiona said, as she and Carrie caught up.

'My dad and I have been up here a lot since we came. Exploring,' David explained.

'Does your dad work in Cliffbay?' Jenny asked, hoping her feet were not going to slide from under her and send her crashing into David's back.

'Oh, er, sort of,' David said. 'He's always busy . . . Look, here's the beach. We're almost down.'

As soon as Jenny's feet touched the beach she sprinted forward, shouting for Jess.

Orla bounded alongside her, keen for a game. The sea was pounding into the shore and dragging itself back again noisily. Orla suddenly stopped scampering about excitedly and stood quite still. Her ears pricked and she lifted one paw, looking hard into the distance. Jenny followed her gaze and saw a dark speck over near the cliff. Orla's nose quivered. Then she barked sharply and set off at top speed.

'There!' David said with satisfaction. 'Orla's found him. I'll bet she has.'

'I can't see anything,' Fiona said.

'Neither can I,' Carrie agreed.

Jenny began to run on ahead, wishing she had worn her trainers instead of sandals. The wind whipped her hair across her face, making it difficult to see. She was beginning to think that Jess must have hurt himself. That would explain his absence. She ran faster.

Jess yapped excitedly when he saw Jenny coming. At his feet Jenny could see a dark shape, bulky in outline and about the size of a man's boot. Orla, streaking ahead of her, reached Jess first. Her tail was rigid as she stalked up to the strange dog and sniffed him all over. Then, she relaxed and her tail began to wag. Jess wagged his tail, too, but he didn't move. It looked to Jenny as though Jess was guarding something.

Jenny slowed to a walk. Her heart was thumping from her effort. 'Jess! What is it?' she shouted. Still Jess didn't move.

'He's not hurt, is he?' panted David, jogging up beside Jenny.

'No,' Jenny frowned in concern. 'It's just that he won't leave that spot. He seems to be guarding something. That must be the reason. He's never disobedient.'

They covered the last few metres together. Jess's

16

tail thumped harder as Jenny approached. 'Oh, Jess!' Jenny began. 'What have you got there?' A large bird was lying on the sand between Jess's front paws. Jenny's hand flew to her nose. The smell that came off it was powerful and turned her stomach. A big wave came thrashing up the beach and rolled the bird around. Jess put his paw onto its dead body and held it firmly.

'Look!' Jenny said urgently. 'Jess wants us to see what he's found. It's a dead puffin . . . and it's covered in something!' She kneeled in the sand and peered at the poor bird. 'Oh, no! It's oil!' she exclaimed. Jess lifted his paw and nudged it gently towards her.

'Yes, Jess,' she told him gently. 'I can see it. Good boy.'

'What is it?' Carrie asked, arriving with Fiona.

'A puffin, coated in black oil,' David told them. 'It's dead.' Jess looked down at the bird and barked. Orla barked in reply. David walked off towards the tide line.

'Oh, gosh,' Carrie put her hand to her mouth.

'What a pity,' Fiona said, sadly.

'It *is* oil!' David called to the girls. 'It's lapping along the edge of the beach.'

Carrie looked at Jenny, who looked at Fiona. 'There must have been an oil spill from a tanker somewhere up the coast. All the birds on Puffin Island might be in danger!' Carrie breathed.

'Jess was trying to warn us,' Jenny said, her eyes wide. 'That's why he wouldn't leave the bird. He wanted us to know what's happened.'

'Hadn't we better do something?' Fiona asked.

'Yes,' David said. 'We should go back to Cliffbay for help.'

'Let's go, then,' Jenny said. 'And quickly!'

## 2

'Come on, Jess,' Jenny said, stroking his head. Jess put his nose into the palm of Jenny's hand. His tail thumped rhythmically against her leg. 'Well done – you're a clever boy.'

'Come on.' David was agitated. 'Let's get moving.' He looked at Carrie, who had sat down on the beach. Wearily, she got up. 'My dad's got a motor-boat,' he went on. 'I'll ask him if he'll take me out to the island to check if there are any birds in trouble. We could all go, if you like.' He looked a bit shy.

'Out to Puffin Island?' Carrie asked.

David nodded.

'Yes,' Jenny smiled.

'My dad's got a boat too,' Carrie told David. 'But he's not at home today, so he can't help.'

'But we'd like to help, if your dad will take us,' Jenny said. She looked at Carrie, who nodded. 'What about you, Fiona?'

'Yes, I want to come too,' Fiona replied firmly. 'I think Jess is brilliant,' she added, rubbing the Border collie's ears.

'Come on, then,' David urged them again. 'We'd better hurry.'

The wind whipped at their clothing as they walked back across the beach. They went in the opposite direction to the cliff path, heading quickly for the fishing village of Cliffbay, at the heart of which lay a small harbour. Jess and Orla ran ahead.

Carrie seemed to be struggling to keep up with the others. She was out of breath again. 'I told my mum I was just going out for a short walk with you, Fiona and Jess,' she gasped to Jenny. 'If we do go out on David's father's boat, I'll have to ring her and let her know.'

'There's the public call box,' Fiona said, pointing,

as they reached the crest of the hill at the harbour wall. 'Shall we ring the coastguard and tell them what we've found first?'

'Yes, the sooner the better,' Jenny agreed. 'Who's got some coins?'

'Me,' Carrie said.

'You won't need any money,' Fiona told her, holding the door open. 'Those sort of important numbers don't cost anything.'

On the wall inside the phone box was a list of emergency services that could be contacted free when you dialled 999. Jenny checked quickly and, under Police and Ambulance, she found Coastguard.

She held the black receiver to her ear and waited impatiently to be put through.

Outside the phone booth, Jess was getting to know Orla. They were walking around each other, sizing one another up, doing a lot of sniffing and tail-wagging. David was sitting astride a low wall, re-tying his shoelaces.

The phone at the other end was picked up.

'Hello?' Jenny said into the receiver. 'Is that the coastguard? Oh . . . he's busy is he?' Jenny made an exasperated face at Fiona and Carrie, who were listening at the door of the phone box. 'A message? Um, yes, please, well, I just wanted to report that I'd seen oil on the beach at Cliffbay today, you see . . . Oh, you know about it! Oh, that sounds bad. Yes, OK, thank you. Bye.'

'What did they say?' Carrie demanded.

David got down and came over. They huddled round Jenny.

'A tanker ship further up the coast *has* spilled its oil. They don't yet know how much but it seems fairly bad. They've already started trying to clean it up.' Jenny reported.

'Oh, that's awful,' Carrie said sadly.

'Wow,' said David. 'Let's go and see if we can help. If that puffin we found had oil on it, then it must be spreading quickly down the coast.'

'It's not only the birds who'll suffer,' Fiona said. 'What about the fish, and the shellfish and things . . .' she trailed off.

'I'll try Mr Palmer, the vet, first,' Jenny said. 'He'll know what to do.' She found the surgery number in the phone book and dialled. The phone was picked up straight away.

'Palmer's Veterinary Surgery,' said a woman's voice. 'Good morning.'

'Hello?' Jenny said. 'Is Mr Palmer there, please? This is Jenny Miles speaking.'

'Hello.' The receptionist's voice was friendly. 'I'm afraid Mr Palmer isn't here at the moment, Jenny. He's been called out. Is there a message?'

'No, it's all right. Thank you,' Jenny said.

'Have you a problem?' the voice asked.

'No, no problem. It's just that I . . . we . . . found a dead bird on the beach covered in oil. I wanted to tell him about it,' Jenny said.

'Ah, yes,' the receptionist said. 'We know about the oil spill. In fact, Mr Palmer has gone out to investigate the situation. But thank you for the information. I'll pass it on, all right?'

'OK, thanks. Bye.'

'Bye, Jenny.' The phone went dead. She stepped

out of the phone box and faced the others.

'What is it?' Carrie said. 'Any news?'

'Tom Palmer isn't at the surgery today – he's been called away – to help the birds, the lady said.'

'Well, let's go then, shall we?' David urged.

'I'll just ring my mum,' Carrie said, feeling in her shorts pocket for a coin. She went into the phone box.

'My house is only a few minutes walk from here,' David said. We can give the dogs a drink and leave them there, if you want. Orla doesn't like going in the boat,' he added.

'Jess does,' Jenny said firmly. 'He'll come with me.' Jenny smoothed Jess's silky ears. He was panting and his tongue looked dry. The sooner they got to David's house, the better.

'Mum says it's OK to go to Puffin Island,' Carrie said, coming out of the phone box. 'She knows about the spill. It's been on the local news. Apparently, everyone's rushing about trying to help.'

'Right, then,' said David, bending to clip on Orla's lead. 'Follow me.'

Fiona hurried after David and Carrie followed more slowly behind. Jess was already waiting at Jenny's side. 'Come on, boy,' she said. 'Let's catch up with Carrie.'

★ ★ ★

David's house was a whitewashed bungalow with a carefully kept, rectangular garden. It was partly fenced, but in places the fence had fallen down and was in the process of being mended. Jenny had noticed the place before, when it had been empty and its garden hopelessly overgrown. Now, patterned curtains fluttered at the open windows and the flower borders were a riot of colour. She and Jess, with Carrie and Fiona, followed David and Orla up to the front door.

'Um, can you wait out here?' David said uncomfortably, not looking at them.' I'll go and find my dad.'

Jenny exchanged looks with Carrie and Fiona. She thought it was a bit odd of David not to invite them in but, noticing that Carrie still looked a bit washed out and would probably be grateful of a rest, she turned towards the garden.

'Let's sit over there,' she said, pointing to a patch of grass.

Carrie gave a long sigh. 'Phew! It's hot,' she smiled.

'Nice garden,' Fiona commented, looking around.

Jess lay down on the manicured lawn. He was still panting but his eyes were bright and alert. Jenny guessed that he knew something was up and was enjoying being involved.

'Isn't it funny that David made us wait out here?' Carrie whispered, frowning suspiciously at the front door. 'Why do you think he didn't want us to go inside with him?'

'Maybe he's got something to hide . . .' Fiona suggested.

'Oh, I'm sure!' Carrie teased. 'He and his dad are probably smugglers . . .'

At that moment, the front door of the house opened and David came out, carefully carrying a plastic bowl of water for Jess. The collie ran to David, lifting his nose eagerly to the cold, fresh water.

'Thanks,' Jenny said, as Jess began to lap thirstily.

'My dad's been on the phone to the SSPCA,' David told them. 'They've agreed to send someone over to Puffin Island as soon as they can but, right now, they're all very busy up the main spill higher up the coast. Even the Puffin Island warden has gone out there. Dad'll take us over to the island – he says they're glad of all the help they can get.'

'Great.' Jenny got to her feet just as Jess barked sharply once, as a man appeared in the doorway of the bungalow.

'Good afternoon!' He had a booming voice. 'I'm John Fergusson, David's father.'

'Thanks for taking us out to the island, Mr Fergusson,' Jenny said. 'I'm Jenny Miles. These are my friends Carrie Turner and Fiona McLay.' Carrie and Fiona said hello, together.

Mr Fergusson was a tall, thin man with grey hair. He wore a yellow waterproof jacket. 'Good sailors, are you?' he asked.

'Yes, I am,' Carrie answered. 'I often go out in my dad's boat. He runs trips to Puffin Island in the summer.'

'I'm not bad either,' Fiona said.

'I'm OK,' Jenny added.

'Right. Sounds like the birds on the island might need help,' Mr Fergusson said. 'Sad business. Let's go then, shall we? That dog coming too?'

'Yes,' Jenny spoke up. 'This is Jess. He'll come . . . that is, if you don't mind.'

'Not at all,' said Mr Fergusson, as he led the way to his garage.

The boat was a sleek and powerful craft, called *Hadrian*. With the help of the others, Mr Fergusson jammed every available bit of space with the equipment they would need for the rescue of wild seabirds. He packed a heap of stacked cardboard boxes, a pile of old newspapers, a blanket or two, and an assortment of gloves – from rubber gloves to thick fabric gardening gloves and some woolly winter mittens.

Jess jumped into the boat, finding a narrow space to sit down at Jenny's feet. She sat squeezed up next to Carrie, who was beside Fiona. David sat with his father in the front of the boat.

'Remember,' Mr Fergusson warned, 'these birds may bite, so don't think you can just pluck them off the beach without protecting your hands, OK? Also, oil is toxic. If you get some on your hands, don't put them near your eyes or mouth.'

'Absolutely not,' Carrie grinned, looking in mock horror at her fingers.

Jess put his front feet up onto the edge of Jenny's seat and looked out as they headed towards the open sea. The wind blew his ears flat on the top of his head. He lifted his nose to the sea air and wagged his tail.

'You OK with Jess back there?' Mr Fergusson shouted, gripping the wheel.

'Fine,' Jenny shouted in reply, though the wind seemed to whip the words right out of her mouth and throw them into the air. She was beginning to wish that she had followed Carrie's example and rung home to let Ellen Grace know what was happening.

'OK?' Carrie asked her, as Jenny frowned.

'I should have phoned to say where I was going, like you did,' Jenny admitted.

'Don't worry, Jen,' Carrie said. 'If Mrs Grace worries about you, she'll ring my mum, you know she will.'

'Yes, you're right,' Jenny said, smiling at her friend.

Mr Fergusson eased the boat to the left and, ahead of them, they could see the shadowy outline of Puffin Island in the distance. The cloud was low and the wind was churning up little white waves across the sea. The boat slapped against the water. Jess got a mouthful of salty spray. He sneezed violently. Everyone laughed.

'Oh, poor Jess,' Jenny said, putting her arm round him to steady him as he tried to wipe at his eyes with one paw.

'Are you girls pupils at Greybridge?' Mr Fergusson asked, half turning so they could hear him in the back.

'Yes, we are,' Jenny replied.

'Fortunate for David, then, that you met before school starts. Good to know a few faces in a new place,' he said.

'Do you like Cliffbay, Mr Fergusson?' Jenny asked.

'So far,' he said cautiously. 'I'm a keen

conservationist and I like birds. So Cliffbay will do nicely.'

'Where did you live before you came here?' Fiona yelled, to make herself heard.

John Fergusson looked at his son, then half turned to look at Fiona. 'Different places,' he replied. 'All over.'

Fiona glanced at Jenny, who shrugged. It seemed difficult to get any straight answers out of either David or his father. Jenny was beginning to find them both a bit mysterious.

'Nearly there!' said David. The island was right ahead of them now. It was a rocky outcrop with just a few trees and a shingle beach sloping down to the sea. Mr Fergusson slowed *Hadrian*'s engine and they eased in closer to shore.

'Oh . . . look!' said Jenny. David stood up and looked out. The sea lapping against the island had streaks of oil on it. Slicks of oil rode on the water in patches.

'Oh, no,' Carrie breathed. 'The poor puffins!'

'I can't bear it,' Fiona said, in a small voice.

'The slick is drifting in from the east – and Puffin Island is right in its path,' Mr Fergusson reported, shaking his head. He switched off the boat's engine and let the tide take him in.

'There's a harbour round the other side of the island,' Carrie told him.

'This will be quicker,' Mr Fergusson assured her.

David jumped out and hauled the keel up over the stones. It made a grating noise that sent shivers up Jenny's spine. As she got to her feet, Jess jumped over the side of the boat. He landed in the shallow water then bounded excitedly up the beach.

Jenny leaped out and looked around her. It was a pitiful sight. Already some of the birds had fallen victim to the oil snaking up the beach. A few puffins, their pale grey and white feathered chests coated in black oil, were struggling around in panic. Even the colourful stripes of their beaks were covered.

She recognised some sleek, fat, white bodies as gulls, and gannets – with their dagger-shaped beaks opening and closing soundlessly and their big black feet slapping around in bewilderment on the oily beach. Black guillemots were bunched together miserably, too weary from their struggle even to move away from the strangers who had arrived in their haven. One was walking round in a circle, dragging its wing.

'Mr Fergusson!' Jenny shouted. 'What can we do to help?' But Mr Fergusson was striding away to inspect the extent of the damage and didn't reply.

Carrie and Fiona stood beside her.

'Look,' David pointed. 'A grey plover. It's dead.'

The bird lay at David's feet. A swirl of oil came up the beach in a rush of sea. When the sea drew back, it left its ugly mark on a patch of pale gold stone.

'Oh, poor thing!' said Carrie.

Fiona peered at the bird. 'How horrible,' she said sadly.

'Let's unload those boxes and things,' Jenny said urgently. 'There are live birds that need our help! Now!'

## 3

David clambered aboard *Hadrian*. Already his jeans were wet up to the knees but Jenny was relieved to see that he didn't seem to mind, or even to notice. He seemed as determined as she felt to help the birds.

Jenny, Fiona and Carrie stood in a line below the hull of the boat, reaching up for the boxes, blankets, gloves and newspapers that David unloaded. Jess stood watching the operation with interest.

'You're doing a great job,' announced Mr

Fergusson, striding back towards the boat. 'Let's get everything out of the boat and away from the water.' He stooped to lift their supplies out of the hull and take them higher up the beach. Jess picked up a glove, and followed him, dropping it helpfully at his feet. 'Good boy!' David's father said approvingly. 'I trust Jess will behave himself? He won't worry the birds?' he asked Jenny.

'No way!' Fiona said, loyally.

'He's a sheepdog,' Jenny explained. 'Even though he's not really a working dog, he's got good instincts. As well as that, his nature is gentle and caring.' She felt proud of the Border collie. 'We strapped bottles of milk to him once, to get the feed out to the weaker of the orphaned lambs in the fields. He did a brilliant job of being a surrogate mum.' She felt certain Jess wouldn't harm the birds, some of which were now battling for their lives.

'Where do we begin?' Carrie asked, dusting the fine sand off her palms. Jenny, too, was impatient to start.

'By lining the cardboard boxes with newspaper to provide warmth,' Mr Fergusson advised. 'Then, go round the island picking up the birds, gently and carefully, from behind. Put them into the boxes as quickly as you can. Most boxes will take at least two birds, some will take three. Close the lids to make it as dark as possible.'

'Why?' Jenny asked. 'I mean, why does it have to be dark?'

'So they won't be scared?' Fiona suggested.

'Well, yes, but mainly it helps to stop them trying to preen the oil off their feathers. It's toxic and if they swallow it, it'll kill them,' he explained. 'Generally, they don't preen themselves in the dark.'

David handed round the boxes while his father talked. He was frowning with concentration, working quickly. Jenny, Carrie and Fiona began stuffing the newspapers into them.

'Right,' Mr Fergusson went on. 'Let me give you a few more pointers. The birds needing help will be found above the strand line, all the way round the island. They will have been washed in from the sea during high tide, early this morning.'

'There are still some birds out at sea,' Fiona noticed, pointing.

Mr Fergusson nodded. 'The ones that have come into shore have done so because they can't stay afloat,' Mr Fergusson explained. 'The oil removes the waterproofing on their feathers. If they stayed out in the water, they would drown. With oil on their wings, they are unable to fly, either. In this situation they only leave the sea when they're really desperate. The water is their natural habitat and where they feel safest.'

'Oh, poor things,' said Carrie.

'Your father seem to know a lot about saving birds,' Jenny whispered to David.

'He once worked as a volunteer for a wildlife hospital,' David explained, as he tore newspaper into strips to fit it snugly into a small box.

'So, they only come ashore when they're in *real* trouble?' Fiona asked.

'That's right,' Mr Fergusson replied. He passed round the gloves. Jenny was given a thick pair of gardening gloves. They were huge. She wondered how she was going to keep them on her hands.

'Now,' Mr Fergusson said, 'we'll take as many birds as we can, OK? Bring the boxes back to the boat when they're full. It's probably going to be necessary to make a second trip to the island, once we've got the first lot back to the mainland.'

Jenny picked up two of the lined boxes. She looked at Jess, who looked back at her.

'Stay, Jess,' Jenny said. The collie lay down and put his nose on his paws and gave a little sigh.

'Good boy,' Jenny told him. 'You know it's best if you wait here, don't you?' Quickly, she bent to stroke his silky head and Jess stayed perfectly still. Jenny smiled. Her father was always amazed at the way the young Border collie was so perfectly in tune with what she expected of him. Jenny never doubted Jess for a moment.

She looked around her. Carrie and Fiona were following Mr Fergusson across the beach. David had gone off round the island in the opposite direction. Wanting to make sure she gathered up her first wild seabird in the correct way, Jenny decided to stick close to Mr Fergusson. He seemed to be an expert at these things. She ran to catch up.

'It's a razorbill,' Mr Fergusson was saying, as Jenny drew close. He was looking at a bird on the shingle. The seabird's wings were spread stiffly and it blinked small eyes covered in oil.

'Poor old thing,' Mr Fergusson said, as he crouched and crept towards it, then made a swift grab from behind. The bird squawked. Mr Fergusson held it firmly but gently between the palms of his gloved hands. It twisted its neck, trying to sink its beak into his fingers. Jenny's heart turned over for the poor, terrified creature. Mr Fergusson plunged it down into the box and secured the cardboard flaps over its head.

'I can do that!' Carrie said. 'Nothing to it.' She grinned at Jenny, who gave her a watery smile. Carrie was always so positive and cheerful, but that was far from the way Jenny was feeling right at this moment. She looked at her hands, thinking about how determined the bird had been to bite.

'There,' Mr Fergusson straightened. 'There's room for a couple more birds in this box, so . . . off you go. Get busy!' he said firmly, clapping his hands playfully. Jenny started.

'Right,' she said. 'Right, Mr Fergusson.' She looked longingly after Carrie, as she wandered away with her boxes, wishing that they could work as a team. She loved Carrie's sparky company and had missed her while she was ill at home. But, she reasoned to herself, there were only five of them, and many more birds needing to be discovered and helped. She picked up her boxes. Fiona picked up hers.

'Let's spread out, then,' Jenny said.

'Yes,' Fiona agreed, and headed towards the summit of Puffin Island.

Jenny spotted a small gull hunched miserably on a stone. It was shaking its small head, which was covered in oil. She began nervously to sneak up on it. The bird made no attempt to fly off, even though her sandals crunched noisily on the shingle as she approached.

The gull felt light in her hands. The wings were

thick with oozing black oil that coated the gloves and seeped through to Jenny's fingers. In spite of the gloves being so hefty, and so big for her, she was glad she had them on. Mr Fergusson had said that this foul-smelling oil was poisonous for the birds – what harm might it do to her if she got it on her skin, she wondered? She laid the bird gently in the box. As she closed the lid, the oil from her gloves smeared across the flaps.

'Ugh!' she said, making a face as David came up. 'This is disgusting.'

David was holding a large cardboard box against his chest. 'I've got three birds in mine,' he told her. 'They're crammed in pretty tight, poor things. Have you been over on the other side, by the rocks? There are loads there.'

'No,' Jenny said. 'I'll have a look now.' She carried the gull carefully, hating the feel of the small, sharp stones and the slimy oil that came in through the sides of her sandals. She guessed she would have to throw them away when she got home.

'You coping?' called Mr Fergusson, struggling with a frantic gannet.

'Um, yes,' Jenny replied. 'This is awful, isn't it?'

'Not as bad as it might be,' he said gravely. 'I've seen worse. Puffin Island hasn't been badly affected, luckily. The slick is further up the coast. Who knows what damage it might do up there.'

'Can they scoop it out of the sea?' Jenny asked, adding, in a sudden spark of anger: 'They should make the people responsible for spilling it clean it up!'

'They try and disperse it with chemicals,' Mr Fergusson said, shaking his head. 'But oil slicks do a lot of damage the moment they hit. Everything in the sea, from periwinkles to shrimps, anemones and even rare sea grasses, could be wiped out by a big spill of crude oil. But . . .' he sighed, 'we have to hope for the best.'

Jenny looked out across the sea. She imagined the oil, as thick as chocolate, spreading slowly towards the little island, and the birds, opening and shutting their beaks, as if calling for help. Her eyes stung with tears.

Carrie passed by with a box pressed against her thighs. The lid was lifting as the bird inside struggled to be free. 'I've got a cross one in here, Mr Fergusson,' she called.

Jenny noticed that Carrie looked exhausted. Her face was as white as a sheet and there were shadows like bruises under her eyes.

'It should settle down in a minute or two,' Mr

Fergusson called after her. 'But I'd put a stone on the top of the box.'

Jenny hurriedly scooped another stricken bird off the beach and put it in with her gull, then caught up with Carrie, who was on her way back to where *Hadrian* was moored.

'I'm tired,' Carrie announced. 'I think I'll get on the boat and have a little rest.'

'Oh,' Jenny said, disappointed. 'It's not like you to give up so soon. We're doing such a good job.'

'I just want to sit down for a bit. I won't be long,' Carrie replied.

'But these birds need our help now!' Jenny said heatedly. 'Otherwise they may die!'

Carrie let out a sigh. 'OK! All right, Jenny. You win. Honestly, you're such a nag at times,' she said.

'I am not!' Jenny returned, feeling hurt. Carrie wasn't behaving like her usual self at all.

'It's quite easy to catch them, isn't it?' Fiona said, as Jenny and Carrie came up to the boat.

The interruption put an end to the argument. Jenny nodded and smiled weakly at Fiona. She suddenly felt embarrassed about the way she had reacted to Carrie. She had got caught up in the momentum of the rescue and, forgetting Carrie was ill, felt annoyed that she wasn't her usual enthusiastic self. It wasn't like her friend just to give up on something because she felt like it.

When Jess spotted Jenny, he stood up and wagged his tail hard. She called to him and he bounded over joyfully, lifting his nose to sniff at the box she was carrying. She laid it down beside Carrie's and Fiona's, then made a fuss of him.

Carrie put a large stone on the lid of her box. 'I'm going back to look for more birds,' she said, in a determined voice.

'That's the spirit,' Jenny teased. But Carrie didn't turn round and make a funny face at her as Jenny had thought she would. She just walked away.

'I think we've got enough to make a first trip back now,' Mr Fergusson decided, as he added his box to the row. 'We'd better start loading them aboard.'

'Oh, but I haven't filled my second box yet!' Jenny pleaded.

'All right, Jenny. 'Go and see what you can find as quickly as you can. OK?' Mr Fergusson said.

'Wait here for me, Jess,' Jenny said urgently and ran down the beach with her box. She decided to head towards the rocks where Carrie was going. There were bound to be plenty of seabirds trying to take shelter there. She slowed to a jog, feeling her legs begin to ache with tiredness. It had been a long day. She would give anything to stop and have a cold drink.

Ahead of her, she could see Carrie on the rocks. Her friend was feeling her way carefully – trying – Jenny guessed, not to slip on the oil. She hoped Carrie wasn't annoyed with her. She hadn't meant to sound like an old nag. When she caught up with her, Jenny decided, she would say she was sorry.

She saw Carrie spread out her arms, as if for better balance. Then, suddenly, she disappeared from Jenny's view. One moment she was there, and the next, she wasn't. She waited to see if Carrie would appear again, but she didn't. Her heart began to hammer in her chest.

'Carrie!' Jenny shouted and started to run towards the rocks. 'Where are you?' She looked back for somebody who would help. Mr Fergusson . . . David . . . Fiona? But they were aboard *Hadrian*, engrossed in stacking the birds.

Jenny reached the rocks. She slowed and stepped cautiously onto the jagged surface, slimy with thick, black oil. There were pools of it forming in the crevices. She put out her arms for better balance and stared around her.

Carrie was lying face down. The oily sea licked at

her outstretched arm. 'Carrie!' Jenny screamed. But Carrie didn't move.

Stumbling and sliding, Jenny went towards her friend. The sea rushed in to cover the rocks, making it impossible for Jenny to see where next to step. She paused, her heart pounding so hard she could hear it. Carrie hadn't moved, in spite of the cold water splashing up against her, touching her with the oil. *Could she have struck her head when she fell? Might she drown?* Jenny thought frantically.

'Carrie!' she shrieked again. She couldn't move any faster. The waves on the rocks and the oil made it too dangerous to hurry. Then, suddenly, Jenny heard a welcome sound. She looked up.

Jess was flying across the beach towards her. His ears were up and his tail streamed out behind him in the wind. He was barking as he ran.

'Jess! Oh, Jess,' sobbed Jenny. 'Good boy! Come, come quickly . . .'

Jess must have sensed by the tone of her voice as she called to Carrie that something was wrong. Now, he sprang onto the rocks, his claws gripping where Jenny's sandals wouldn't hold. He found a passage towards her. Jenny's heart nearly stopped beating when she saw him stagger under a powerful wave. Then he was beside her. She pulled off her glove and stroked his head gratefully.

'Jess,' she told him firmly. 'Go and get help. Get Mr Fergusson, or David . . . or Fiona. Good boy! Go!' Jess put his head to one side, listening. He looked first to where Jenny was pointing back at the beach, then back at her face. 'Quick, Jess!' Jenny said again.

Jess sprang off the rocks and ran back towards the boat. In the distance, Jenny could see Mr Fergusson jump from the deck of *Hadrian* onto the beach. He stooped to roll up his trouser legs. Jenny saw him look up as the wet, oily dog came streaking towards him. He straightened up. Jess let out a volley of sharp barks, then turned and ran back towards the rocks.

Mr Fergusson put up a hand to shade his eyes from the glare and peered in the direction the dog was running. Jenny waved her arms frantically and a few seconds later he caught sight of her, waved back, and then began to run.

'What is it?' he shouted as he got nearer.

'It's Carrie,' Jenny yelled back. 'My friend . . . she's unconscious. You've got to help her, please!'

# 4

Jenny felt the relief surge through her. Help was on the way. As the next wave pulled back off the rocks, she quickly covered the last couple of metres to where Carrie was lying. She was surprised to find her friend curled up on her side, looking quite peaceful, as though she had chosen this spot to have a sleep.

Jenny bent down and put a hand on her shoulder. 'Carrie!' she said, urgently. 'Carrie . . . are you all right?' Carrie's eyelids fluttered and she gave a small groan.

'What's happened?' Mr Fergusson was out of breath from his dash down the beach. His voice was gruff with alarm. He was staggering around on the rocks, trying to keep his balance and peer at Carrie at the same time. Jess stood firm, gripping the rocks with his claws, his tail still and his ears flat. He whimpered.

'I think . . . well, she just fell down,' Jenny said, miserably. 'I don't know what happened – if she collapsed, or just slipped.'

'What's the matter?' Fiona shouted, from the beach.

'Stay where you are,' Mr Fergusson ordered Fiona. 'You and David keep an eye on the birds.' He lifted Carrie, who slumped against him, just as a large wave came swooshing up the rocks, showering them both with cold water.

Carrie coughed, then blinked and opened her eyes. She looked at Jenny's worried face, and frowned with confusion, as if trying to remember where she was. 'Sorry,' she said, shyly, as Mr Fergusson pulled her to her feet. 'I took a tumble . . . tripped, or something.'

'Oh, Carrie!' Jenny breathed. 'You gave me such a fright! How do you feel?'

'Well, that wasn't the most comfortable bed!' Carrie said, sounding more like her old self. 'But I'm OK.' She looked down at her legs, which were covered in cuts and scratches. Jess put his nose gently into the palm of Carrie's hand.

'Hello, Jess. Yes, I'm all right now.' Carrie managed a giggle as Jess's tongue darted out to lick at her bare legs. They were caked with salt and traced with blood. Her white shorts were ripped and streaked with oil.

'It was the dog who let me know something was up,' Mr Fergusson said, admiringly. 'He's an intelligent animal, I'll say that.' Jenny put her hand out to Jess and stroked him proudly.

Mr Fergusson kept a firm hold on Carrie's upper arm as he helped her off the rocks. Then Jenny slipped her arm round Carrie's waist and walked with her up the beach back to the boat. She was trembling all over and Carrie laughed.

'You're shaking like a jelly in a high wind, Jen. It's *me* who should be doing the shaking!'

Jenny was overcome with relief that her best friend was safe. She felt awful for having spoken sharply to Carrie earlier. 'Are you OK? I mean, *really* OK?' she asked quietly.

'Fine,' Carrie replied. 'Now, stop fussing. I tripped, that's all. I must have banged my head or something. It's nothing. Oh, hello, Fiona . . .'

'Oh, your legs!' Fiona gasped, seeing a trickle of blood snaking down Carrie's calf. 'Did you fall?'

'Yep,' Carrie said cheerfully. 'Tripped over a wave.' She chuckled, but Jenny noticed that she was still very pale.

'Right,' said Mr Fergusson, 'Let's have you all in the boat now and we'll head for the mainland. I want to get these birds to the vet.'

Every centimetre of *Hadrian*'s hull was occupied by boxes containing birds. Jenny, Carrie and Fiona were crushed into the back of the boat, Jess at their feet. Their laps were laden with boxes, some unmoving, some being buffeted by the bewildered creatures inside. David had several boxes at the front with him. As Mr Fergusson opened the throttle and

headed back to Cliffbay, Carrie quietly laid her head against Jenny's shoulder and closed her eyes.

Jenny tried not to mind about being so wet and uncomfortable. She'd noticed her toe was bleeding, too, and now it began to sting. But they'd rescued, and probably saved, a good number of seabirds – and Carrie was safe beside her. That was all that mattered.

She put out her hand and her fingers found the fur of Jess's soft chest. She began to tickle and scratch him and in return he licked her hand lovingly. 'Nearly home,' she whispered. 'And, do *you* deserve a treat!'

When *Hadrian* was secured at her mooring, Mr Fergusson transferred the birds to the back of his van. 'I'll take you straight home, young lady,' he said to Carrie, climbing into the cab. 'Then we must hurry these birds to a vet. They'll be needing treatment as soon as possible.'

'What sort of treatment, Mr Fergusson?' Fiona asked.

'They need to drink,' he told her. 'They'll be dehydrated, and also very cold. They need rehydration and a heat lamp, or a warm room in which to recover.'

'Will you be going back to Puffin Island for more birds, Dad?' David asked.

'We'll see. One of the specialist agencies should be on the job pretty soon,' Mr Fergusson replied. 'They may not need our help.'

Carrie seemed to doze off again as they drove, saying nothing when Jenny gave David's father instructions on how to find the Turners' home. She sat up just as they arrived at Cliff House, and Mr Fergusson pulled up beside Mrs Turner's brightly painted mini.

Carrie opened the door of the van. 'Thanks, Mr Fergusson, bye everyone,' she said with a smile.

Jenny moved to climb out. 'I'll come in with you . . .' she began.

'No,' Carrie spoke firmly. 'No you won't. Those birds in the back need your help. My mum's here for me.'

'But . . . you're not well,' Jenny said.

Carrie pushed her coppery hair out of her eyes and straightened her shoulders. 'Go to Mr Palmer's surgery!' she pleaded. 'I'm *fine*.' She guided Jenny back into the van and closed the door. Then she stood back and waved as Mr Fergusson pulled away.

Jenny craned her neck to look back at Carrie. Mrs Turner had come out of the house. The warm smile of greeting vanished from her face when she saw the state of her daughter. She put her arms round Carrie who, in turn, buried her face in her mother's shoulder. As they drove away down the street and Jenny lost sight of them, she didn't know why – but she just couldn't shake off a feeling of real worry for her friend.

Tom Palmer, the vet, was a big man with a loud voice, but Jenny had always liked him. It had been Mr Palmer who had given Jess the chance to lead a normal life. He had performed the operation that had straightened out the puppy's crippled leg. Over the months, Jess's leg had got progressively stronger, so that now, the slight limp he had had since being a pup was barely noticeable.

'Jenny!' Mr Palmer beamed, and removed the stethoscope that was swinging from his neck. 'How nice to see you. How are you?'

'Hello, Mr Palmer.' Jenny smiled. 'I'm fine, thanks,' she replied, despite the fact that she was feeling so tired she was almost seeing double and her stomach was growling with hunger. 'This is Mr Fergusson. He took us out to the island and we helped him to rescue some seabirds that . . .'

'The birds are in the back of the van,' Mr Fergusson

said hurriedly, interrupting Jenny. 'They need seeing to, and pretty quick I'd say.'

'Ah, yes,' Tom Palmer frowned. 'Nasty business. It was a South American oil tanker, I believe. I've been told its engines failed, and the ship was dragged round by the tide onto some rocks. The hull split open.'

'What happened to the people on the ship?' David asked, his eyes wide.

'They're being taken off by the lifeboats,' Mr Palmer said. 'We're hoping the full might of the slick doesn't move this way, though there is bound to be some damage.'

'It was Jess who discovered an oil-covered puffin on the beach at Cliffbay this morning,' Jenny told him. 'So really it's him who let us know about the spill and made us go out to the island to see if we could help.'

'Ah, a fine young dog, is that Jess,' smiled Tom Palmer. 'Where is he, by the way?'

'He's out in the van,' Fiona said. 'He's been brilliant.'

'What about these birds, then?' David's father asked.

'Bring them in, Mr Fergusson, if you don't mind. And, well done – all of you.' Mr Palmer smiled, putting a gentle hand on Jenny's tousled head. 'From the look of you, it's been a long, hard day.'

David followed his father out of the surgery. Fiona trailed wearily in their wake. 'Let Jess in, too, lass,' Mr Palmer said kindly, to Jenny. 'He'll be needing a drink, I'll bet.'

'Thanks.' Jenny grinned and then ran to release Jess from the back of the van and bring him inside.

A room had been given over to the emergency treatment of wildlife that had suffered from the oil spill. To Jenny's amazement, even a small seal pup was snoozing under a lamp. Tom Palmer and his two assistants had used all the available equipment to heat the room. Makeshift barricades had become holding pens for an assortment of sea creatures. Heat lamps shone their eerie red glow onto shivering birds.

Jess, with water dripping from his muzzle, walked about peering into the pens, his nose twitching with the smell of the oil.

'What a hero, you are, young Jess!' said Mr Palmer, patting his side. Jess's tail thumped happily on the floor.

Mr Palmer handed out gloves to everyone and they helped him to put the birds into the appropriate pens. 'My,' he said admiringly, 'you've done a good job here. These birds would certainly have died if you hadn't been there to help.'

Jenny grinned at Fiona, who grinned back.

'What will happen to the birds now, Mr Palmer?' Fiona asked.

'They'll need about twenty-four hours to rehydrate and to get warm,' he told her. 'Then, those that live will be taken to the special centre run by the SSPCA to be cleaned. We haven't got the equipment needed for that here, you see, and a new place has just been opened in Graston.'

'Oh, yes, I read about that in the paper,' Jenny said. 'But shouldn't all that horrible oil be washed off straight away?'

'No,' Mr Palmer assured her. 'Being cold and thirsty will kill a bird more quickly than the oil will. This first step is vital for their survival. Someone will be coming along from the SSPCA to check on this latest lot in a minute, I expect.'

'No need for us to hang around, then?' Mr Fergusson said. 'It's been a long day.'

'No need at all, thank you. And I should think someone is on their way back to Puffin Island for more casualties even now.' Tom Palmer smiled. He reached down and smoothed Jess's coat. 'Good boy! A fine job . . .'

'I'll take you two home,' Mr Fergusson said to Jenny

and Fiona. 'Then I'm going to have a much needed cup of tea!'

'Thanks, Mr Fergusson,' Jenny said. She took a last look at the birds they had rescued. She hoped they *would* survive and that soon they would be released back to an oil-free Puffin Island. 'C'mon Jess,' Jenny called.

Fiona practically fell out of the van when they reached Dunraven, the McLays' home. She mumbled a goodbye to Jenny and David and thanked Mr Fergusson for the lift.

'See you, Fi,' Jenny said. Then she told David's father how to get to Windy Hill. Jess began to bark as they approached the farm gates.

'He wants his dinner!' David laughed.

'He's always pleased to be home.' Jenny smiled.

Fraser Miles was loading hay bales onto a tractor when Mr Fergusson's van pulled up. There were bits of straw in his dark hair and his wellington boots were caked in mud. He looked up and a grin spread across his face. 'Hello, love,' he said warmly, opening the door to let Jenny out. He ruffled Jess's ears as the collie came up to greet him. 'You look as though you've done three rounds in the ring with a champion boxer!'

'Oh, Dad, what a day we've had! We went out to Puffin Island with Mr Fergusson to save the birds from the oil . . .'

'How do you do?' Mr Miles said, putting out his hand. 'Thanks for bringing Jenny home. I heard from Ellen, who spoke to Mrs Turner, that you'd gone off on some adventure.'

'Hello,' Mr Fergusson took the outstretched hand. 'No problem.'

'I've heard about the oil spill. Nasty business. Did you save any birds then, Jen?' Fraser Miles asked with a grin.

'Yes, loads!' Jenny said proudly. 'Jess discovered a puffin covered in oil down on Cliffbay beach, so we knew there was a problem. Mr Fergusson took us out there in his motor-boat and showed us how to catch the birds. We've left the ones we rescued with Mr Palmer.'

'Well done, lass!' Jenny's dad said. 'You're new around here, aren't you?' he asked David's father.

'Yes, we moved in a week or so ago,' Mr Fergusson said. 'This is my son, David.' Fraser Miles nodded and smiled at David, who smiled back. 'We've taken a house at Cliffbay.'

'You're here on holiday here, then?' Mr Miles asked pleasantly.

'Uh . . . no, we're going to see how it goes . . .' he trailed off.

Fraser Miles looked puzzled. An awkward silence hung over them.

'Um, would you like a cup of tea, Mr Fergusson? David?' Jenny put in brightly, but hoping they would refuse. She was exhausted and desperate to get indoors to feed and groom Jess, and to have a shower. And now all the excitement was over, she realised how hungry she was.

'No, thanks,' said Mr Fergusson. 'We'll be off now. Nice to meet you.'

'See you at school, David,' Jenny said.

'Yes, on Monday.' He nodded.

'Thanks again,' Mr Miles said, as David and his father climbed into the van.

'By the way,' Mr Fergusson called, from the driver's window. 'That's a great dog you've got there.' Jess's tail thumped against Jenny's leg.

'Thanks!' she shouted, as the van drew away.

'There's something odd about Mr Fergusson,' Fraser Miles mused.

'Hmm, I think so too. But I can't think what it is,' Jenny agreed. She stretched and gave a sigh. *Perhaps Fiona is right*, she thought. *Perhaps we should be suspicious . . .*

But she was far too tired and hungry to give it much thought and calling Jess, Jenny gladly let herself into Windy Hill.

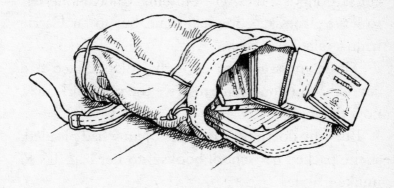

# 5

The moment Jenny arrived in her classroom on Monday morning her eyes wandered hopefully to Carrie's desk. She looked for the usual unruly head of red hair bent over a haphazard pile of books. But no laughing blue eyes looked back at her, and the desk itself was as neat as a pin.

Jenny sat down slowly at her own desk and gave a big sigh. She'd been trying to speak to Carrie since Mr Fergusson had dropped her home after the bird rescue three days ago. The Turners' had installed an answer machine on their telephone line and all Jenny could get was a metallic-sounding voice asking her to leave a message. She had done, but so far Carrie hadn't called her back.

'Three messages are enough,' Ellen Grace had advised. 'You don't want to drive the poor girl crazy, now do you?'

'But why doesn't she ring me?' Jenny had pleaded, as she packed her school books into her bag. 'It's so unlike Carrie.'

'I can't help you there, Jenny,' Mrs Grace had said kindly. 'Perhaps she's not well and her mother wants her to rest. That's simple enough, isn't it?'

'Yes, but usually Carrie would phone me back,' Jenny had said, feeling a bit hurt. 'I am her best friend, after all.'

Mrs Grace was wonderful, and had largely filled the enormous gap left in the heart of the family after Jenny's mother had died, but she didn't understand her in quite the way her mother had.

'No,' Jenny had insisted, 'I must've upset Carrie in some way. That's got to be the reason.'

'I'm sure you haven't, Jenny,' Ellen Grace had said, coming over to give Jenny a hug. 'Best friends are not that fragile. Especially not Carrie. She's a fighter, isn't that what you always told me?'

*Yes*, Jenny acknowledged to herself miserably, as she sat at her desk hoping Carrie's face would appear in the classroom doorway. *Carrie's a fighter, all right. So, where is she? What's happened to her?*

'Hello.'

Jenny jumped. David Fergusson stood there with his schoolbag over his shoulder, his dark hair neatly combed and flattened across his head. He looked different to the last time Jenny had seen him, with the wind whipping his hair round his face and the salt dried in patches on his cheeks.

'Hello,' she said brightly.

'Um, do you know where I should sit?' David asked, looking round awkwardly. 'I've been told to use Carrie Turner's desk for the day.'

'Oh!' Jenny started. 'Does that mean Carrie isn't coming in to school today?' She didn't know why she had asked him. Why would he have the answers that she didn't?

'I expect so . . .' David trailed off.

'It's this one,' Jenny said absently, pointing to the desk beside hers. She watched as David lifted the lid of the desk and look about inside, fitting his own few books in and around Carrie's.

'Where's Carrie?' Fiona asked, coming straight over from the doorway.

'Don't know,' Jenny mumbled. 'Sick, maybe?'

'I tried ringing her yesterday,' Fiona said. 'They've got an answer machine now.'

'Well,' David said, 'she did fall on the rocks, remember? Maybe she's not feeling too good because of that.'

Fiona perched on the edge of Jenny's desk. 'Are you OK?' she asked, leaning in close. 'You look awful.'

'Thanks,' Jenny said, then she smiled. 'Sorry, Fi, I'm just worried about Carrie.'

'Why? I mean, OK, so she tripped on the rocks but . . .'

'I think she's cross with me,' Jenny confided.

'But why?' Fiona was interested. 'What's happened? Did you have a fight?'

'No . . . but when we were out on Puffin Island I nagged her to keep working. She was tired and she wanted to rest but I begged her not to. I wasn't very nice . . .' Jenny trailed off, ashamed of herself.

'Ah, Carrie wouldn't mind about *that*!' Fiona dismissed Jenny's fears. 'She's not one to bear a grudge. She's always so . . .' she narrowed her eyes, trying to find the right word to describe Carrie, '. . . happy-go-lucky!' she finished.

'That's what I mean,' Jenny whispered. 'Then, if

she isn't upset with me, why hasn't she phoned? I've left loads of messages.'

Fiona was considering this when the bell rang. 'I'll talk to you at break,' she hissed and went to her own desk.

Jenny opened her maths book. Her eyes were swimming with tears and she wiped them away angrily. She was missing Jess, that was it. Coming back to school after having spent so many happy days at home with him was always hard. As she had left for the bus without him this morning, his face had been a picture of despair. Just thinking about it made her sad.

'Can I borrow your ruler?' Penelope James asked her, on the other side. Jenny looked up.

'Sure,' she said. Then, forcing a smile, she decided to put Carrie – and Jess – out of her mind and get on with her maths.

When school finished for the day, Jenny was torn between rushing home to be with Jess and going to visit Carrie. She was troubled by Carrie's silence and badly wanted reassurance.

'Do you want me to come with you?' Fiona asked. She was trying to be kind and Jenny was grateful. For a long time, Fiona had been her enemy and her spiteful tongue had taken away Jenny's confidence.

'Thanks, Fi, but I'll go alone, if you don't mind,' she smiled. 'I'll talk to you tomorrow, OK?'

Fiona nodded as Jenny swung her bulging schoolbag onto her shoulder and hurried off to catch the bus to Cliffbay.

Jenny walked quickly from where the bus dropped her to Cliff House. Mrs Turner's mini was parked in the drive. That was a good sign – they must be at home. She wondered why she felt so nervous. Even if Carrie *had* been offended by her remarks on Puffin Island, she wasn't going to eat her!

Jenny rang the bell. It was opened almost immediately by Mrs Turner. Jenny stared. Carrie's mum didn't look her usual groomed self. Her hair hadn't been brushed and it looked dirty; and the bright lipstick she normally wore was missing, making her face appear pale and tired.

'Hello, Jenny,' she said, sounding subdued.

'Hello,' Jenny stammered in her confusion. 'Um . . . I've come to see Carrie. I wondered if she was sick, because . . .'

'She's not very well, actually, Jenny,' Mrs Turner said. 'In fact, she's resting right now – so I won't disturb her, if you don't mind.'

'No, of course . . . I was worried . . .' Jenny finished.

'Yes, well – don't be!' Mrs Turner snapped. Then her voice softened. 'I'm sorry, love. We'll get in touch with you . . . soon, all right?'

'All right,' Jenny repeated, bewildered. Why wouldn't Mrs Turner let her go up and see Carrie? She stepped back and looked up at Carrie's bedroom window. She almost expected her friend to be peering down at her, her nose flattened against the pane, making a ghastly, comical face. But the lilac curtains in Carrie's window were drawn.

'Bye,' she said, in a small voice, looking back at Mrs Turner. But the door had already been shut. Mrs Turner had gone back inside.

Jenny walked slowly back to the bus stop. Nothing felt right. She was convinced, more than ever, that Carrie just didn't want to see her. She must have decided that Jenny wasn't worth having as a friend and was trying to avoid her.

She struggled not to cry as the bus jolted along the rough road towards the stop near Windy Hill. She trudged her way to the gate and was so wrapped up in her misery that she failed to see Jess streaking across the farmyard towards her – until he was leaping up joyously, his front feet on her chest, licking at her cheeks and making her laugh.

'Jess! Oh, darling Jess! You're my friend, aren't you? My *best* friend! I missed you today, too!'

Inside the big kitchen, Jenny slung her schoolbag on the floor. Mrs Grace was slicing onions, a large brown pot of tea on the table in front of her. 'There's juice in the fridge, Jenny,' she said. 'How was the first day back at school?'

'Carrie wasn't there,' Jenny said, not really answering the question. 'I went to her house after school and her mum said she wasn't very well.'

'There!' Ellen Grace said triumphantly. 'What did I tell you?'

'It still shouldn't stop her from *ringing*,' Jenny said mutinously. 'She's not at death's door!' She poured herself a glass of orange and rummaged in the tin for a biscuit. 'I'm going to take Jess for a walk, now,' she said.

'Any homework?' Mrs Grace asked, raising an eyebrow, being playfully stern.

'Not on the first day back!' Jenny slid out of the door, Jess at her heels.

Jenny headed towards Darktarn Keep, the place she always went to when she wanted to be alone with her thoughts. From up there on the knoll that overlooked Windy Hill, she could see all the way down into Cliffbay, and across the sea to the shadowy outline of Puffin Island.

The late afternoon sun was warm on her back as she walked. Jess ambled along at her side, his tongue lolling happily. But suddenly, the collie stopped, and lifted a paw. He sniffed the air.

'What is it?' Jenny asked him.

The answer arrived in the form of Orla, David's Border collie. She rushed up to greet Jess, her tail wagging. David was ambling along on the path, swinging a stick.

'David!' Jenny called. 'Hello.' She waved. Concerned as she was about Carrie, she was determined to be friendly.

'Hi,' he said, coming over.

'Hello. How did you enjoy your first day at school?'

'Oh, it was OK,' David said, watching Jess playing with Orla. 'I miss my mates, you know . . . from my other school.'

'I looked for you on the bus today. I went down to Cliffbay this afternoon,' Jenny said warmly.

'My dad fetched me,' David said. 'First day and all that.'

'Why did you have to move to Cliffbay?' Jenny asked, as she fell into step beside him.

David's face darkened. He brushed a lock of hair out of his eyes. 'Oh, my father's . . . um . . . it's a business thing, you know.' He changed the subject. 'Look, I was going to go to the SSPCA centre at Graston, that place where they've taken the birds we saved. To see how they're doing. Do you want to come?'

'Oh!' Jenny said, surprised. 'Yes . . . but, do you think it's OK to just drop in? Will they mind?'

'Nah!' said David, grinning. 'We rescued them, didn't we? We've got a right to know if they survived.'

'OK, then,' Jenny smiled. 'Do you know where to go?'

'Yeah, my dad showed me. It's not far,' he answered.

David was quiet as they walked along. Jenny found it difficult to get him to talk much about his life before he came to Cliffbay. Whenever she asked a direct question, David managed to ask a question of his own. She found herself telling him all about Jess's birth.

The SSPCA centre was a small, purpose-built hospital for injured wildlife. There was a reception area with a circle of comfortable chairs and a table with magazines on it. 'It's like the dentist,' David whispered. He had left Orla tied up outside. Jess had come in with Jenny.

At the desk, a young woman was tapping away at a computer keyboard. Her blonde hair was held back in a ponytail and she had a scattering of pale freckles across the bridge of her nose. Jenny guessed she was about twenty years old. She looked up when Jenny approached and took off her reading glasses. 'Can I help you?' she asked pleasantly.

'My name's Jenny Miles,' Jenny began. 'My friend David and I helped to rescue some birds from Puffin Island at the weekend. We wondered how they were.'

The woman got up. 'Would you like to come through and visit our patients?' she smiled. 'You'd be very welcome.'

Jenny grinned in surprise. 'Thank you,' she said, watching as the receptionist came round the desk.

When the woman saw the collie, who was lying down, worrying a burr out of the fur on his paw with his teeth, she bent down to stroke him. 'Hello, gorgeous,' she said. 'You'll have to wait out here, I'm afraid.' Then she looked up at Jenny and David. 'I'm Sarah, by the way. Sarah Taylor.'

Leaving Jess resting comfortably in the waiting-room, Jenny and David followed Sarah through a pair of double doors and down a linoleum-floored corridor. The room she took them to was enormous, made up of a series of pens for the recovering birds. Hanging on the wall, above some shallow tin baths, was a selection of what looked to Jenny like coiled garden hosepipes. The room was very hot.

'Phew!' said David, looking around. 'It looks more like a torture chamber than a hospital.'

Sarah laughed. 'I hope not! Most of the birds you brought in are doing very nicely, thank you! She pointed to the pipes roped up against the wall. Those are high-pressure hoses. We use them for washing the oil off the birds.'

Jenny walked about, peeping in the birds. They were huddled under heat lamps, some with their heads tucked under their wings. There were no traces of oil on their feathers now.

'I heard about your rescue,' Sarah said admiringly. 'Well done. But, there were five of you, weren't there?'

'Yes,' Jenny told her. 'David's dad, and my friends Carrie and Fiona were with us. Only Carrie fell when she was out on the island and she's been sick ever since.'

'Really?' Sarah sounded concerned. 'That's a shame. What's wrong with her?'

'I don't really know,' Jenny confessed. 'She's my best friend but I haven't been able to see her yet. Her mum says she needs rest and shouldn't be disturbed.'

'I can see that must be very worrying for you, not knowing what's going on,' Sarah said gravely. She seemed very understanding and Jenny warmed to her immediately.

'Do you work here all the time?' she asked Sarah.

'Well, I'm a volunteer,' Sarah replied. 'That means I come when I'm needed – and I'm learning as I go along.' She smiled. 'There's a small team of people who come in when a crisis like this one arises. That's why we're always very grateful when people like you and your friends want to help.'

'Oh, we'd love to help – any time,' Jenny offered. 'I'm sure Carrie and Fiona would love to come along too.'

'Well, I'll tell you what, why don't you all come in when Carrie's better? It would be nice to meet her. And your other friend too, of course.' Sarah smiled.

'Thanks,' Jenny said, surprised again. She had imagined that she and David would be allowed just a glimpse of the birds, before being hurried out of the centre. Sarah was making them feel very welcome.

The young woman glanced at her watch. 'It's almost time for the night-time assistant to come in for the next shift,' Sarah said. 'So, I'm off home in a moment. Come back again when you can, all right?'

'Yes,' Jenny said, smiling. 'Thanks, we will.' She would tell Carrie about Sarah and the centre. Tomorrow at school, when Carrie was back. Carrie would love it here and it would be sure to cheer her up. Jenny could hardly wait for the next day.

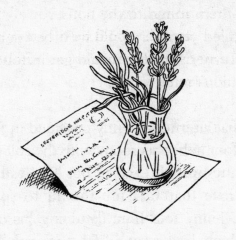

**6**

When Carrie didn't appear at school the following day, Jenny began to feel a sense of dread. Her lessons passed in a blur. She couldn't find a grain of enthusiasm for anything.

'She must be really sick,' Fiona said gloomily, at breaktime. 'Too sick even to come to the phone.'

'Oh, don't,' Jenny begged. 'I can't bear to think about it.'

'I know!' Fiona said, suddenly sounding cheerful. 'Why don't we buy some chocolates – her favourites

– and take them round to the house?'

Jenny smiled wanly. 'No, Fi, we'd better not,' she said. 'Mrs Turner said *they* would get in touch with *us*. We shouldn't interfere.'

At home that afternoon, Jenny confided in Jess. She sat on the floor in her bedroom, with the collie curled against her, resting his head in her lap. 'It's hard for me to believe that Carrie's too ill to speak on the phone,' Jenny told him, flattening his ears and watching them spring back. 'If I were sick, I'd ring her. I mean, she must know how worried I am.'

Jess looked at Jenny, his head cocked to one side, his soft brown eyes full of understanding.

'I'm so glad I've got you!' Jenny said, kissing the top of his soft white nose. Without Carrie around, Jenny was feeling particularly alone. Her nineteen-year-old brother, Matt, hadn't made it back to Windy Hill for two weekends in a row now. He was away in England on a field trip and Jenny didn't know when she would next see him.

Mrs Grace was there, of course, and she had listened patiently to Jenny going on about Carrie for three days now. Her father, who had noticed Jenny's glum face, had dismissed her fears with a confident chuckle. 'The sort of friendship you have with Carrie Turner is not going to dissolve overnight because of a few harsh words spoken under pressure, lass,' he said. 'I promise you that.'

Jenny didn't know what to think any more. 'Maybe I should write to her,' she said to Jess, who, alerted by the brighter tone in her voice, stood up and looked around the room expectantly. It made Jenny giggle. 'Silly boy,' she said. 'Oh, well, that's enough brooding. A letter is too formal, anyway. Let's go and see what's for supper.'

Jess barked his approval.

The geography lesson had started when Carrie appeared in the classroom the next day. Jenny looked up, overjoyed, as Carrie came across to her desk.

'Sorry I'm late,' she said to the teacher, who nodded and smiled. Carrie slipped in behind her desk and propped her chin in her hands. She didn't even glance across at Jenny but looked straight at the blackboard, where Mrs Johnson was drawing a map.

Jenny felt an ache deep in her chest. That proved it! Carrie must be cross with her.

She tore a piece of paper from her notebook and scribbled: *Welcome back. I missed you*, on it. She slipped it onto her friend's desk. Carrie was smiling at David, now sitting at the desk to her left. Jenny's ache worsened.

Then Carrie looked over and smiled. 'Thanks,' she whispered, waving the tiny note. Almost as quickly, she turned her attention back to the blackboard.

Jenny was relieved and puzzled all at once. Carrie seemed . . . somehow . . . different. It was as though someone had blown out the spark that made Carrie who she was. This was a quieter Carrie, a Carrie held in check by some mysterious, invisible force. Even her eyes seemed to have lost their strong, sparkly blue colour, and faded to a wishy-washy pastel. What *was* going on?

When the bell went at mid-morning break, Jenny went straight to the part of the school grounds where she, Carrie, and sometimes Fiona, usually met. She sank onto the grass and waited. Each minute seemed to tick by like an hour.

'Where's Carrie?' Fiona asked, joining her.

'I don't know,' Jenny said carefully. 'She had her art lesson, but I thought she would meet us here at break.'

'Well, then, if she's coming to meet you she can't be cross with you, after all?' Fiona said.

'No,' Jenny agreed, not feeling at all sure of this. 'She didn't seem it.'

'Here she comes now,' Fiona said. 'Hi, Carrie!'

Jenny felt a hot flush creep into her face. She wanted to talk to Carrie alone. Now Fiona was here, she wouldn't get the chance.

Carrie, who usually came belting up the field singing the latest pop song, was walking slowly towards them. 'Hello,' she called, smiling.

'Are you better?' Fiona rushed in. 'Have you seen the new history teacher? He's Italian!'

'I've been worried about you,' Jenny said softly, annoyed with Fiona for prattling on. 'What was the matter?'

'Ugh! Some bug,' said Carrie, dismissively. 'Have I missed loads of work?'

'Yeah, loads,' said Fiona unhelpfully. 'Did you throw up?'

'Fiona!' Jenny said. She suddenly felt protective of Carrie. It was normally Carrie who kept an eye on Jenny. She realised she was peering closely at her friend, looking for signs that Carrie wasn't annoyed with her. All she could see was a calm, ashen face. There were no clues at all.

'Yes, I did, if you must know,' Carrie was saying to Fiona.

'Carrie . . .' Jenny began, but her sentence was interrupted by the bell. Break was over already. 'Meet here at lunch-break?' she asked hopefully.

'Um . . . no,' Carrie was vague. 'I'll be going home at lunch-time today. My mum's coming to fetch me.'

'Oh!' Jenny was stung. There would be no opportunity to talk to her friend at lunch-time. Jenny didn't know how much longer she could bear it. She looked at Carrie. Her pale, weary face showed no emotion but her eyes challenged Jenny. *Don't make a fuss*, they seemed to plead. *Don't say anything. Leave me alone.*

Carrie must have seen the hurt in Jenny's face. 'Can I borrow your books? To catch up on notes?' she asked.

Jenny was relieved. 'Yes, of course,' she said.

'Thanks,' Carrie said, and began to walk away. Jenny looked at Fiona helplessly.

'Well!' Fiona said, after Carrie had gone. 'She wasn't exactly friendly, was she? Maybe you're right, after all.'

Jenny nodded, preoccupied with her own thoughts. She realised she hadn't told Carrie about the SSPCA centre, and meeting Sarah. There was so much Jenny wanted to say. She was longing to have a chance to talk – really talk – to her friend.

Jess was especially affectionate when Jenny got home.

He wouldn't leave her side, sitting beside her when she sat, putting his nose gently into her hand or his paw into her lap. 'I'm OK, boy, really I am,' Jenny reassured him. But the collie seemed to sense the depths of Jenny's sadness and his eyes were dull.

'Why don't you go over and try talking to Carrie?' Mrs Grace suggested.

Jenny felt a stab of guilt. Poor Mrs Grace had been so kind. Jenny was certain she was sick of looking at her miserable, moping face. But she couldn't help herself. 'I've tried that, remember?' she said. 'Mrs Turner turned me away.' She was interrupted by a voice from the door.

'Hello, love.' Fraser Miles had taken off a wellington boot and was hopping around on one sock. 'You look as though you've just lost your best friend,' he joked.

'Dad!' cried Jenny, wounded by the remark.

Fraser Miles's face flooded with guilt. 'Oh, Jen!' he said, mortified, and pulled off the other boot. He padded over to her. 'Forgive me, lass. I was only joking – don't tell me this thing with Carrie is still going on?'

Jenny nodded, her eyes filling with tears.

'Something's up,' Mrs Grace told him, slipping a comforting arm round Jenny's sagging shoulders.

'And it's clear Carrie won't share whatever's troubling her with Jenny.'

'Would you like me to try and talk to Mrs Turner?' Fraser asked.

'No!' Jenny said quickly. 'Thanks, but that would make me look desperate. I have got other friends . . . I suppose,' she trailed off. It was unthinkable, losing Carrie as a friend.

'Go over there!' Mr Miles urged. 'Go and hammer on the door and ask what's going on. Haven't you got an excuse for a visit?'

Jenny's face brightened. She suddenly remembered the school work. Jess, looking at her and pricked up his ears. 'Yes, that's it. I promised her she could have a look at my school books – the work she missed when she was away. That's the perfect reason to go round. After all, she did ask for my help,' she said.

'Well, then . . .' said Fraser, relieved to see Jenny more determined. 'I think this calls for a cup of good, strong tea, Ellen!'

'I'll put the kettle on,' Mrs Grace said, smiling.

It began to rain just as Jenny left the house to visit Carrie. It was grey and showery, which suited Jenny's mood. Jess walked solemnly beside her, his tail out straight. He seemed reluctant to bound ahead in his usual fashion, preferring to keep pace with Jenny.

The sky was the colour of an old bruise by the time she reached Cliff House. Rain was pelting at her from every angle and she ran, trying to dodge it, until she arrived in a rush at the front door. She was soaked, but pleased about it. Surely Carrie's mum couldn't turn her away in this weather.

'Oh, Jenny,' said Mrs Turner, matter-of-factly, opening the door. 'It's you.' She peered out, as though she had only just noticed the change in the weather. 'Gosh, just look at that rain! You'd better come in. And Jess too . . . come through into the kitchen.'

Jenny stepped into the hall and slipped off her shoes. She wiped her wet face with the flat of her hands. 'I've brought these books for Carrie,' she said, taking a plastic bag from inside her coat and following Mrs Turner.

The kitchen was brightly lit. Jenny loved the colours in the room. Carrie's mum was an artist and had brought the walls to life with warm, bright shades of deep yellow and strong green. It had always seemed a happy room to Jenny.

'Here, Jess,' said Mrs Turner. The collie trotted over and sat down while she rubbed him all over with an old towel. 'What a puddly day,' she said, and sighed.

'How's Carrie?' Jenny asked, looking down at her feet.

'She's in her bedroom,' Mrs Turner said, avoiding the question. 'I'll go up and see if she wants a bit of company, shall I?'

Jenny and Jess were alone in the kitchen. Jess lay down and put his nose on his paws. He gave a big sigh. 'It's all right, Jess,' Jenny whispered. 'There's bound to be an explanation for all this, you'll see.' She put a comforting hand on his head and looked around her.

There was a bunch of lavender in a little glass vase on the table in front of her. Under it was a letter. It was lying open, and the words 'Dr Ian David' caught Jenny's eye. Rather guiltily, she leaned forward to read it, looking first at the letter heading across the top of the page. It was from Greybridge Hospital.

Jenny scanned the typed letter quickly, knowing she had no right to do so. The brief words confirmed an appointment for Carrie to attend a clinic during the following week. That was all. Jenny felt her heart tighten in her chest. Hospital! Then Carrie was more sick than she was letting on. Jenny quickly replaced the vase and sat back in her chair. She felt herself tremble slightly. She heard Mrs Turner coming down the stairs.

'You can go up and see her, if you like,' Carrie's mum said, from the door. 'Leave Jess here with me. I'll bring up some drinks. Coke?'

'Yes, please. Thank you,' Jenny said, in confusion, picking up the carrier bag. Now that she was at last going to confront her friend, she felt tongue-tied with nerves.

'Jenny?' Mrs Turner said softly, as Jenny headed for the stairs. 'Don't stay too long, will you?'

Jenny stared at her. Then she remembered her manners. 'No, of course not, Mrs Turner,' she said. 'I won't stay long.'

The door to Carrie's room was closed. Jenny knocked lightly.

'Hi,' Carrie called, from the other side.

Jenny eased the door open and peered around it. 'Hello,' she said, as cheerfully as she could. 'I've brought you the books you wanted.'

Carrie was lying on her bed. She was propped up against several pillows, her feet crossed at the ankles. Her hair was loose, spreading around her in a cloud of red and making her face look a ghostly white by contrast. She was holding a comic in her hand.

'You shouldn't have bothered to come over in this rain,' Carrie said vacantly. 'It could have waited.'

Jenny sat on the chair in the room and looked at her friend. She couldn't think of what to say. In the awkward silence, Jenny thought she was going to cry. *Just say what you've come to say, Jenny*, she told herself. But her courage failed her.

'How are you . . . feeling?' she eventually asked Carrie.

'Fine,' Carrie replied, too quickly.

'Really?' Jenny pressed her.

'Oh, for heaven's sake!' Carrie said irritably. 'Stop looking at me like that.'

Tears stung Jenny's eyes and spilled down her cheeks. She couldn't hold them back any longer. A

great sob escaped from her. It sounded awful in the quiet of the room. She covered her face with her hands, hot with emotion.

Carrie said nothing. She didn't move.

'Carrie,' Jenny mumbled, through her tears. 'Please tell me . . . talk to me. Tell me what's wrong. What *is* it?'

## 7

Carrie swung her legs off the bed and sat facing Jenny. She pushed her springy hair behind her ears and gave a huge sigh. 'Oh, Jen,' she said, mournfully. 'I'm sorry for shutting you out.'

'Really?' Jenny asked hopefully. 'You've been so . . . different . . . at first I thought I'd upset you . . .'

'No, it's not that. It's just that I'm *angry* – at the whole world!' Carrie shouted, making her hands into fists and punching wildly at her pillow. Jenny was startled.

'But what's happened?' she said again. 'Please, you must tell me.'

'Well, OK,' Carrie said. 'But promise not to tell another living soul, right?'

'Right,' said Jenny. Her mind was racing, wondering what terrible thing Carrie was going to tell her. Surely, whatever illness she had, she could be made well again?

'Before I came to live here I was very ill,' Carrie said. 'Then I got better – but now the sickness has come back.'

'What kind of sickness?' Jenny wrinkled her nose and frowned.

'Leukaemia. Acute lymphoblastic leukaemia, to be precise. Cancer of the blood. It makes you feel rotten,' Carrie finished. She lay back on her bed and gazed up at a photograph of a basket of tiny kittens, pinned on the wall.

'But can't the doctors do something?' Jenny asked, thinking of the letter she'd seen on the kitchen table.

'They're trying,' Carrie told her. 'It isn't an easy thing to cure.'

'But you'll have to go into hospital?'

'Maybe,' Carrie said. 'You see, the cancer attacks the white blood cells, which are called lymphocytes, inside the marrow of your bones. I may have to have some new marrow to replace the sick marrow – that is, if they can find some for me.'

Jenny frowned at her friend. She was obviously very knowledgeable about this confusing illness. 'Why didn't you tell me you'd had it before?' she asked.

'I was trying to forget about it,' Carrie told her. 'I thought it was all behind me and I'd never have to think about it again. It was a horrible time,' she added.

'How did you catch it?' Jenny said.

Carrie smiled. 'You don't *catch* cancer!' she said. 'You just get it.'

'But how does it make you feel?' Jenny voice had a tremor in it.

'Tired – because I've got so many white blood cells being made in my bone marrow,' Carrie explained. 'It's bad to have too many of them, you see. They break down the marrow in your bones and seep out into your blood.'

Jenny chewed at a fingernail. There were so many questions going round in her head. She felt bewildered and afraid. 'You're going to get better . . . soon, though, aren't you?' she asked Carrie.

'Who knows?' Carrie shrugged and looked up at the ceiling.

'Who *knows*?' Jenny repeated, blinking. 'You mean, you may *not* get better?' The terrible truth of what she was hearing was beginning to sink in. Carrie didn't answer her.

'I don't want anyone to know, OK? Not even Fiona,' she said firmly.

'But . . . why not?' Jenny asked, faintly.

'I don't want people feeling sorry for me, that's why,' Carrie told her. She sat up again, frowning fiercely.

In a trice, Jenny was out of her chair. She threw her arms round Carrie and hugged her tight. 'You *are* going to get better!' she said. 'Of course you are. Think of all the wonderful medicines there are in the world today.' She spoke into Carrie's ear, their cheeks pressed together.

Carrie hugged her back. 'I'm scared, Jen,' she whispered.

'Carrie,' said Jenny, facing her. 'There are so many people who love you and want to help. We'll all help you! And I'm sure you're going to get better.'

Jenny didn't feel as confident as she sounded. Her words seemed hollow in her ears and inside, her tummy was churning with fear. What if Carrie didn't get better? Jenny realised, with a little shock, that she was going to have to be the strong one of the two of them, from now on. No more leaning on bright, devil-may-care, Carrie. Carrie would need Jenny's strength and support. She was going to have to be the positive one in the friendship to see her through.

'So many people love you,' she said again, '. . . and, look, here's one of them now!'

The door to Carrie's bedroom had been nosed open. Jess's head appeared in the crack. He peeped through hesitantly.

'Jess!' said Carrie, laughing. 'Hello, boy!' Jess bounded into the room, his tail wagging furiously. He pranced about, delighted to have discovered Jenny.

'Has Jess found his way up there to you?' called Mrs Turner from the stairs. She came into the room. 'I went outside to hang some washing on the line and he was out of the kitchen and upstairs in a moment.'

'It's nice to see him,' Carrie said, hugging the collie. She smiled at her mother as Jess licked her hand.

'Here are your drinks.' Mrs Turner put two glasses of Coke on the bookshelf. She turned and looked anxiously at Carrie and her face brightened. 'You look more cheerful!' she smiled at her daughter. 'I'm glad you came, Jenny.'

Jenny squeezed Carrie's hand. 'So am I,' she said.

\* \* \*

Jenny remembered to tell her friend about the SSPCA centre and what Sarah Taylor had said, and then she left Carrie to rest.

Walking up the lane through Graston towards Windy Hill later, Jenny gave in to her tears. She had been cheerful when she had said goodbye to Carrie but now there was no one about to see or hear her crying.

The first lights of early evening were coming on in the houses dotted about the hillside. Storm clouds were still glowering in a low, dark sky, though the rain had gone. Her shoulders shook as she walked and her throat ached from her sobbing. Jess, his tail drooping, slunk along at her side. From time to time, he pushed his cold, wet nose into the palm of her hand. 'I'm all right, Jess,' she stuttered. 'I'm just sad about Carrie.' The Border collie whined and hung his head.

Jenny wiped her eyes on her sleeve as she went through the gates of the farm. Ahead of her she saw her father, carrying a bale of straw into the big barn. She followed him in. It was gloomy inside and she was glad of it. She didn't want him to see her red, tear-stained face. 'Hi, Dad,' she said in a small voice.

Fraser Miles looked round. 'Jenny, love!' he said.

'How did your visit to Carrie go?'

Nell, Jess's mother, was sniffing her puppy all over, curiously identifying the strange places he'd visited. Jess's tail thumped in greeting, then he hurried over and lay quietly at Jenny's side. She had slumped onto a nearby bale.

'Ah . . . didn't go well?' Fraser Miles frowned. He titled Jenny's chin with his finger and looked into her troubled face.

Jenny crumpled. 'Oh, Dad,' she wept, 'Carrie wasn't cross with me. It's just that she's ill — she's got . . . leukaemia!' She blurted out the news that Carrie had made her promise to keep to herself.

'What?' Mr Miles was startled.

Jenny nodded miserably. 'Will she get better?' she pleaded, knowing that her father couldn't know the answer to this.

He sat down beside Jenny and put an arm around her. He had gone quite pale. 'There's always a chance, lass,' he said softly. 'But it might mean a long, brave fight.'

'She asked me not to tell you, or anybody, but there are so many questions I want answered. I didn't want to ask her too many,' Jenny said.

'Well, there are things that can be done,' Fraser Miles said. 'For a start, there is a type of treatment called chemotherapy. That's using special drugs that fight the abnormal cells growing in the body. That's what cancer is.'

'Carrie said something about getting some new bone marrow?' Jenny said.

'A transplant, yes,' Mr Miles nodded. 'I don't know a lot about it but I know that the doctors have to find someone whose bone marrow will be exactly the same as Carrie's. Then they take it out of the healthy person and put it into her.'

'But if nobody *knows* Carrie's sick, how will they be able to offer her their bone marrow?' Jenny wailed. 'I mean, could I give her some of mine?'

'Well, that's a noble thought,' Jenny's dad squeezed her shoulder. 'And a brave one, too. But I expect the right match of marrow is likely to come from people in Carrie's immediate family.'

'You won't tell anyone?' Jenny asked him. 'I promised her . . .'

'No, it will be our secret. And if you need to talk to someone other than Carrie about it, you'll come to me, won't you?' Mr Miles hugged her.

'I'm sorry that I'm not being more help to you on the farm,' Jenny said.

'I don't expect it, lass. You've got your own problems, just now,' her father replied.

Jess whimpered, looking up at Jenny with liquid brown eyes. She put out a hand to him. 'I've got you,' she said to her father, 'and I've got Jess. I'm a very lucky girl.'

Jenny was preoccupied during supper and hardly said a word. If Ellen Grace noticed, she didn't comment. 'I've made up a marvellous dish of leftover bits and pieces for Jess,' she told Jenny, brightly. 'Had a good old clear-out of the fridge. He'll have a feast tomorrow.'

Jenny smiled her thanks. 'I'm tired,' she said. 'I think I'll go to bed.'

'I'll let Jess out last thing, shall I?' Fraser Miles asked. He blew her a kiss. 'Sleep tight,' he said and winked. Jenny was glad she'd confided in her father. The news about Carrie was too much for her to bear all alone.

She walked slowly up the stairs to her bedroom. Her bedside lamp, with its creamy yellow shade, gave the room a lovely, lemony warmth. Jenny had chosen to have the walls painted yellow again when Windy Hill had been restored after the fire, and she was glad. It was a cosy, cheerful colour. A photograph of her beautiful mother stood in a frame on her desk, replacing the one she'd had of her as a young girl that had been charred to cinders. How she wished it were possible to tell her mother about Carrie, and to ask her what to do.

There was a faint scraping at the door. When Jenny opened it she found Jess was sitting outside, looking up at her lovingly, his tail swishing gently against the carpet on the landing. 'Oh, Jess,' Jenny smiled, her heart melting. 'Do Mrs Grace and Dad know you've come up here?'

The collie slipped quickly into the room and lay down on Jenny's carpet. His coat smelled of heather, and rain, and there was mud on all four of his white feet.

She sat on the floor beside him, and put an arm round his neck. 'I'm glad you're here,' she told him, smoothing his ears. Jess rolled over onto his back, all four feet in the air, so Jenny could tickle his tummy.

'You know, I'm going to be the best friend to Carrie *ever*,' Jenny said. 'I'm going to show her that she needn't be scared all on her own. Mum always said that sharing a problem halves it. You can help too, Jess. We've got to make her see that she doesn't have to hide away – and we've got to find somebody with healthy marrow in their bones to give to her.' Lying upside down, Jess blinked his caramel-brown eyes at her knowingly.

Jenny was suddenly more tired than she'd ever felt before. Her eyelids began to close. She slid down onto the carpet, curling up next to Jess, and closed her eyes. The warmth of the dog and his soft fur was comforting. She could feel Jess breathing.

'I don't know what I'd do without you,' she murmured, and fell asleep.

# 8

Sunlight slanted in through the gap in Jenny's curtains and woke her. She heard the crunch of boots on gravel in the farmyard below her window. Curled up in her duvet, she recognised her father's long, low whistle, as he put Jake and Nell through their paces, shepherding the young sheep to the field for grazing. These were familiar and comforting sounds, and they filled Jenny with a sense of security.

Then she became aware of another sound. A gentle snuffling, muddled with a more strenuous snore. She sat up, surprised, and looked to the floor. Jess was stretched out on his side, sleeping deeply. His back legs twitched and his nose quivered. He gave a grunt, then sighed.

'Jess!' whispered Jenny. 'How on earth did you manage to stay in here all night long? If Dad finds out . . .' Jess lifted his head. He blinked dopey eyes at her, then sat up and yawned. Stretching luxuriously, he reached out with a wet tongue to lick Jenny's cheek. She giggled. 'Good morning to you, too, sleepyhead.'

'Jenny?' There was a gentle tapping at the door.

'Ooh, quick!' Jenny said to Jess. 'Here's Mrs Grace . . .' The door opened.

Mrs Grace stepped into the room as Jess was trying to disappear under Jenny's bed. Only his tail stuck out. 'I can see you,' she said, trying not to smile. She turned to Jenny, 'Your father discovered you both asleep up here last night and decided to leave Jess with you. I can't think why . . . but don't think you're going to make a habit of it.' She chuckled.

'Oh, we won't, Mrs Grace,' Jenny grinned. 'Will we, Jess?' Jess popped his head out from under the bed. They could hear his tail thumping on the floor under the mattress.

'Up you get, love,' Ellen Grace said, opening Jenny's

curtains. 'You've had a little lie in – and you're going to be late for school if you don't hurry.'

Jess ran to the door and looked back at Jenny, his tail going from side to side. She laughed. 'Jess wants that feast you promised him last night,' she said, jumping out of bed.

Mrs Grace nodded. 'Don't be long,' she called, as she left the room.

Jenny ran lightly across the landing to the bathroom. Then, she remembered Carrie and her heart squeezed tight in her chest. 'Carrie!' she whispered, to herself. Carrie, too, would be waking up now – but to another day of feeling unwell, and frightened, and having to hide it. Jenny grabbed her toothbrush. Her friend needed her. There was not a minute to waste.

On the way to the hall for assembly, Jenny managed to get Carrie alone. 'At breaktime,' she said, 'will you meet me somewhere other than our usual place?'

'What for?' said Carrie, glumly.

Jenny couldn't get over the change in her friend. Her energy and enthusiasm had drained away. The vitality and curiosity she had so envied in Carrie had gone.

'Just meet me, will you?' Jenny smiled. 'Outside the history room, OK?'

Carrie nodded, and looked down at her feet. Jenny felt a surge of triumph. At least she wouldn't have to worry about Fiona, and possibly David, tagging along, and would be able to talk to Carrie openly.

Carrie was waiting when Jenny arrived at their meeting place at lunch-time. She was picking at a packet of crisps. 'I'm never even hungry any more,' she announced, as Jenny came over and sat down. Carrie held out the crisps. 'D'you want these?'

'Thanks,' Jenny took them. She noticed that Carrie's eyes were wet. 'Are you OK?' she asked.

Carrie shook her head. 'We've had some bad news,' she said. 'Some friends of my mum and dad have been tested to see if the marrow in their bones matched mine . . .'

'And . . .?' Jenny was staring at Carrie, her hopes were high.

'They don't,' she said. 'Marrow has to be genetically compatible . . .'

'What?' Jenny said. 'What's that?'

'Matched exactly to my own marrow, to fit in with mine, you know. But it doesn't.' Carrie sighed. 'Neither Mr nor Mrs Bailey's.'

'Could I have a go?' Jenny said, her eyes shining. 'You know I *would* . . . what do you have to do?'

'You have to have your blood tested, first. Then, if the tests show that it's any good to me, you go into hospital for a bit. They stick a needle into your hip and pull out some marrow, then test it. It's called aspiration,' Carrie explained.

Jenny winced. 'Ouch,' she said, then regretted it. 'Oh, but I'd do it, Carrie,' she added quickly, loyally. 'If it would help you to get better.'

'You get these neat little puncture marks in your skin, just like a vampire bat has feasted on you,' Carrie said, showing a spark of her old sense of humour.

Jenny laughed.

'But there's got to be a perfect match of cell tissue,' Carrie went on, 'or my body will reject it.' It sounded complicated to Jenny.

'Isn't there anybody else you could ask to give you some of their marrow?' she asked. 'Some of the other people in your family, maybe?'

'Tried them all,' Carrie stated. 'The last time I was sick, we tried them. There is something called a register of donors – a place where anyone can just go in and give their blood and marrow for testing. Then it's kept in a kind of bank for sick people who might need it.'

'And?' Jenny urged. 'Have you been to this bank?'

'Yes,' Carrie sighed. 'There is nothing in there that's a match for me.'

'But there must be!' Jenny cried.

Carrie shook her head. 'Everyone has to die,' she reasoned, though her lower lip was wobbling. 'I'll just die a little sooner, that's all.'

'You're not going to die!' Jenny said. 'You're not! That's why you've got to tell everyone about your sickness, Carrie. The more people that know about it, the more people there will be to help you.'

'I suppose you're right,' Carrie said quietly. 'I've definitely felt better since I told you about it.'

Jenny smiled. 'And it'll get difficult to pretend, won't it?' she asked. 'People would wonder about you, and whisper and things. It's best to tell them.'

'I will have to go into hospital soon to have my next drug treatment, anyway. So I won't be at school for days at a time. Also, my hair will probably fall out. It did last time,' Carrie said.

Jenny tried to imagine Carrie without her lovely mop of coppery red hair and began to cry.

Carrie put an arm round her. 'Don't cry, Jen,' she said.

'It's OK. We're going to find someone to give you their bone marrow,' Jenny said through her tears, with as much determination as she could. 'We *are*.'

'Yes,' said Carrie, smiling. 'Yes, you're right. There might be a chance. You'll help me, won't you?

As the bell went for the end of break Jenny hugged her, reluctant to let her go.

Jenny told Mrs Grace about Carrie's sickness. Remembering the way Carrie had tried not to give in to her tears when she had spoken about dying made Jenny cry all over again.

'Oh, Jenny, love,' Mrs Grace said sadly, putting her arms round Jenny and holding her tight. 'It's always a very frightening thing when someone we love is so ill. You feel hopeless, don't you?'

'That's it,' sobbed Jenny, burying her face in Mrs Grace's shoulder, 'that's exactly how I feel. All sort of hopeless inside. I want to do something to help, but I don't know what.'

'Well, it sounds to me as though you're doing just what Carrie would want. You're being positive and showing her you care. That's a good start,' she said. Mrs Grace smoothed Jenny's hair.

It felt lovely and made her a bit calmer, as though she didn't have any more tears to cry. It wasn't the same as it might have been talking to her mother, but Ellen Grace was kind and Jenny was beginning to feel the housekeeper really cared about her. She realised that working at Windy Hill wasn't *just* a job for Mrs Grace any more. It was her father, herself, and Matt and Jess, that mattered to her. Shyly, Jenny wound her arms round Mrs Grace's neck. She kissed her lightly on her rosy, scented cheek. 'Thank you,' she said. 'Thanks for being here.'

Then Jenny pulled away and took the handkerchief Mrs Grace offered her. She blew her nose. There was a slight noise and she looked up at the door to see her father standing there. He was smiling.

On Friday Carrie was absent from school again. Jenny knew that she had gone into hospital for her chemotherapy. She had even given Jenny permission to ask the teacher to announce to the class that she had leukaemia and to explain what the sickness was.

'There is every chance that Carrie will get well,' said Jenny's form teacher, 'but I want to ask you all for your understanding. I expect you to be gentle and kind and not make Carrie feel awkward or alone. She will need the support of all of us.'

'Can we catch it from her?' Fiona asked Jenny later, miserably.

'You don't *catch* cancer, silly,' Jenny retorted, remembering Carrie's words. 'You just get it.'

'Carrie hasn't even been to see the birds down at the centre yet,' David remembered gloomily.

'Neither have I!' Fiona said. 'I'd like to go.'

'Then we'll go, shall we?' Jenny said, trying to be cheerful and strong for Carrie's other friends. 'Let's go today after school and see how they're getting on.'

'Oh, OK. Meet you on the cliff path at, say, four o'clock?' David agreed. He forced a smile.

'Yes,' Fiona nodded. 'I'll be there, too.'

Jenny decided to leave Jess at Windy Hill. A bird hospital was no place for a collie, even though Sarah Taylor had welcomed him warmly the last time he'd been there. Jenny knew that Jess would behave perfectly, as always, but she didn't want any of the birds to be frightened.

She changed into jeans and a sweatshirt, ran a brush through her honey-brown hair and took the stairs two at a time. Down in the kitchen, Mrs Grace was grating cheese onto a plate. She looked up. 'Are you off somewhere, Jenny?'

'Down to that bird centre place, with David Fergusson and Fiona. I thought I'd leave Jess behind, but I want to spend a little time with him first,' she said. Jess, who was lying just beneath the table on which Mrs Grace was now slicing through a loaf of chunky wholemeal bread, looked up as she spoke and put his head to one side.

'Sorry, Jess,' Jenny stroked him. 'But you'd only have to stay in the waiting-room, like last time.'

'Have a sandwich before you go?' Mrs Grace suggested. 'I'm making a heap of them for your father.'

'Where is he?' Jenny asked, taking one from the plate and biting into it. 'Hmmm, yum,' she mumbled, her mouth full.

'Up in the top field,' Mrs Grace told her. 'Several of the ewes are close to having their lambs now.'

'The first spring lambs!' Jenny breathed. 'Oh, and I've been so wrapped up with Carrie I've hardly spent any time out in the fields.'

'Well, we've had fine weather,' Mrs Grace said, pleased. 'It should be a good lambing this season.' Ellen Grace had grown up in the region and so she knew that the harsh Borders climate could be tough on newly-born lambs.

Jenny whistled and Jess's head shot up. 'Come on, boy,' she said, swallowing the last mouthful of her sandwich. 'Race you to the top field.'

★　★　★

# THE DISCOVERY

Jenny found her father examining a heavily pregnant ewe.

'You win, Jess!' she yelled, as she reached the fence to the field moments after the collie. She was out of breath and her tummy ached, and even Jess's sides were heaving as he panted. Mr Miles waved and Jenny climbed over the stile to join him. Jess squeezed under the wire and kept to her heel.

'It's nice to see you up here, lass,' smiled Jenny's dad. He let go of the sheep, and it ambled off, bleating, to the rest of the flock.

'I came to say I'm sorry for not showing more interest in the lambing. It isn't that I don't care about the farm any more. It's just that I've been so busy thinking about Carrie,' Jenny said.

'I know that, love,' Fraser Miles smiled. 'Being a good friend to someone who needs you is more important than being a good farmer's daughter.' He sat down on the slope, his big wellington boots stretched out before him and crossed at the ankles. He patted the grassy mound beside him.

Jenny joined him, leaning against his woolly jumper and sighing. 'Our teacher told the class about Carrie today,' she said, plucking the flecks of straw from his sleeve. 'Don't you think it's better now that everybody knows?'

'Aye, I do,' her father agreed, 'Far better than living with a secret.'

'A terrible secret,' Jenny said in a small voice.

Fraser Miles slipped an arm round her. 'It's not been an easy time, Jen love,' he said quietly. 'Mum . . . going . . . then the fire, and that unfortunate business with Marion . . .'

'Don't remind me!' Jenny shuddered. She hated to think of the horrible time when Marion Stewart had tried to poison Jess. The estate agent was a friend of Fraser Miles and she had come to stay at Windy Hill while Mrs Grace had been in Canada. Marion hadn't liked Jess, who had shown an unusual hostility towards her. She had wanted him out of the way – and had almost succeeded. But ultimately, Jess had revealed to everyone Marion's true colours. Jenny reached out for Jess, and pulled him closer. She could not imagine a life without her beloved dog.

'I'd better go,' she said, jumping up. 'I'm meeting David and Fiona and we're going down to the SSPCA centre. Can I leave Jess here with you?'

'Of course you can,' grinned Mr Miles. 'He can learn a few more lessons from his mother and father. See you at suppertime, love?'

'Yep,' said Jenny. 'Now, stay there, Jess. Good boy.'

The collie's face fell. His ears went down and he put his chin on his paws.

'She's coming back!' Jenny heard her father laugh, as she went off down the hill.

Even though it had been several days since the tanker's accident, oiled birds were still being found along the coast, and brought in to the SSPCA centre by concerned volunteers. The holding pens were full of recovering birds, huddling together, shivering, under the heat lamps.

Jenny, David and Fiona were taken through to the room with all the hosepipes, where they found Sarah Taylor washing a furious-looking puffin.

Sarah hardly glanced up as she greeted them. 'He's not enjoying this one bit, poor mite,' she said sympathetically.

Fiona covered her eyes as the high-pressure shower blasted against the bird's chest, parting the feathers to the pink skin beneath.

'Isn't that water too hot?' David asked, amazed at the steam coming off the bird. 'Won't it burn it?'

'No,' Sarah assured him. 'The water needs to be really hot, as hot as the bird can bear, to loosen and soften the oil. That's the only way we can get it off.'

'What about using soap?' Jenny asked, feeling

desperately sorry for the poor puffin.

'We do use soap,' Sarah said. 'We wash as much oil as we can off first, then use a special detergent, like washing-up liquid. Then the bird is rinsed again, in soft water, to make certain that all the soap is out of its plumage.'

'How long does it take for them to recover?' Fiona asked, peeking at the struggling bird through a gap in her fingers.

'Usually about a week or two,' Sarah said. She was massaging the liquid soap into the feathers of a small, outstretched wing. The puffin kept turning its head, trying to grab her glove with its beak. 'But, sadly, some don't make it.'

'Oh, that's such a shame,' Jenny said.

'Well, we do our very best to save them,' Sarah told her. 'We feed them a gourmet diet – sand eels and best quality sprats – to build them up. They have a swimming-pool too, to make them feel at home.'

'Then, when they are fat and healthy again, what then?' David wanted to know.

'The SSPCA has the job of returning them to the sea,' Sarah smiled. 'Actually, some of the birds you brought in are just about ready to go back. Ah . . . here's Debbie, coming to help me to get this little fellow dry and warm again. There!' Sarah handed the dripping puffin to an assistant, who had come over with a towel. Sarah knelt and began to hose out the porcelain basin, washing the traces of oil and feathers away down the plughole.

'Does anyone want to give me a hand over here?' someone called.

'That's Kim,' Sarah explained. 'She's taking some birds out to the pool. Do you want to help her?'

'Yes please!' David said and hurried over.

'I do, too, please,' Fiona followed David. Before Jenny could move, Sarah spoke.

'How's your friend? Carrie, is it?' she asked.

'Not too good,' Jenny said. She squatted down beside Sarah. 'I've found out what was wrong with her. She's got leukaemia.'

Sarah drew in her breath sharply. She stopped what she was doing and gave Jenny her full attention. 'What shocking news. Poor girl,' she said softly.

'She doesn't mind my telling,' Jenny added. 'She's decided it's best if people know. You see, Carrie needs a bone marrow transplant to get well. Only, she hasn't found any new marrow that fits in with hers.' Jenny's face darkened. She felt a stab of fear, just thinking about Carrie.

Sarah sighed and gave a little shudder. 'I'm so sorry,'

she said. 'I know exactly how helpless and afraid you must feel.'

'Really?' Jenny said, surprised. How could Sarah know? she wondered.

'My younger sister.' Sarah was almost whispering. 'She had leukaemia, too.'

'Did she . . . get better?' Jenny asked.

'No, Jenny, she didn't,' Sarah said. 'She died. Nearly a year ago. I tried to help her. I donated bone marrow, but the match wasn't right.'

'Oh, that's awful,' said Jenny, wondering if the match of one person's marrow to another could ever be right. It didn't seem very likely.

'I'd like to meet Carrie – really I would,' Sarah said, changing the subject. She stood up. 'You will bring her in to the centre, when she wants to come?'

'Definitely. She'd like that,' Jenny said.

'I must get on with my work now,' Sarah smiled. 'It was nice to see you again, and to meet Fiona.'

'I'd better be getting back home, anyway,' Jenny said. 'I'll go and find the others.'

'OK, Jenny,' Sarah said. 'They're out through that door over there, at the pool. I really must stop chatting and get working. Thanks for coming in to see us.'

'We'll come again,' Jenny said.

'Oh, by the way – which hospital does Carrie go to, do you know?' Sarah asked.

'Yes, it's Greybridge Hospital,' Jenny said. 'Why?'

'No reason,' Sarah said, picking up a gannet and striding across to the sink. 'Bye for now.'

# 9

Over the next ten days, Jenny had more than enough to keep her busy. When she wasn't at school, or doing her homework, she divided her time between visiting Carrie and helping her father with the lambing.

In the middle of all the rushing around, Matt, Jenny's brother, came home for the weekend. She was helping Mrs Grace pack up a basket of food to take up to her father in the top field, when Matt's motor-bike roared into the courtyard. His smiling face appeared round the kitchen door.

'Matt!' cried Jenny. 'You made it! Where's Vicky?' Vicky was Matt's girlfriend. She was doing the same course as he was at Agricultural College. Matt slung his bag and helmet to the floor and ruffled Jenny's hair.

Jess was leaping around in excitement, getting under Matt's feet. 'Whoa! Steady boy!' he told the collie, rubbing his ears affectionately.

'Welcome home, Matt,' smiled Mrs Grace: 'Your dad *will* be pleased to see you!'

'Sorry I couldn't get back sooner,' Matt said, making a face. 'We all had to go on this field trip. There was no way of getting out of it.'

'Where's Vicky?' Jenny asked again.

'She's gone home to visit her mum and dad,' Matt told her, helping himself to a slice of cold meat from the chopping board. 'How's the lambing going?'

'No problems, so far. There are eight lambs in the lambing barn, all doing well,' Jenny reported. She realised she sounded a little flat. She gave her brother a bright smile.

'You look terrible, Jen.' Matt was frowning at her. 'Dad been working you hard, instead of me?' he joked. His blue eyes twinkled at her.

'Oh,' said Jenny vaguely, 'it's not that. It's just we've been having a . . . . bit of a sad and difficult time lately.'

She reached for Jess, who was never far away. From under the table, he put his nose into her lap.

'What's this?' asked Matt, coming round and sitting beside Jenny. He peered into her face. 'Hey, what's up, little sis?' He looked concerned.

'I'll just take this lot out to the field, Jenny love,' Mrs Grace said, quietly. She lifted her basket. 'You have a chat with your brother. It *is* nice to have you home, Matt,' she added, and closed the door behind her.

'Carrie's got leukaemia.' Jenny said slowly.

'Oh . . . no,' Matt said. He looked stunned and was silent for a several seconds. 'That's nasty. Really nasty. Poor kid. Is she responding to treatment?'

'You mean the drugs?' Jenny asked. Matt nodded.

'I think so. She spent her second day in hospital this week. I've been visiting her at home each day. She feels sick most of the time so she can't go to school.'

'There's a good chance then – is there – that she'll get well again?' Matt said hopefully.

Jenny shrugged. 'Don't know, really,' she said. 'You see, Carrie had leukaemia before she came to live here. The drugs made her better that time. But now the sickness has come back.'

'Oh, poor girl,' Matt said.

'She needs a bone marrow transplant, Matt. Her own bone marrow is so damaged it can't mend itself. I want us all to be tested – you, Dad, Mrs Grace, even Vicky – all of us – to see if our marrow matches Carrie's,' Jenny was passionate. 'Will you do it?'

Matt blinked at her. She was squeezing his arm. 'Me?' he said. 'Us? But isn't Carrie more likely to find a match for her marrow among members of her own family?'

Jenny shook her head. 'She's tried all of them,' she said.

'Well, um, what does Dad say about this?' Matt wondered.

'I haven't asked him yet,' Jenny said. 'But I told Mrs Turner – and she's very grateful for the offer. At the moment, the doctors are looking through the register of donors – those are people who give their blood and marrow into a bank – to see if they can find anyone to match Carrie's.'

Matt gave a long, low whistle and sat back in his chair. 'Well, let's see what this donor bank turns up, shall we? If nothing comes of it, then, I'll get tested.'

'Thanks, Matt,' Jenny hugged him. 'I knew you would.'

'Right,' said Matt, standing up. 'I'm going to have a wash and get changed and then I'll go and give

Dad a hand with the ewes, OK?'

'OK.' She grinned.

Thoughts were racing around in Jenny's head. She took a moment to groom Jess's coat. His long fur had become tangled in places and he had a clump of burrs in his tail. Jess looked up as Jenny showed him the brush, then, obediently stretched out on his side on the kitchen floor. He gave a patient sigh.

'Yes,' Jenny chuckled. 'I know you're not particularly fond of being in the beauty parlour, but you're a mess!' She began to comb out his long hair and Jess rolled onto his back, allowing her to brush his tummy.

'Good boy,' she said, kissing the top of his nose. Next she tackled his knotty tail as he lay upside down. Jess sneezed, then cocked his ears. Suddenly, he rolled over and jumped up, giving a series of excited little yaps.

'What is it?' Jenny asked, as Jess shook himself all over. 'Don't think you're going to fool me into letting you off being groomed because . . .'

'Hi!'

Jenny looked round. Carrie was at the door.

'Carrie!' Jenny threw the brush aside. It went clattering across the floor. She leaped up and hugged her friend. Carrie was smiling, though her skin was ashen. She wore a French beret, set at a jaunty angle. Her hair had been cut short.

Jenny tried not to show her surprise. 'I like your hair.' she grinned at Carrie. 'It looks great.'

'Suits me, doesn't it?' Carrie spun around, her arms outstretched, pretending to be a fashion model.

'Why have you come? It's great to see you! How are you feeling?' The questions tumbled out. It was so good to see Carrie when she wasn't lying down looking bored.

'I'm feeling a bit better,' Carrie said. 'So I've come to see the lambs. Mum dropped me off.'

'We've got eight, or nine . . . I've lost count,' Jenny told her. 'Come on, let's go and see.'

Jess streaked ahead of Jenny, his tail waving happily as he bounded across the yard. Nell and Jake, Jess's parents, were dozing against the big barn in the morning sun. Nell looked up, and thumped her tail in the dirt in greeting. Jess nuzzled his mother under her ears, then looked around for Jenny.

'In here,' Jenny said, holding the door open for Carrie.

It was warm inside the barn. The only light came from the weak spring sunshine, slanting in through the cracks in the timber roof and criss-crossing on the straw on the floor. It smelled of freshly cut grass and lanolin, a combination Jenny loved. Fraser Miles had used the big bales of hay to make partitions for the pregnant ewes, providing a cosy and safe environment for the lambs to be born in.

'Why aren't they having their lambs out in the field?' Carrie asked, as the ewes turned their curious yellowy eyes on her.

'Sometimes Dad brings the first-time mothers in here,' Jenny replied. 'It's easier to keep an eye on them at night. Look!'

A lamb had been born moments before Jenny and Carrie had come into the barn. The ewe, her sides still heaving with her effort, had turned to investigate the tiny bundle that had slipped from her and was now lying still in the straw. She began to lick gently at it, rolling it over with her nose and lifting its tiny tail to inspect it all over.

'Oh that's amazing,' breathed Carrie, her hands clasped to her chest. 'Look how tiny it is! How sweet.'

'She's establishing a bond with her baby,' Jenny told her. 'If he ever gets separated from his mother out in the field, she will be able to find him.'

'Another successful birth,' said Fraser Miles, stepping up quietly from the shadows of the back of the barn. 'Hello, Carrie lass,' he added, warmly. 'How are you?'

'I'm OK, thanks, Mr Miles,' Carrie said. Fraser Miles stepped over into one of the hay bale partitions. Gently, he lifted a tiny dozing lamb – born, Jenny guessed, the day before. The little black head was still floppy and weak. He held it out to Carrie.

'Ah, it's so sweet,' she said, taking it into her arms. She stroked its curly coat. The lamb bleated pitifully, calling to its mother. Its tongue was pink against the coal-black of its face. 'You're gorgeous,' Carrie told the lamb. She sat down in the straw with it and put her finger gently into its mouth. The lamb began to suckle, making Carrie giggle.

'Any news, love?' Mr Miles asked gently. Jess had sidled up quietly. He lay down between Jenny and Carrie, his ears flat, head erect, his nose quivering, watching the tiny lamb with the dedication of a well-trained sheepdog. Jenny felt proud of Jess's strong instinct.

'Not really,' Carrie said, keeping her eyes on the lamb in her lap. 'I'm going to have a bone marrow transplant, if they can find someone whose marrow matches mine,' Carrie told him. 'They're still looking for a donor.'

'Right, lass,' smiled Fraser Miles. 'You'll keep us posted, won't you? On how it all goes – and if you need anything, any help . . .' he trailed off, looking uncertain. Then he brightened. 'Jenny, why don't you take advantage of the fact that Carrie is feeling better and take her to see those birds you rescued from Puffin Island?'

'Good idea!' cried Jenny. 'Can you come, Carrie?'

'Not today,' Carrie said. 'But I could go tomorrow. Are they open on Sunday?'

'Yes,' Jenny said, eagerly. 'Seven days a week.'

'I'll ask my mum, but I'm sure it'll be fine,' Carrie said. She bent over the tiny lamb. Its wobbly head was nodding sleepily. She smoothed its curly brow and smiled.

Jenny felt hopeful, looking at her friend. There was now a faint spread of colour in her cheeks. Perhaps there was a chance that she would soon be completely well again. In the meantime, there was tomorrow at the SSPCA centre, and introducing Sarah Taylor to Carrie, to look forward to.

# 10

Jenny woke up on Sunday feeling happier than she had for a long time. She was going to spend time with her best friend, away from Carrie's bedroom. She felt sure it would cheer Carrie up and take her mind off her illness for a while.

It was a brilliant day. The sky was clear and blue. Looking out of the window of her bedroom, she saw Matt herding the ewes out of the barn, getting them ready for the field. The lambs skittered about on their spindly legs, trying to keep up with their mothers, making a dreadful racket.

Nell and Jake were crouched in position, circling, ever-watchful, waiting to spring forward and ease the lambs back into line should they break free from the group. Jenny never tired of watching the dogs work. How she would love to reward their loyalty by bringing them into the house on a cold night and cuddling them up on a blanket beside the Aga stove. But rules were rules, she knew that. Nell and Jake were working dogs, not pets.

She thought of Jess, who'd be wanting his breakfast. Jenny dressed quickly, and hurried downstairs.

'He couldn't wait,' announced Ellen Grace, smiling. 'It was the smell of the bacon frying that did it.' Jenny burst out laughing. Jess had his nose in an enormous bowl. Without looking up, he wagged his tail hard. Then, having licked the last traces of egg and bacon from the dish, he rushed over to Jenny and licked her bare knee.

'Ooh! An eggy good morning kiss! Thanks, Jess,' she said with a giggle.

'Your father said to tell you that twins were born in the night,' Mrs Grace said.

'Oh, how lovely,' Jenny grinned. 'But I haven't time to see them this morning.'

'No, Carrie should be here soon,' Mrs Grace

remembered, glancing at her watch. 'How nice for you both to be out and about – just like the old days.'

'I'm so pleased she seems to be better,' Jenny said, putting a rasher of bacon between two slices of bread.

'Jenny,' Mrs Grace's tone was cautious. 'Remember that Carrie might have days when she's not feeling so good, won't you? It won't always be like this.'

'How do you mean?' Jenny frowned.

'Well, she'll have to have further treatment at the hospital. The drugs they give her will make her sick again,' Mrs Grace was gentle.

'I know,' Jenny sighed. She came over and gave Mrs Grace a hug. 'I won't get my hopes up too high, I promise. Or, at least, I'll try not to.'

Just then, Mrs Turner's flower-painted mini pulled into the drive, driven by Mr Turner.

'Here she is,' said Ellen Grace, as Jenny pulled away and dashed outside.

'Hello, Carrie,' she called. Her friend was wearing her woollen beret again. She was smiling, Jenny saw with relief, but she stayed in the car. 'Hello, Mr Turner.'

'Hello, Jenny,' he said, getting out. 'Do you fancy being driven down to the SSPCA centre? I'd like to get a look at these birds you rescued for myself.'

'Yes,' Jenny said. 'But, can Jess come? I hate to leave him and they don't really mind him being there.'

'Sure,' said Carrie's father. 'You jump into the back with him.' Jess looked at Jenny expectantly. He put his head to one side.

'In you get,' she instructed. Mr Turner pulled his seat forward and Jess slithered into the back.

Jenny got in beside him. 'Bye, Mrs Grace,' she called. Ellen's face appeared at the kitchen window. She blew Jenny a kiss and waved to Carrie.

'Have a good time,' she called.


'This is Carrie Turner,' Jenny told Sarah. Carrie grinned at the young woman and stuck out her hand.

'Nice to meet you,' she said.

Sarah shook hands. 'Hi, Carrie,' she said. 'I'm a bit filthy,' she added, looking down at her soiled, wet clothing. 'We've had a couple of very angry birds in the shower this morning!'

'You're doing a great job,' Mr Turner said. 'May I look around?'

'Sure,' Sarah said. 'We've had a good recovery rate since the oil spill. You'll find the more active birds out in the pool, over that way.' Sarah pointed.

'Thanks,' said Mr Turner, wandering away.

'How are you feeling?' Sarah had turned to Carrie.

'Jenny tells me that you have leukaemia.'

Jenny's heart turned over. Wasn't this just a bit too direct? Would Carrie be cross that Sarah knew? But, to her relief, Carrie smiled. 'Yes, that's right,' she said. 'But we're going to fight it, aren't we, Jen?'

'That's the spirit!' grinned Sarah. 'Now, are you two up for a bit of hard work?'

'Yes!' Jenny and Carrie spoke together. Carrie's eyes were bright.

'A few of the volunteers are taking some of the birds back to Puffin Island today. There are only traces of the oil left now, so it's quite safe. And I'm happy to report that they're well enough to go back to sea!' Sarah told them. 'Do you want to go along?'

'Oh, please!' Jenny begged. 'We'd love to . . . wouldn't we, Carrie?'

'Love to what?' said Mr Turner, coming over.

'Dad,' Carrie began, 'Sarah says some of the birds we saved from Puffin Island are ready to go back home today. Can we go along and see them set free? Please?'

'Yes, well, I expect so, if we take it gently, Carrie,' he said, quietly. 'We can go in our own boat, and follow the SSPCA boat out there, OK?'

'Oh, great,' Sarah was pleased. 'You've got your own boat!'

'Can Jess come too, Mr Turner?' Jenny asked. He grinned and nodded in reply. Jess was waiting in the reception room.

'Are you coming?' Carrie asked Sarah. Jenny could see Carrie had warmed immediately to Sarah.

'Um, no,' Sarah said. A shadow crossed her face. She glanced away. 'I've got an appointment, which I can't miss,' she said. 'But you go along, and you can tell me all about it when I next see you.'

'Oh . . .' Jenny was disappointed.

'I'll take you to where the birds are being loaded into our boat. You can meet Jack and Karen, our helpers. Then, just follow them out to Puffin Island.'

'Thanks,' Mr Turner said.

'I should say thank you to you!' Sarah laughed, linking arms with Carrie and Jenny. 'You did a great job bringing those birds to us the way you did. You've saved their lives. You deserve to see them go back to their island. Now, come with me.'

'I'll just go and get Jess,' Jenny said, and darted away to the reception area. Jess was lying down, his nose on his paws. He rushed towards Jenny when he saw her, and, as usual, greeted her as though he hadn't seen her in months.

'You're a good boy,' she told him. 'We're going out on the boat, Jess! Come on! Let's catch up with the others.' Jess barked, then trotted along at Jenny's side.

Outside, a trailer was being loaded with a cargo of boxed birds. It was hooked up to a van, marked with the logo SSPCA. Jenny spotted the two helpers, dressed in waterproof clothing and rubber-soled shoes. Carrie and Mr Turner were watching the operation with interest.

'This is Jenny Miles,' Sarah introduced her,' And Jess . . . this is Jack Castle and Karen Keane.'

'Hello,' Jenny said shyly. She and Carrie watched for a bit, then, Mr Turner suggested they set off to the quay at Cliffbay.

'We'll meet you there,' Jack said pleasantly.

'Have a good day!' Sarah said. 'I hope to see you again, soon.' She smiled at Carrie, who smiled back warmly.

Mr Turner drove them down to where his boat lay bobbing on a gentle swell of calm sea.

'Lovely day for a trip out to the island,' he said. 'Feeling all right, Carrie?'

'Yep,' Carrie said gamely. She adjusted her beret, and climbed into the boat. 'I'm glad it's calm, though,' she said. 'What a lovely, friendly person Sarah is,' she added.

'A charming girl,' Mr Turner agreed. He started

the engine and the boat began to shudder and shake.

'There they are!' Jenny said, pointing. 'There's Jack and Karen, and the SSPCA boat.' Jess looked too, to where Jenny was pointing. He lifted his nose to the wind, then jumped up onto the wooden seat that ran around the insides of the boat and settled comfortably.

'You're a real old sea dog at heart,' Jenny told him, ruffling his ears.

Mr Turner waved to Jack, then the boat began to lift and fall as it swung out towards the open sea. The early morning mist and the bright sunlight made it difficult to see the outline of Puffin Island, but Mr Turner knew exactly which direction to go.

'Those birds are going to get a happy surprise,' Carrie said. 'I'll bet they thought they would never see their little island ever again.' Jenny sat close to Carrie, watching her protectively. She didn't want Carrie to get too tired, or start to feel seasick.

'It's going to be great to watch them when they suddenly realise they are home, and free,' Jenny thought out loud.

Carrie nodded but didn't reply. She was quiet while the boat ploughed along through the water. From time to time, her eyelids started to close, then she opened them quickly and gave a little shake.

Jenny said nothing, but her heart ached for her friend. How wonderful it would be if the doctors could find someone whose marrow matched Carrie's. Looking at her, Jenny wondered how much longer Carrie could wait.

'Nearly there,' she said, as Puffin Island came into view. Jess had been lying down. Now, he sat up and his tail began to swish happily from side to side.

When the boat had been safely anchored, Mr Turner disembarked, then he lifted Carrie down onto the shore, holding her in his arms like a baby. Jenny and Jess jumped onto the beach. Jenny's instinct was to dash across with Jess to where the SSPCA boat was unloading the boxes of birds, but she stopped herself. Carrie couldn't dash anywhere. When Mr Turner had put his daughter down, Jenny walked slowly, beside her. Jess seemed to sense this and he, too, walked sedately next to Jenny.

'Most of the oil has gone,' she said, looking around her. 'Isn't that great?'

'I can still see a few little patches of it,' Carrie said.

'You know, Puffin Island was very lucky to have escaped the major spill further along the coast,' Mr Turner said. 'The result of a spill near this bird sanctuary could have been a disaster.'

Jack and Karen had reached Puffin Island before

them. They had already lined up the boxes along the shoreline. As Jenny drew closer, she could see the cardboard was shifting about eerily on the shingle as the healthy birds inside struggled for their freedom. There was the sound of pecking, and the occasional squawk and call.

'Ready?' said Karen, to Jack.

'I certainly am,' he grinned. They began to open the flaps of the boxes.

Within seconds, the alert and frantic heads of a variety of birds – scoters and guillemots, puffins and razorbills – were popping up comically from their boxes. Beaks opened, heads swivelled, bright eyes blinked, wings flapped – and the boxes toppled over as the birds began to break free. Half running, half flying, they made for the sea, cawing and calling in panic.

Jenny was thrilled by it. She looked around for Jess and noticed that he had crouched low, and was inching forward, circling, his head moving from side to side, trying to keep an eye on the scrabbling, fleeing birds.

'Oh, Jess!' Jenny collapsed with laughter. 'Don't worry about it! These aren't sheep, they're birds.'

'That's his instinct coming out,' observed Mr Turner. 'You can't keep a good sheepdog down!'

'You're a sweetie,' said Carrie, patting his head.

Some of the birds had spread their wings and taken to the sky. They wheeled around, their beaks opening and closing, as though celebrating their freedom. Others were bobbing about in the waves, ducking their heads gleefully into the water.

'What a marvellous sight,' said Mr Turner.

'They're so happy to be back!' Jenny said. She was thinking how Carrie might have reacted to this scene before she'd become ill. The old Carrie would have whooped and shouted with joy; she would have done cartwheels across the sand. This Carrie stood watching quietly, her thin arms folded across her

tummy, a fixed, sad smile on her face.

'Come on, love,' said Mr Turner, putting a gentle hand on her shoulder. 'We'll get you home, now. Let's say our goodbyes, and get back in the boat.'

Carrie nodded. 'I'm so glad we came,' was all she said.

Back in Cliffbay harbour, Jenny helped Mr Turner to lock up the boat and pull the awnings down over the deck. Carrie sat down on a patch of grass, her arm round Jess's back. Her hand moved gently across his coat but her expression was blank and sad. Jess sat looking at her, as if he, too, was perplexed at the change in her.

'I'll bring some schoolwork round to your house this afternoon, if you like,' Jenny said brightly.

Carrie smiled and nodded and they got into the car. She was silent all the way home. Jenny didn't know what to say, so she said nothing. There was little point in forcing a merry conversation just for the sake of it.

As Mr Turner came slowly through the gates of Windy Hill, Jess barked happily.

'Looks like you've got a visitor,' observed Carrie's father.

Jenny peered out of the window of the mini as

they came to a stop in the yard. A car she hadn't seen before was parked there.

Carrie's head was resting against the back of the seat, and she sat up. 'Who?' she asked, without much interest.

'I don't know . . .' Jenny began, as the kitchen door opened.

Ellen Grace came out onto the top step. Jenny could see right away that she had been crying. Her heart squeezed tight in her chest. Standing behind her was Mrs Turner. Matt and Mr Miles were standing at the kitchen window. Jenny was relieved to see that her brother was smiling broadly. But, what on earth had happened? Why was Carrie's mum here? Why was everyone looking out for them?

'Let's get you out,' said Mr Turner, helping Carrie from the back of the car. 'It looks like your mother's here to meet us. Fraser must be having a little party . . .' Jess slipped past Carrie and up the steps.

'Mrs Grace, Mrs Turner . . .' Jenny ran forward. 'Is anything the matter?' Mrs Turner ran past Jenny and over to the car. She put her arms around her daughter and gave her a long, tight hug.

'We've had some news,' she told Carrie, her eyes filling with tears. 'Some wonderful news. Come inside, all of you.'

Jenny stood in the doorway of the kitchen and gaped. There was Sarah Taylor sitting at the pine table as though she was a regular visitor at Windy Hill. She was smiling gently, fussing Jess, who had gone over to greet her.

'Hello, Sarah!' Jenny said, surprised. 'Well, gosh . . . how . . . what . . .?'

'Perhaps,' Mr Miles said, 'we ought to let Sarah explain.'

'Good idea,' Matt piped up.

'I'll make some more tea,' said Mrs Grace.

Sarah went over to Carrie who was holding her mother's hand tightly, frowning in confusion.

'I've had some news today – from my doctor,' Sarah started. 'And I couldn't wait to share it. So I found out where the Turners live and then Carrie's mum and I came over here to find you all.' She took a long, shuddering breath.

Carrie stared at her, bewildered. Jenny had started to think that they had won an award for rescuing the birds.

'You see . . .' Sarah paused. 'My bone marrow is the exact match for yours, Carrie . . . And I'm going to be your donor.'

'What?' shouted Jenny, making Jess's ears prick up. He hurried over to her side and put up his paw.

142

Carrie sat down suddenly on the nearest chair, blinking.

'I was tested a year ago,' Sarah explained. 'It was when my sister was ill with leukaemia. I wanted to donate some marrow then, but I wasn't the right match for her. I was bitterly disappointed and, after Katie died, I felt as though I had failed her. Anyway, for a while, I couldn't face having any reminders of what had happened and so I withdrew my name from the National Register – that's the bank where they keep all donors on file. Then I heard about you, Carrie. And, as the test was already done, and you and I have the same doctor, all that had to be done was to check to see if my marrow was compatible with yours.'

'And it is?' Carrie said slowly, obviously struggling to take in what Sarah was saying. 'It really is?'

'It's a perfect match!' Mrs Turner cried, throwing her arms round Mr Turner's waist.

He put his cheek on the top of her head and squeezed his eyes shut. 'How can we begin to thank you, Sarah?' he said. His voice came out as a croak.

'I'm so pleased to be able to help.' Sarah smiled. 'I felt so . . . hopeless, when my sister . . .' She broke off, as Carrie reached up and gave her a hug.

'Thank you!' Carrie whispered. Then, looking

round, Carrie caught Jenny's eye. She rushed over and grabbed Jenny round the waist. 'I'm going to get well! I'm going to get better!' she chanted, dancing Jenny around the kitchen. Jess barked gleefully, his tail going in circles.

'Mind that teapot!' warned Mrs Grace, loudly, wending her way through the noisy crowd with her tray. Jenny looked at Carrie. Two bright spots of pink had appeared in her cheeks, bringing her face alive, and her eyes flashed with a sparkle Jenny hadn't seen in days. She didn't know whether to laugh or cry with relief and happiness.

Mrs Grace had found room for the tray on the table. Jenny saw her take a tissue out of her sleeve and dab at her eyes. She went over and gave her a hug.

'A happy day!' sniffed Ellen Grace. 'What a *happy* day, Jen, love.'

'It is,' Jenny said, kissing Mrs Grace on a cheek wet with tears of joy. 'One of the very best.'

# THE
# GIFT

*The Gift*

**Special thanks to Ingrid Hoare**

Text copyright © 2000 Working Partners Ltd
Created by Working Partners Ltd, 1 Albion Place, London W6 0QT
Illustrations copyright © 2000 Sheila Ratcliffe
Jess the Border Collie is a trademark of
Working Partners Limited

First published as a single volume in Great Britain in 2000
by Hodder Children's Books

# 1

'What's this?' Jenny Miles glanced down at her feet, then into the warm brown eyes of Jess, her Border collie. 'It's a toy, Jess. Who does it belong to?'

Jenny looked around, but she and her dog were alone in the fields above Cliffbay. Her sweeping gaze took in the distant, red rooftops of Windy Hill, the sheep farm where she lived in the village of Graston.

Jess dropped the toy on Jenny's shoe. It was the battered remains of a doll. Then the collie took it gently into his mouth, tossed it aside and pounced on it with both front paws.

'Oh, I know!' Jenny laughed. 'I forgot to bring your *ball*, is that it?' She ruffled the sleek fur on his head, then picked up the toy and threw it – overarm – with all her might. Jess raced after it, barking happily.

Jenny grinned at him. *I should have remembered your ball*, she thought, feeling guilty. She had been so wrapped up in thinking about Carrie, she had overlooked the fun Jess often had on his walks with a tennis ball. Her thoughts switched again to her friend.

Jenny had recently found out that Carrie Turner had leukaemia – a type of cancer that was affecting her blood. She and Jenny had been best friends since one day at school when Carrie, her green eyes ablaze, had taken Jenny's side in an argument with Fiona MacLay. Jenny hadn't dared to hope that the new girl, a bubbly and confident redhead, would want her as a friend. She could hardly believe it when Carrie had invited her out on a day trip to Puffin Island. Their friendship had gone from strength to strength. Now Carrie was facing a frighteningly uncertain future, and Jenny was trying to do everything she could to help her.

Jenny looked over at Jess. The collie had given up trying to make the doll bounce and had decided to roll on it instead. He yelped with pleasure as he wiggled about on his back, all four of his white feet up in the air. Jenny burst out laughing.

'First sign of madness, laughing at nothing, all on your own.'

Jenny started and looked behind her. 'Oh!' she said. 'You scared me, David.'

David Fergusson grinned and stooped to let his Border collie, Orla, off her lead. 'Sorry! Have I missed something funny?' he asked, pushing his curly dark hair away from his eyes.

'I was laughing at Jess,' said Jenny, watching Orla bound towards her playmate.

David and his father had moved recently to Cliffbay, and David had joined Greybridge Senior, Jenny's school. He was a secretive boy, and hard to get to know, but Jenny liked him as much as Jess liked Orla.

David's face suddenly clouded. 'How's Carrie?' he asked. 'She's missing quite a bit of her schoolwork, isn't she?'

'I don't think she's feeling well enough to worry about school,' Jenny said gravely. 'But she's cheerful and full of hope,' she added brightly. 'Did you know she's found someone who is going to donate their bone marrow to her?'

David wrinkled his nose. 'Yes,' he said, 'but I'm not exactly sure what that means.'

'It's called a transplant,' Jenny explained, walking in step with David behind the dogs. 'The doctor can put healthy blood into Carrie's sick blood to try and make her better. Only, the blood they put into her has to be *exactly* the same type as her own, or her body will reject it.'

'I see . . . I think . . . but what exactly is *marrow*?' David looked puzzled.

'Bone marrow is the tissue which makes the blood cells,' Jenny said knowledgeably, adding: 'Carrie's explained it all to me.'

'When will she have this . . . transplant?' David asked.

'First, she has to have very high doses of a drug, a treatment called chemotherapy,' Jenny said. 'It's to destroy the sick bone marrow and make way for the new, healthy marrow. But it's not very pleasant and it makes Carrie feel sick.'

'Poor Carrie,' David muttered sympathetically. He picked up a stick and hurled it, sending it flying. Orla sprinted after it. Jenny's eyes followed its path and she saw Fiona McLay strolling towards them.

Fiona waved. Her younger brother Paul was racing along with his Border terrier puppy, Toby, who was snapping playfully at his ankles.

'Hello,' Jenny called.

Jess had disentangled himself from his game with Orla and the two dogs hurried over to sniff Toby in greeting. Jess and Orla's tails swept from side to side in welcome, while Toby's compact little body shuddered with excitement. His stump of a tail wiggled happily.

Fiona came over to Jenny and David. 'Have you heard?' she began, her eyes wide. 'Carrie's going to have an operation to make her better . . . that lady from the SSPCA centre is going to give Carrie some of the marrow from inside her bones!'

'Yes, we know,' David said, as though he had known for ages.

'Sarah Taylor came up to Windy Hill to tell us,' Jenny said, her eyes shining. 'She's so kind – as well as brave!' she added. There had been a bleak and frightening period when it had looked as though no suitable match for Carrie's marrow would be found. Then they had met Sarah.

'Who *is* Sarah?' Paul asked. 'Do I know her?' The little boy was out of breath from his race with Toby.

'I don't think so,' Jenny said. 'She works at the

wildlife hospital. She met Carrie when we took those oil-covered birds from Puffin Island there for help. Remember?'

But Paul had lost interest and wandered away to find a stick for Toby.

David found a stone, and lobbed it at the trunk of a nearby tree. 'Bullseye!' he said.

'Carrie's not feeling well at all,' Fiona stated glumly. 'I wish we could do something to cheer her up.'

'Me too,' Jenny said. She watched the three dogs playing.

Jess was leading Orla in a merry game around the field. He streaked through the grass, leaping effortlessly over anything in his way. Orla was close on his heels, her pink tongue lolling. Toby was lost from view, swallowed up by the tall spring grasses, as he bobbed gamely along behind.

It gave Jenny an idea. 'I know what we could do!' she said suddenly. Fiona and David turned to her and even Paul looked up, alerted by the excitement in her voice. Jenny paused until she was certain that she had the full attention of her companions. 'Let's organise a sponsored walk!'

'A *what*?' said David.

'What for?' Fiona asked, frowning.

'A sponsored walk . . . to show Carrie how much

we care!' Jenny said triumphantly. 'We'll get all of Graston – and Cliffbay too – out walking – for miles! There'll be a prize at the end of it . . . and we'll ask everyone to give the money they raise to cancer research, or something.'

'Hey,' Fiona said slowly. 'That's not a bad idea. Carrie would know then that the whole village is thinking about her.'

'It sounds as if it might be a bit far. Will Toby make it?' Paul asked, looking doubtfully at Toby's short legs.

'I'm sure he will.' Jenny smiled.

'We'll have to plan a route first, then let everyone know. We could put up a poster at school,' Fiona suggested.

'We've got a computer at home, with a new colour printer. My dad's got plenty of free time because he doesn't work . . . well, not at the moment, anyway. I'm sure he'll help us.' David sounded enthusiastic. But suddenly he frowned and looked searchingly at Jenny. 'Doesn't Carrie mind everyone knowing that she's ill?'

'She did in the beginning,' Jenny said. 'But she's fine with it now. She thinks it's easier to tell people. Just imagine what might have happened if I hadn't told Sarah about her leukaemia! She might still be looking for the right person to give her their bone marrow.'

'You're right.' Fiona shuddered. 'Oh, poor Carrie! Let's go home and talk about our plans for this sponsored walk straightaway, shall we?'

'Let's go to my house,' David said, taking Orla's lead from round his neck. 'We'll go there first and ask my dad if we can use the computer.'

Jenny nodded and smiled. She felt her spirits rise. At last she would be doing something positive to support her friend. Keeping busy would make the waiting for Carrie's transplant, and its result, so much easier.

Jess trotted over and sat down at Jenny's feet. He put his head to one side. His sides were heaving with the effort of his energetic play with Orla and Toby. He held up a dirty white paw and Jenny took it gently. 'Yes,' she murmured. 'You can take part too. Jenny and Jess Miles – we'll make a great team.'

'Come on!' David had gone on ahead. 'Let's get moving.'

The wind began to tug at Jenny's fair, shoulder-length hair as she walked with her friends across the field. The farm she lived on, with her father, Fraser Miles, and their housekeeper and friend Ellen Grace, had been perfectly named. It *was* on a windy hill, and it was the place that Jenny loved best in the world.

The sloping acres, that were given over to the blackface sheep Fraser Miles farmed, had originally belonged to Jenny's mother's family. When Sheena Miles had died tragically and suddenly, Jenny's dad had been more determined than ever that Windy Hill would survive, not only as a thriving business – but as a happy home for Jenny and her brother Matt.

'Is Matt coming back this weekend?' Fiona asked, cutting into Jenny's thoughts.

'Yep, he should be,' Jenny replied happily. Nineteen-year-old Matt was away studying at agricultural college, but he liked to spend his weekends at home on the farm. Jenny was always pleased to see him. 'No doubt Mrs Grace is getting ready for Matt by spending today cooking a mountain of food.' She giggled.

It hadn't been easy to accept the idea of Ellen Grace coming to live at Windy Hill. At first, it had seemed to Jenny that, somehow, her mother was being replaced. But over the past couple of years, Mrs Grace's wise and gentle presence had made her a valued member of the family.

Jess trotted along, obediently keeping pace with

Jenny's heel. Fiona and Paul took turns holding Toby on his lead.

'Here we are,' said David, when they reached the small white bungalow he shared with his father. The neat little garden was surrounded by a picket fence. As David swung open the gate, Orla slipped past him and round a flowering bush, before making a protective dive for an old bone lying on the lawn. Her lead became entangled in a low-lying branch.

'Hang on!' scolded David irritably, stooping to untangle it. 'Jess isn't even interested in that smelly old bone. Neither is Toby.'

Jenny was first to follow David through the gate and she smiled at the sight of her friend, on his hands and knees, grappling to free Orla. She looked at the front door, painted a bright blue, and noticed a note pinned there. She stepped up to read it.

*Douglas — I had to go out. Be back around 5.30. Dad.*

'Douglas?' Jenny said. She turned to see David striding up the garden towards her. 'Who's Douglas?' she asked, wrinkling her nose.

David blushed. He reached round Jenny and quickly tore the note from the door. The drawing pin that secured it flew off and hit the stone step with a little pinging sound. Crumpling the paper in his hand David stuffed it into his jeans' pocket. 'It's . . . er . . . a name, a silly *pet* name that my father calls me. Nothing else.'

Jenny was taken aback by his defensiveness. 'That's fine,' she said quietly, as Fiona and Paul came through the gate. 'I was only wondering.'

'Is your dad at home?' Fiona asked.

'No,' David said, looking flustered. 'But it's best if I talk to him on my own, later. I'll let you know what he says.'

## 2

In the kitchen at Cliff House, Carrie was pouring Coke from a big plastic bottle. 'I'm glad you've come,' she said, grinning at Jenny and Fiona. 'Sundays can be so boring when you're stuck at home.'

'How are you feeling?' Fiona asked.

'Awful, most of the time.' Carrie made a face. 'It's the chemotherapy. But at least I don't have to worry about maths and geography and tests and . . .'

'Lucky you!' Fiona interrupted.

Jenny shot a glance at Carrie and saw that she hadn't minded Fiona telling her she was lucky. *But really*, Jenny thought, *Carrie is far from lucky*. She would much rather have to face a maths test, every day for the next six months, than have a single moment of Carrie's leukaemia.

She took a longer look at her friend. Against the vibrant yellow and green of Mrs Turner's cheerful kitchen, her face was chalky pale. The woollen beret on her head was set at a jaunty angle, letting a few remaining wisps of the flame-red hair – once Carrie's most striking feature – escape. She watched Carrie set out the glasses and rip open a big bag of crisps. There was a muddy yellow bruise on the back of her hand from the drug treatment she'd been having. Every time Jenny saw her friend she couldn't get over how brave she was.

'You're quiet,' said Carrie, peering into Jenny's face. Then she looked under the table at Jess. 'And so are you, for a change.' She darted out a hand to the collie's cold and quivering nose.

'Jess misses you,' Jenny smiled.

'I miss him, too,' she said. 'I miss going for walks. And you wouldn't believe it, but I even miss being at school.'

'Do you really?' Fiona said, amazed. 'Seriously?'

'Seriously.' Carrie smiled at her friends. 'How's David?'

'Weird,' said Fiona immediately.

'Weird?' Carrie raised her eyebrows at Jenny.

'Tell her what happened yesterday, Jenny,' Fiona prompted.

'It was nothing, really,' Jenny said, sipping her drink. 'It was just . . . strange.'

'Strange how?' Carrie demanded, holding out her hand for Jess to lick her salty fingers.

'Yesterday morning, we were out walking and decided to go back to his house. Anyway, I got there first, with Jess, and I found a note pinned on the door . . .'

'It was to *Douglas* – from Dad!' Fiona squeaked.

'David said it was a pet name his father had for him. Douglas, I mean. But he went all red and cross because I'd seen the note before he did,' Jenny explained.

'Let's call him Douggie, then – if we want to tease him.' Carrie giggled.

'No, don't,' Jenny said gently. 'He seemed really upset about it. I don't know why.'

'It's a silly nickname for someone called David,' Fiona said. 'Dave or Davey would make more sense.'

'Maybe he was christened Douglas but his family

have always called him David,' Jenny suggested. 'You know, some people are called by their second names.'

'Ah, but maybe,' said Carrie, speaking in an eerie whisper, 'the Fergussons are not who they say they are. Maybe they're a couple of criminals, on the run from the police!' Her eyes narrowed in playful suspicion.

'Don't make up scary stories,' Jenny pleaded, laughing. 'I'm sure it's just a name from when he was younger that he doesn't like any more.'

'Well, I agree with Carrie,' Fiona said. 'I'm sure there's something funny going on in that bungalow.'

'What were you doing at his house, anyway?' Carrie asked.

'It all began with Jenny's brilliant idea,' Fiona said.

'Well, *I* think it's a brilliant idea. You might not!' Jenny smiled, but before she could go on, the door to the kitchen opened and Mrs Turner came in. She was holding a plastic laundry basket of newly-ironed clothes. A warm, lemony smell came into the room with her.

'All right, Carrie love?' she asked anxiously. Carrie gave her mother the thumbs-up sign. 'Is she being a good hostess, girls?' Mrs Turner smiled at Jenny and Fiona. With her free hand she smoothed Jess's head, sticking out from under the table.

'Yes, thanks,' Jenny said, eyeing Mrs Turner's outfit discreetly. Carrie's mum was an artist and Jenny loved the clothes she wore. She wasn't afraid of vibrant colours and she always looked bright and interesting. Today she was wearing a calf-length dress of scarlet and lilac stripes. Her red hair was loosely tied back with a yellow ribbon.

'Did your brother make it back this weekend, Jenny?' Mrs Turner asked, as she began to make preparations for supper.

'Yes,' Jenny said happily. 'And Dad was especially glad to see him. We're really busy on the farm at the moment,' she explained. 'Matt came in from the fields very late last night, and went out early this morning, so I've hardly had a chance to see him yet.'

'I expect Matt will find time for you before he has to go back to college,' Mrs Turner said, taking some carrots over to the kitchen sink.

'What about this brilliant idea of yours, then?' Carrie tugged at Jenny's sleeve, changing the subject. 'Go on, don't keep me in suspense.'

'Oh, yes.' Jenny eased her foot out from under Jess. The collie had fallen asleep under the kitchen table, with his head cushioned on her shoe. 'Well,' she began, 'I thought it would be fun to organise a sponsored walk through Graston and on, down to

Cliffbay and back, in a loop.'

Carrie blinked at her. 'Why?' she said, resting her elbows on the table and propping her chin in her hands.

'To raise money for charity – a cancer charity, I mean. What do you think?' Jenny's eyes were bright.

'I think that's really sweet of you,' Carrie smiled. 'But I don't think anyone will go for it. Why would anyone want to trudge all that way just because of a horrible illness?'

'Because it will be great fun!' Fiona said enthusiastically.

'We could take Jess, and Orla,' said Jenny, trying to interest Carrie in her idea. 'There'd be prizes for the first people to reach the finish – and *think* how much money we could collect.'

'It's a wonderful idea,' Mrs Turner said softly, coming to stand behind Carrie's chair. She smiled warmly at Jenny. 'It *would* be fun to go walking on a beautiful spring day, and it is for a very good cause.'

'What cause?' Carrie asked, turning to look up at her mother.

'Well,' Mrs Turner said, 'Sarah Taylor told me that her sister Katie spent time in a little hospice near Greybridge. I think it would be great if we could raise some money and give it to the people who run the place.'

'What's a hospice?' Fiona asked.

'It's a home for people who are too ill to stay in their own homes,' Mrs Turner explained.

'Oh,' said Fiona.

'That's a great idea!' Jenny said, thrilled.

'OK, then,' Carrie said, suddenly grinning at Jenny. 'Let's organise a sponsored walk. What do I have to do?'

'Nothing,' Jenny smiled. 'Except help us to design the poster. David's father's got a computer with a printer, so we thought we'd print quite a few posters and put them up around Graston. There are still a lot of details to be sorted out.'

'That will give me something to think about,' Carrie said.

'When are you coming back to school?' Fiona asked, draining the last of her drink.

'I don't know,' Carrie replied. She rubbed her eyes. 'Mum says it depends how I feel.'

Mrs Turner glanced at her wristwatch. 'I think you should rest now, Carrie,' she said softly.

'Oh! Yes.' Jenny stood up and Jess immediately came out from under the table. His eyes were glazed with sleep. He shook himself and yawned. She smoothed the top of his head. 'We'll get going, then.'

'Thanks for coming,' Carrie said, as Mrs Turner walked with Jenny and Fiona to the front door. 'And say hello to "Douggie" for me!'

Jenny wagged a playful finger at her friend. '*Don't* call him Douggie!' she chided, then giggled.

Jenny and Fiona cycled up the hilly lane from Cliffbay to Graston. Jess loped along easily beside them. Jenny was always pleased to see the collie keep up so effortlessly. There had been a time when she had wondered if Jess would ever walk without a severe limp, let alone be as strong and sure-footed as he was now.

Jess had been the runt of a litter born to Fraser Miles's beloved sheepdog, Nell. Jenny had been heartbroken when her father had suggested that the newly-born puppy, whose tiny, twisted leg hung uselessly, be put to sleep. Some spark of determination that Jenny had seen in the puppy's pleading eyes had made her beg for his life. Her father had relented, in spite of his belief that there was no room for a non-working dog on a busy sheep farm. So Jess had stayed, hand-reared by Jenny, and when he was older and stronger, an operation had all but completely mended his damaged leg.

Jenny was lost in memories of Jess as an adorable puppy, when Fiona braked abruptly at a fork in the road. 'Bye, Jenny. See you tomorrow at school,' she said.

'Bye, Fi. Don't forget to think about the details of our walk, will you?'

'I won't.' Fiona put a hand out towards Jess. He looked up at her and wagged his tail gently. Then, she cycled away towards Dunraven, the neighbouring farm to Windy Hill.

Jenny's tummy rumbled with hunger as she headed home. She could already see the grey stone farmhouse sitting solidly among the undulating fields, facing a sweep of sea. A rocky mound rose up behind Windy Hill and, perched on its crest was the ancient ruined keep called Darktarn – Jenny's favourite place to go when she wanted to be alone with her thoughts. She would have liked to go up there now, and think about the walk, and Carrie, but she was too hungry.

She dismounted and began to wheel her bike up the unmade track to the farm's gate. In the paddock, adjacent to the small shearing barn, Matt's stallion, Mercury, was rubbing his glossy shoulder up against the trunk of a tree. He skittered when he heard the wheels of Jenny's bike crunching into the gravel.

The big horse tossed his mane and threw back his head, whickering and snorting in welcome.

'Oh no,' warned Jenny, as Mercury cantered up to the fence and stretched his sleek nose towards her. 'I haven't anything for you. Not even a peppermint. Sorry.'

She cupped the palm of her hand round his velvet-soft muzzle and looked into the large, liquid eyes of the horse. Mercury's smooth lips opened and closed, making a soft snapping sound, as he searched hopefully for a small titbit. Jenny chuckled. 'Silly old boy.'

Two years ago, Jenny's mother Sheena had been killed riding Mercury. She had fallen and broken her neck. Fraser Miles, struggling with his shock and his grief, had immediately sold his wife's horse, and had hoped never to see the animal again. But many months later, Matt had come across Mercury at the livestock market in Greybridge. Knowing that Mercury's fate was to be shot if he wasn't bought that day, Matt had taken pity on his mother's beloved horse and brought him back to Windy Hill.

Rubbing the little white smudge between the horse's eyes, Jenny wondered how she could ever have been so angry with Matt for having rescued Mercury. The horse had suffered greatly away from

# THE GIFT

Windy Hill. The once-proud stallion came home broken both in health and in spirit. It had taken months to rebuild his confidence and make him well again.

'It wasn't your fault,' she whispered to Mercury, kissing his warm cheek. 'I know that now. I'm sorry if I ever had any bad thoughts about you. Only, we miss Mum so much, you see . . .'

Jenny broke off. The face of her mother came up brightly in her mind, making her chest tighten and ache. Sometimes the pain of having lost her was so great that Jenny could hardly bear it.

She heard the porch door to the kitchen open. Jenny turned to see Ellen Grace come out onto the top step and put a hand up to her eyes to block out the glare from the sinking sun.

She spotted Jenny at the fence to Mercury's paddock and called over to her. 'Time to eat, Jenny,' she called. 'Are you hungry?'

Jenny felt the pang in her chest ease a little. Her voice rose on the wind. 'Yes,' she yelled. 'I'm starving. I'm coming!' She took up her bicycle and began to wheel it hurriedly towards the house. 'Come on, Jess.'

But Jess was already bounding up the track towards Mrs Grace, his tail wagging furiously.

# 3

As Jenny propped her bike against the wall of the shed, she looked up at the sky. All around her it was streaked with stripes of luminous pink and soft grey, and she saw a first small star that had popped out above the sea. It was a beautiful sight, and she could make out the gentle bleating of the ewes and their lambs in the barn as they began to settle for the night. Feeling contented, she kicked off her shoes in the porch and flung open the door to the kitchen.

Matt and her father were seated at the big pine

table under the window. Jess was standing on his back legs, his tail thumping noisily against the leg of a chair. His front paws were on Matt's lap. 'Hey! You crazy dog,' Matt was laughing. 'Your paws are filthy. Hello, Jen. Can't you control this animal?'

'Hi, everyone. Jess, down!' Jenny commanded and the collie looked round and obediently crawled under the table. 'He's only pleased to see you,' Jenny grinned. 'Me, too!'

Matt half-rose and leaned towards Jenny for a hug. 'Sorry, I haven't had a chance to spend much time with you. Some of us have to work, while certain little princesses I could name snooze away Sunday mornings undisturbed . . .' he teased.

'Not true!' said Jenny indignantly. 'I was up early working too – on my history assignment.'

Matt patted her on the head. 'I'm only joking!' he laughed.

'How's Carrie, lass?' Fraser Miles poured himself a glass of water from the jug.

'Quite cheerful, today,' Jenny said, pulling a chair up to the table.

'Have you washed those hands?' Mrs Grace asked, frowning.

Jenny looked at her palms. There were traces of dirt on them – from Mercury's coat, she guessed. She smiled at Ellen Grace and went over to the sink.

'Carrie hasn't got much of her lovely red hair left, except for a few strands, and she looks even thinner,' Jenny reported. 'But she's still her fun self!'

'I expect she's much more hopeful now that a transplant has been arranged,' Mr Miles said, making room on the table for a big earthenware casserole dish that Mrs Grace had brought from the oven.

'Oh, yes,' Matt put in. 'Dad told me about the operation. Has Carrie been given a date for it yet?'

'No,' Jenny said, sitting down. 'But I think it will be quite soon.'

Mrs Grace served each of them in turn. Steam from the delicious-looking meal curled into the air. The room was fragrant with the scent of baking apples and sweet pastry. Fraser Miles broke off a hunk of bread from a home-made loaf and raised his glass. 'Ellen,' he said, 'this is wonderful, as always. Thank you.'

Jenny giggled. It was unlike her father to be so formal. But Mrs Grace raised her own glass, and gave Jenny's father a shy, girlish smile. Jenny giggled again, and Matt nudged her with his foot under the table.

'Hey!' she glared at her brother and he frowned at her.

'Mmm, thanks Mrs Grace,' Matt said, smiling

warmly, ignoring Jenny. 'This is delicious.'

Jenny began to eat, and glanced furtively across the table at Ellen Grace. She wore a marine-blue blouse and skirt Jenny hadn't seen before, and a pair of tiny gold earrings. She couldn't remember the last time she had seen Mrs Grace wearing anything other than her practical little work pinafore, covering a T-shirt and old jeans. She looked positively radiant. Jenny wondered with a little stab of guilt if today was perhaps Mrs Grace's birthday. In her head, she began to calculate the date. 'September . . .' she said aloud, without thinking.

'What about it?' said Matt.

'That's when your birthday is, isn't it, Mrs Grace?' Jenny looked closely at her.

'Yes, love, it is,' she replied, surprised. 'Ages away. Why?'

Jenny shook her head. 'Oh, no reason,' she said. 'I was just checking.'

'More rice, Jenny?' Mrs Grace asked.

'Yes, please. Oh, I haven't told you about my brilliant idea!'

Jenny had suddenly remembered the sponsored walk. Her dad, Matt and Mrs Grace gave her their full attention. Jess ventured out from under the table, encouraged by the excited tone of her voice. He sat beside her chair, and rested his cheek against her thigh.

'Fiona, David and I, and Carrie, are going to organise a sponsored walk to raise money for the hospice where Sarah Taylor's sister stayed when she was sick with leukaemia,' Jenny explained.

'Really?' Fraser Miles looked up from his plate.

'Don't make it *too* strenuous,' Matt groaned.

'That's a lovely idea, Jenny.' Ellen Grace smiled. 'And Carrie's keen on it?'

'She thought it was a great idea – eventually. She couldn't see the point of it at first. But, really, I just want everyone to know about Carrie's illness, and about how brave and strong she's being . . . and the nicer and kinder people are to her, then the better it'll be for her!' Jenny finished her sentence in a rush of emotion. Her cheeks felt hot and her eyes were suddenly stinging. She looked down at Jess, and put a hand to his soft chest. He licked her arm with a warm, loving tongue.

Ellen Grace put her hand on Jenny's shoulder and rubbed it soothingly. Very quietly, she said: 'And how brave and strong *you're* being, love.'

'Have you worked out the details of this walk, Jen lass?' Mr Miles looked up. He had been mopping up the last of the gravy on his plate with a piece of bread.

'It's got to be ten kilometres, tops,' said Matt firmly. 'No more, or people won't go for it.'

'How much can we ask people to pay, Dad?' Jenny asked.

'You could ask for a minimum of ten pence a kilometre. But I think you'll find that most people will be willing to pay more.'

'I think you're right, Fraser,' said Mrs Grace. 'Especially as it sounds like fun, too.'

'We're going to design some posters and paste them up all round Graston. I'm sure loads of people will want to take part when they hear about Carrie, and—' Jenny broke off, startled by the sudden, shrill ringing of the telephone.

'Now, who can that be calling on a Sunday night?' Mrs Grace looked at her watch. She put her knife and fork together on her plate.

'I'll go, Ellen.' Fraser Miles got up from the table, smiling at her. He patted her arm affectionately as he squeezed between the wall and her chair. Jenny caught Matt's eye and he raised his eyebrows at her.

'We had twins lambs born last night, Jen,' Matt said, helping himself to some more vegetables.

'Ah! Good. How lovely. Are they both doing all right?'

'Yep, two strong little lads,' Matt grinned.

Fraser Miles voice carried from the hall where he was speaking. 'Mr Fergusson? Yes, hello! How can I help you?'

'Perhaps David has left his homework a bit late, and wants some help from you, Jenny?' Mrs Grace whispered. Jenny shrugged, and listened to what her father was saying.

'Well, I'm sure it wouldn't be a problem. Of course, I'd like to check with Mrs Grace, my . . . housekeeper. But I feel sure she won't have any objections. Would you hold on for just a minute, please?'

'What is it?' hissed Jenny, when her father put his head round the door to the kitchen. Jess blinked and pricked up his ears.

'It seems that Mr Fergusson has been called away suddenly, on urgent business. He can't leave the lad alone in the house and there's nowhere for him to go. Would you mind if he came and stayed here at Windy Hill for a while, Jenny? Ellen?'

'Oh!' Jenny was surprised.

'I wouldn't mind a bit. He can have Ian's old room!' Ellen seemed pleased.

'Jen? Do you mind?' Her father looked searchingly at her.

'No, I don't mind,' Jenny replied. She supposed it wouldn't be any different to having Mrs Grace's nephew, Ian, around the farm. He had spent quite a long time with them while his parents were setting up home in Canada, and it had been all right.

'That's settled then.' Fraser Miles grinned. 'I'll go and tell Mr Fergusson.' He went back into the hallway.

'What's David like?' Matt asked.

'David? Oh, he's a nice boy,' Mrs Grace said kindly, collecting up the empty plates. Jenny stood up to help her.

'Yes, he is nice,' she said.

'You can put him to work on the farm,' Matt suggested, grinning.

'Matt!' Jenny scolded. 'He's got schoolwork to do. Loads of it, like me.'

'David can stay with us, Mr Fergusson,' Jenny heard her dad say. 'No problem. Tomorrow? Yes, I'm sure that's fine. OK, then. No bother. Goodnight.'

'Would you like a piece of apple pie?' Mrs Grace smiled as Fraser Miles came back into the room.

'Hmmm, is that what I can smell, Ellen? My favourite! You're spoiling us.'

'Dad?' Jenny was frowning. 'Did Mr Fergusson say what business it was that had called him away?'

'I didn't ask him, Jenny,' her father replied. 'Why?'

'It's just that only yesterday David told me and Fiona that his father didn't have any work to do. He said that his father would be able to help us print out some posters on his computer for our sponsored walk.' Jenny was puzzled.

'Perhaps this is something that isn't really work at all,' Ellen Grace suggested, as she sliced into the crust of the pie. 'It might have to do with family, or something.'

'Maybe someone's died,' Matt said helpfully. 'And it's a funeral. He has to go.'

'That's silly,' Jenny said. 'Why wouldn't he just say so then? Why talk about urgent business?'

'It doesn't matter anyway,' Mr Miles said gently. 'It isn't any of our business where he has to go, or why. All I know is that he's very grateful we're letting David stay here at Windy Hill.'

'What does he do, this Mr Fergusson?' Matt asked. 'Is he a farmer?'

'No.' Jenny shook her head. 'He's not. I don't know what he does. A bit of this and a bit of that, David says.'

'Odd,' said Matt, and yawned. 'Well, good luck to

the man and his urgent business. I'm off to bed!'

'We'll just have to draw and colour the posters for the walk ourselves,' Jenny shrugged, adding: 'I'll help you clear away, Mrs Grace.'

'No, Jen lass,' smiled her father. 'Don't you worry about that tonight. I'll give Ellen a hand. You go on and let Jess out for his last walk, then have an early night. You look sleepy.'

Jenny looked at her father. A soft, rather secretive, smile was hovering around the corners of his mouth. He looked very pleased with himself about something. 'OK, thanks,' she said. 'Goodnight. Thanks for supper!'

' 'Night, Jen, love,' Ellen Grace said softly.

Jess followed Jenny to the back door. He bounded through the porch, then stood wagging his tail, barking, as she pulled on her shoes. 'I'm coming as fast as I can!' Jenny chided him, laughing.

Jess ran over to where Nell and Jake, his parents, were dozing beside the barn. It was a warm spring evening, and Nell had made herself a little nest in a pile of discarded straw. Jake was curled up close to her. He thumped his tail in greeting when he saw the younger dog, who briefly touched noses with his mother, before running off into the field.

Jenny straightened and peered into the gathering gloom for Jess. She could just make out the woolly

shapes of the sheep, shuffling around at the fence along the top field, like small wintry clouds. She whistled, and Jess came streaking towards her.

*Jess is more than a working dog*, Jenny thought, *and much more than just a pet. He is, quite simply, the best dog in the whole world.*

Back inside, Jenny discovered that her father and Mrs Grace had gone into the sitting-room. The door was closed but she could hear the distant murmuring of their chatter. She shook out Jess's blanket and then laid it back in his basket.

Matt had come into the kitchen and was filling a

glass of water at the sink. 'What's going on, d'you think?' he said, with a quizzical smile on his face.

'What do you mean, going on?' Jenny frowned, puzzled.

'Dad and Mrs Grace seem . . . different together,' Matt said. 'You know, as though something has changed.'

'Well, Mrs Grace *does* look a bit dressed up this evening . . . and Dad is being especially nice to her. At dinner, I thought for a moment it might be her birthday!' Jenny grinned. 'Oh, Matt! You don't think . . .?'

'Romance is in the air?' Matt frowned. 'Maybe.'

'I guess it would make Dad happy,' Jenny said thoughtfully.

'I'm not so sure,' Matt replied. 'Dad has just begun to settle down and enjoy life again after Mum . . . I think he needs more time.'

'Maybe,' Jenny said. She looked at Jess as he got into his basket and curled up. 'Goodnight, Jess.'

'It's too soon,' Matt said, in a distant voice, as if he were talking to himself. He was still frowning.

'Oh, don't let's think about it now, Matt. We don't know for sure, do we? Besides, there's too much else going on. I'm not going to give it another thought! Let's just wait and see what happens.'

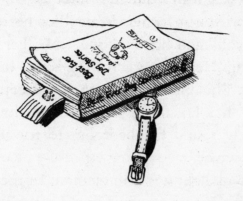

# 4

Jenny slept fitfully. She was deep in the clutches of a series of dreams.

In one, she was standing on the corner of a busy road in Greybridge, pleading with people passing by to sign up for her sponsored walk. In another, she was striding out along a stretch of smooth, tarred road. Carrie walked briskly beside her, a huge smile on her face. But the tar began to melt, and it grew stickier and stickier. The soles of their shoes began to melt into the tar and hold them fast, and Carrie stretched out her hand to Jenny. 'Help me, Jen,' she begged. 'I've got to make it. I've *got* to.'

Jenny cried out in her dream: 'I'm here Carrie. I'll help you!' and her shouting woke her. She sat up, gasping. Her hair was matted across her damp forehead. She blinked and took a deep breath to steady her breathing, then looked slowly and deliberately round her bedroom to try and calm herself down.

A soft pink light was coming in under the edge of her curtains. It was no more than a glow, but it was comforting. There was the photograph of her mother, smiling at her, and one of Jess, about ten weeks old. She pushed back her hair and went over to the window to pull back the curtains. A crescent of sun was starting to show above the horizon but the dawn chill gave her goosebumps. She scurried back into bed.

Monday mornings weren't the same without Carrie being in school, Jenny reflected. She didn't look forward to being there quite as much, although Fiona was a good friend to her. Pulling the blankets up to her throat, Jenny wished for the hundredth time that Carrie's operation had come and gone, and that her friend was better – that things were the way they used to be. The sadness she felt was like a weight, pressing down on her. It was as if it were trying to squeeze all the breath out of her.

She remembered that when Carrie had first been ill, Mrs Grace had given her some advice. 'Conjure up a picture of Carrie in happier days,' she had said, 'and hold on to the image in your mind.' Jenny tried this now, and into her head popped a vision of Carrie at the birthday party of a school friend the previous year. Her coppery hair flew around her face as she danced about, showing off a new dress her mum had bought her, and laughing.

A party! She would give Carrie a party! Jenny sat bolt upright in bed. It would be the perfect end to the day of the sponsored walk. Carrie would love it, Jenny felt sure. There would be streamers and balloons, delicious things to eat, music to dance to, and all of Carrie's friends and family there to wish her well for the operation.

Struck by the brilliance of this idea, Jenny snatched up her wristwatch, which was lying under her reading book on the bedside table. It read 5.45 am. Dad would be up and out in the fields, with Matt, by now. She would go and share the idea with them.

She dressed hurriedly, pulling on a pair of denims and a sweatshirt that was muddy from yesterday's walk with Jess. Then she tore out a page from her school jotter and scribbled a note to Mrs Grace: *I woke up early, so have gone out to see the lambs. Love, Jenny.*

The door to the housekeeper's bedroom was shut. Jenny slipped the note under it and took the stairs to the kitchen two at a time. Jess was curled into a tight little ball in his basket, his soft blue blanket tucked cosily round him. At the sound of Jenny's footsteps he lifted his head and peered sleepily up at her. His chin was propped on the edge of the basket and one eye was partially closed.

Jenny dropped to her haunches and kissed the top of his head. 'You coming, sleepyhead? I'm going out to the fields,' Jenny whispered.

Jess yawned and craned his neck up to the ceiling to stretch. Then, fully awake, he leaped out of his basket and ran to the kitchen door, wagging his tail. Jenny quietly opened the door to the porch and pulled on her wellington boots.

She found her father, with Matt, outside the shearing shed. Matt was shredding bales of straw with a pitchfork and Fraser Miles was putting the finishing touches to a new lamb incubator with a screwdriver. The sheepdogs, Nell and Jake, were lying side by side looking into the field that held over a hundred head of blackface sheep – watching for any movement that might be a signal for them to work. Jess took his cue from his parents, and lay down obediently nearby – his eyes never leaving Jenny.

'Hi!' said Jenny.

'Well, hello, lass!' Fraser Miles looked up in surprise. 'We don't usually see you up and about this early on a school morning.'

'Did you bring up a Thermos of coffee?' Matt demanded.

'No, I didn't,' Jenny replied. 'I've only come for a quick chat.' She peeped into the lambing box. 'No, orphans, Dad?'

'Not so far, Jenny, thankfully.' Fraser Miles grinned. As the lambing season progressed, there were usually a host of unlucky little new-borns whose mothers rejected them, refusing to feed or care for them. This was where the heated, wooden box Fraser Miles was working on came in. Jenny liked to think of it as a little hospital ward, in which the lambs could be kept safe and warm, and be fed by willing nurses, such as herself.

One year there had been so many needy new lambs that Jess had had to be employed as a surrogate mother. He had gone off around the fields with bottles of warm milk harnessed to his sides in an old waistcoat. The collie had done a brilliant job and had earned the admiration of all who heard the story.

'Well?' said Matt, wiping his forehead with a handkerchief, and grinning at his sister. 'Go on then, chat away.'

'Well, listen to this! I thought it would be a great idea to throw a big party for Carrie – after the sponsored walk, I mean.' Jenny sat down on a bale of hay and curled her legs under her. Matt and her father said nothing. 'What do you think?' Jenny prompted.

'I think it's a fine idea, Jen, lass,' Mr Miles said. 'I'm only thinking that Carrie might not feel well enough to dance a jig, you know . . .'

'Then she needn't,' Jenny explained. 'She can sit comfortably and be among all the people who care about her.'

'Sorry to have to be the practical one but what's it going to cost, this big party?' Matt wondered, making a face.

'We can all chip in,' Jenny explained. 'Us, and Mrs Grace and the Turners and the McLays . . . I've got some pocket money saved.'

'You could have it in the village hall,' Matt said, warming to the idea.

'Yes,' Fraser Miles said thoughtfully, 'there's room enough there for a proper knees-up – a ceilidh, even.'

'It will be great fun,' Jenny said, getting up and jumping about excitedly. Jess came to her side immediately, rose up gracefully and put his front paws against her collarbone. She threw her arms round his neck. The more she thought about it, the clearer the picture of Carrie became, spinning around happily in her new dress at Laura Dern's party.

'Whoa!' said Mr Miles, holding up a calming hand. Jenny sat down, slightly out of breath. 'There's rather a lot to organise and sort out, Jenny. All this is going to take time and effort. There's the walk, now the party – and school in-between – not to mention all that's going on on the farm!'

'I can do it by myself,' Jenny promised. 'I won't need your help. I know you've got enough to do.' She jumped up again. 'But you're right, Dad. There is a lot to be done. I'd better get going.'

'See you later,' Matt called.

Jess sprang after his mistress as she raced away across the field, scattering the sheep in her path. After a minute, Jenny slowed to a jog. The pinky-orange sun was sliding higher into a clear dawn sky. It was going to be a lovely day.

There were posters to design and put up, invitations to write and food to plan, and all before Carrie had her operation. Afterwards, Jenny knew, her friend wouldn't be well enough to walk, or to dance.

*This is the best way to show Carrie how much I care about her*, Jenny thought. Her only regret was how little time she had had lately to help her father and brother with the farm. But it couldn't be helped. For the meantime, Carrie had to come first – and there wasn't a moment to lose.

A couple of hours later, Jenny discovered David waiting for her at the gates of their school.

'Hi,' Jenny called, hitching her schoolbag over her shoulder and striding towards him.

'Hi,' David replied, looking a bit awkward. He shuffled from foot to foot. 'You know, don't you, that I'll be coming to your house, later on, to stay for a bit? Is that all right with you?'

'That's fine!' Jenny smiled. 'We've got a room for you. How long is your dad going to be away?'

'I don't really know,' David mumbled. 'But I'm sure he won't be gone long. I'll go home after school and he'll bring me to your place later. OK?'

'That's fine,' Jenny said again, sensing that he wanted to be sure that she *really* didn't mind him sharing Windy Hill. 'It'll be great to have you – and Orla, of course. We'll have fun on the farm – and we can work together on planning the walk and . . . here's Fiona.' Jenny couldn't wait to tell Fiona about her idea for a party.

'Hello, you two.' Fiona hurried over, frowning. She looked tired. 'I haven't finished my homework! That science was so hard and—'

Jenny didn't give her a chance to finish. 'Listen, Fi! I've had a great idea!' She seized Fiona's arm. 'Why don't we give Carrie a surprise party at the end of the sponsored walk? We could do it in the village hall!'

'A party?' said Fiona. 'You mean, like a birthday party?'

'No, it's not her *birthday*, silly. Just a party – to wish her good luck and things with her operation.'

'That's a nice idea,' David said. 'I'd be on for that. But who will supply the music . . . food . . . drinks . . . and pay the bill?'

'We'll have to sort it all out,' Jenny said with determination. 'We've got time.'

'My mum will help,' Fiona suggested.

'We can tell Mrs Turner – in confidence,' Jenny said. 'She'll help.'

'There's the bell,' said David. 'We'd better go in. Let's talk about it more at break.'

As Jenny went into class, she had a little spring in her step. Automatically, she put out her hand to share her feelings with Jess, then realised that he wasn't there. *What a shame that dogs aren't allowed in school*, Jenny thought.

When Jenny got home at four o' clock, Ellen Grace was just leaving Windy Hill.

'It's my friend, Mrs Perry,' she told Jenny. 'She hasn't been well at all, poor thing. I said I'd do her shopping for her.'

Jess was prancing about, delighted that Jenny was home. He found her wellington boots and paraded about with one in his mouth. Jenny chuckled and rubbed his ears. 'Yes, I missed you, too!' she said.

'I won't be back late,' Ellen was edging her way round the dancing collie. 'I must hurry or I won't get to the chemist in time and . . . oh! Look, Jenny, here comes a visitor.'

Jenny looked out of the window. Sarah Taylor was getting out of her car. She waved and smiled at Jenny, then walked to the kitchen door. Mrs Grace got there first and greeted the young woman warmly.

'I'm afraid I'm just off, Sarah,' she explained. 'But Jenny's here. Come on in.'

'Hello, Sarah!' Jenny was pleased to see her, then added: 'See you later, Mrs Grace.'

'Bye, you two,' Ellen Grace said.

Sarah came into the kitchen and peeled off a light blue cardigan. As she smoothed Jess's black ears, her blonde hair swung round her shoulders. She perched on the end of the pine table and smiled at Jenny. 'I heard something about a sponsored walk for charity,' she said. 'Anything I can do?'

'Gosh! People are talking about it already! That's just what I hoped would happen,' Jenny said happily. 'I need as much help as I can get,' she admitted.

'Right,' said Sarah, slipping off the table. 'Then let's get started. Have you got a piece of paper and a pencil?'

Jenny usually gave Jess a long walk when she got home from school but now she settled down at the table to work on making a list of tasks. The collie seemed to sense something important was going on, so he lay down beside Jenny's chair and waited patiently.

'I feel much better now,' Jenny said gratefully, when she'd gone through all the details with Sarah. 'Not so worried about it all.'

'Carrie won't be having her operation for a few weeks yet,' Sarah said, 'so the Saturday we've picked for the walk is the best time. I think we'll be organised by then.'

'I want to give Carrie a party, after the walk,' Jenny said. 'It'll be a secret, so she'll get a real surprise. What do you think?'

'Good idea!' Sarah's face lit up. 'A knees-up might be just the thing to give her a boost before the operation.' She reached over to the little pad of paper and made a few more notes. 'I'll help you organise the party, too, if you like.'

'Thanks, Sarah.' Jenny's smile was radiant. She hadn't liked to ask Mrs Grace for help, and her dad was always so busy. She'd started to wonder how on earth she was going to make sure everything was done in time.

'Mrs Turner suggested that we donate the money we raise to the hospice where your sister stayed . . .'

'Oh, that's such a nice thought. Thank you. They could do with some help up there.' Sarah was beaming.

Jenny looked seriously at her. 'Is she . . . Carrie, going to be all right after the operation?' she asked.

'I can't say that for sure.' Sarah shook her head. 'But it's the best chance she has. The marrow in her own bones is breaking down – but as you know, my own marrow is the perfect match of cell tissue with hers, so it looks very positive.'

'Thank you,' Jenny said simply. 'Thanks for letting Carrie have some of it.'

'I'm glad to do it.' Sarah smiled. 'I'm what is known as MUD in medical terms, and I'm rather rare. MUD is Matched Unrelated Donor.'

Jenny smiled. 'Mud!' she said and wrinkled her nose. 'What's going to happen at the hospital?'

'It's really very simple,' Sarah explained. 'When all the drugs they are giving Carrie have done the job of destroying her damaged marrow, the marrow they get from me will be fed down a little tube and into her. Once the new cells are in Carrie's circulation, they find their own way to the places in the bone where the new marrow should establish itself. Then the doctors will have to check Carrie to make sure that new white blood cells are starting to be produced. If they are, then the transplant will have been successful.'

Jenny felt her head begin to ache. It seemed a lot to take in – and the thought of the operation *not* being successful made her feel sick.

'Well, I'd better be going now.' Sarah stood up. 'And don't worry about the walk or the party, Jenny – we'll make sure that Carrie has a great time.'

Jenny smiled. 'Thanks,' she said again. 'You've been brilliant.'

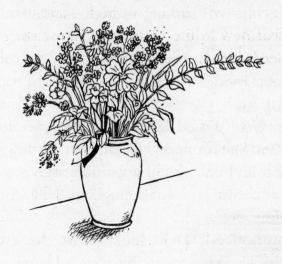

# 5

Just then, there was a soft knocking on the door. Jess went at once to investigate, his tail wagging and his head cocked to one side.

Jenny opened the door and gasped. David stood there, a small, black, bulging sports bag in his hand. 'Oh! David. I'd forgotten . . . the time! Come in.'

Jenny had been so intent on making plans, and talking to Sarah about Carrie, that David's arrival at Windy Hill had gone right out of her mind. There was a minute or two of confusion, as Orla rushed into the kitchen, barking in high excitement.

David stood in the doorway looking uncertain. Then Jenny remembered her manners. 'Let me take your bag, David.' She had to raise her voice to make herself heard.

'*Stop*, Orla!' David bellowed. The collie looked crestfallen. She dropped her ears and sat down. Jess walked round her, his tail wagging briskly.

'That's better,' said Sarah, laughing. 'Hello, David.'

'Hello.'

Jenny noticed David look round the kitchen rather stiffly, taking in the big pine table on which stood a vase stuffed full of wild flowers; the saucepans hung over the Aga range; and the brightly coloured cushions strewn along a wooden bench. It was a homely sort of room. Jenny guessed from the look on David's face that it was a very different kitchen from his own.

'I'm just on my way home,' Sarah told David. 'Jenny and I have been making plans for the walk. I'm sure she'll tell you all about it.' She picked up her cardigan.

'Thanks again, Sarah,' Jenny said.

'Bye.' Sarah smiled and slipped past David, who was still standing just inside the door. Orla was helping herself to a few biscuits left behind in Jess's breakfast bowl. When Jenny had closed the door, she wondered with a pang of guilt if Mrs Grace had had time to make up Ian's old room for David, and she remembered, too, that she had said she would help to prepare it. *Honestly, Jenny!* she chided herself. *This is not much of a welcome.*

'Did your dad bring you?' she asked cheerily.

'Yes, he dropped me at the gate. He was in a hurry.' David seemed hunched up inside his baggy jumper and his eyes darted round the room in a way that Jenny found unsettling. She thought it odd that Mr Fergusson hadn't had time to bring David in himself.

'Mrs Grace – she's our, sort of, housekeeper, and friend – will be back soon. Meantime, I'll take you upstairs to your room, if you like?' Jenny smiled. David seemed so ill-at-ease, she wasn't quite sure what to suggest.

'Yes, OK.' David stopped and took his bag from her. 'Is it all right if Orla sleeps in the kitchen? She's used to that.'

'Yes,' Jenny laughed, 'I'm sure Jess will feel very honoured.'

Jenny led David along the landing to a closed bedroom door. Inside, Mrs Grace had been true to her word, and Jenny found to her relief that she had made up the bed, removed the bits and pieces Ian had left behind in the wardrobe, and even put a few sprigs of lavender in a vase on the bookshelf.

'This is your room,' she told David. 'The bathroom's over there.'

'Thanks,' David said, managing a small smile. 'I'll just unpack my bag, then, OK?'

'Fine,' Jenny said. 'I'll be in the kitchen, doing my homework. I'll show you around the farm, when you're ready, and tell you all about our ideas for the walk, and the party.'

As she walked away down the landing, Jenny heard David firmly close the bedroom door. It made her feel uneasy. He *was* a hard person to get to know. And he seemed to be becoming more secretive as time went on!

Jess was sitting at the bottom of the stairs, looking up at Jenny as she came down. He thumped his tail, and looked across at Orla, who had curled up in his basket.

'Oh, Jess!' Jenny giggled, as she followed his gaze. 'She really has moved in, hasn't she? You're very kind to let her have your bed.' She stroked his silky head and he looked steadily up at her.

Jenny sat down on the bottom step and gave a big sigh. Jess put his nose lightly on her shoulder, edging closer for a cuddle, and her hair closed over his face like a curtain. She hugged the collie and felt a bit better. But there seemed a lot to deal with just now – Carrie, the walk, the party, her father's changing relationship with Mrs Grace, and now David, who was being rather sullen and difficult, too.

Jenny jumped when the telephone rang. She ran to answer it, hoping it might be Carrie. It was Fiona.

'Is he there? Has he come?' she demanded.

'Yes,' Jenny was guarded, thinking that David might appear on the stairs at any moment. She lowered her voice. 'He doesn't seem very happy at all,' she confided. 'His father left him at the bottom of the drive and went off. I mean, he doesn't even know where his son is going to sleep!'

'I tell you, there's something odd about it all,' Fiona sounded certain.

'Well, I'm being as nice as I can,' Jenny said. 'Maybe I can find out a little bit more about him and his dad.'

'Let me know what happens, won't you?' Fiona urged. 'Ring me later.'

'Fi,' Jenny chuckled, 'I'll see you at school tomorrow. I'll tell you then, OK?'

'Well, OK. But ring me if something dramatic happens.'

'Nothing *dramatic* is going to happen, silly,' Jenny whispered. 'Except that I'm going to get into a huge amount of trouble if I don't do my homework! And poor Jess hasn't even had his walk yet. See you tomorrow. Bye.'

'Bye.' Fiona hung up.

Jenny replaced the receiver and felt a little shiver go through her. What if Fiona was right? What if David and his father *were* criminals, on the run from the police? The more Jenny thought about this possibility, the more it seemed likely. There had been very few answers to the questions Jenny had asked about David's life before he moved to Cliffbay; Mr Fergusson seemed a really mysterious character, who was out of work one minute and rushing off on urgent business the next – and he called David *Douglas*! It just didn't add up.

Jenny found herself looking over her shoulder nervously, as she heard the creak of the wooden stairs. David came slowly into the kitchen, a blank expression on his face. For a second, Jenny was tongue-tied. She wished Mrs Grace had been there to make things easier. *This is ridiculous!* Jenny told herself. *It's just my imagination running wild.*

'Do you want to have a look around the farm?' she asked brightly.

David nodded. And then Jess did something that made Jenny feel a lot happier. He went over to David and, very gently, put his nose in the palm of the boy's hand. David, looking surprised, gave Jess a loving stroke, murmuring: 'Hello, Jess. Good boy!'

'Well,' said Jenny, 'that's Jess's way of saying welcome!' Instantly she remembered the way the collie had sensed the evil intent in Marion, a former friend of her father's, who had come to stay at Windy Hill last year. Jess had been wary of the woman from the start – and he had been right. She had ended up trying to poison him for her own selfish gain. Surely Jess's fine instinct would sense if David, in some way, was going to mean trouble for the Mileses?

'Come on, then.' Jenny smiled in relief. 'Let's get going. Jess needs his walk. I'll show you the lambs first, shall I?'

Orla and Jess bounded along as Jenny led the way round the farm. As they walked, Jenny chattered on about the lambing, the dipping and the shearing, pointing out bits of equipment and all the technical terms that she thought might interest David. She told him about Darktarn Keep, and the horse, Mercury. He seemed to relax as he listened, and the strained look on his face finally melted into a smile.

'It's nice here,' he said, looking across the sloping hills to the sea. 'I'd like to live on a farm.'

'You do – for now!' Jenny chuckled. 'You can explore any part of it – and help my dad too, if you want.'

'Thanks,' David said. He rubbed his fingers through his hair. 'Where's your mother?' he asked suddenly.

Jenny was startled. She hadn't realised David didn't know the Mileses' history. 'Um . . . she died . . . in a riding accident, two years ago.' She spoke quietly.

'Mine too,' David mumbled.

'Really?' Jenny was stunned. She had imagined that the absent Mrs Fergusson had married another man, but she had never liked to ask. 'Horse riding . . .?'

'No – in a car.' David looked away, and the shadow Jenny had seen so often crept across his face, darkening his eyes.

'It's horrible, isn't it, losing a mum?' she said simply.

'Yes.' He sighed. 'I've got Orla, though. I got her as a puppy after my mother died.'

'What a coincidence! I got Jess quite soon after my mum died, too,' Jenny smiled.

*He looks so lonely*, she thought. 'Does your father go away often – on business?' Jenny asked tentatively. She opened the door of the lower barn, where the newer lambs were kept until they were strong enough to go out to the field.

David went inside ahead of her. 'Not too often,' he

# THE GIFT

said. 'Half the time I don't know when he's going or why he has to go – or even how long he'll be away!'

'How come?' Jenny frowned.

'Look,' David said, suddenly turning on her. 'I don't want to talk about my father, or what he does, or why. OK? Let's just leave it.' He pushed past Jenny and went over to an enclosure, where he dropped onto his knees in the straw, peering in at the lambs, so Jenny couldn't see his face.

She was so surprised she didn't know what to do. She just stood there, gaping after him. But Jess's cold nose roused her. He was nudging at her, looking up, as if he was trying to tell her something. Then, the collie went over to David, sat down in the straw beside him and held up a paw. David half turned, and took Jess's front foot, with its little white sock, gently in his hand.

*There!* thought Jenny. *Jess is showing me that I should try to understand David. Jess trusts him and so should I.*

She walked to where David was kneeling. 'I'm really sorry,' she said. 'I didn't mean to pry. I won't ask any more questions, OK?'

David smiled sheepishly. 'I'm sorry I got cross. Are these new-born lambs?' he said, changing the subject.

Jenny nodded. 'Do you want to hold one?'

★　★　★

206

When the lights came on in the kitchen at the farmhouse, Jenny and David made their way home from the top field. They found Mrs Grace out of breath, rushing round the kitchen trying to hurry a meal together.

'Oh, David! Hello!' she said. 'I'm sorry I was so long! I wanted to be here when you arrived.' She threw some pasta into a pan of simmering water.

'It doesn't matter, Mrs Grace,' Jenny smiled. 'David's settled in, and I've shown him around. How's Mrs Perry?'

'Not well at all. I ended up by taking her to her doctor. Is your room all right, David?' she asked.

'Fine, thank you,' David replied.

'I'm sorry I didn't see your father, but . . .' She broke off, and her face broke into a beaming smile, as Fraser Miles came striding in through the kitchen door, bringing with him the strong smell of sheep. Jess hurried over to greet him.

'Ah! Hello, David. Welcome to Windy Hill.' Mr Miles spoke warmly, putting out a hand to pat the Border collie.

'Thanks Mr Miles.' David looked a little overwhelmed. He looked from Jenny, to Mrs Grace, to Mr Miles.

Jenny decided it would help if she gave him

something to do. 'Will you help me to set the table for supper?' she asked, going over to a large oak dresser. David followed and Jenny handed him the cutlery as she pulled it out of the drawer. 'There's five of us, so . . .'

'Um, there's just the *three* of you tonight.' Fraser Miles corrected, clearing his throat. Jenny looked at her father, confused.

'How come?' she asked.

'I've decided to take Ellen out . . . to a restaurant,' he finished quietly.

'Then . . . something special has happened! It must have! What are we . . . you . . . celebrating?' Jenny cried, turning to Mrs Grace.

Ellen Grace chuckled as she stirred a cheese sauce. 'Nothing, Jenny. Your father and I just thought it would make a pleasant change, that's all.'

David was standing still, holding the knives and forks in his hand. Quickly, Jenny swallowed her surprise. 'Well, good. That's . . . lovely. We'll be fine, here,' she mumbled.

Jenny suddenly noticed now that Mrs Grace was wearing a new dress, one she hadn't seen before.

'Matt will be in soon,' her father said. 'You can all eat together and watch a bit of telly. I'm going upstairs to change.'

'Fine, Dad,' Jenny said. She took the cutlery from David, feeling a slight flush creep into her cheeks. This was a first – her dad taking Mrs Grace out on a date! And on the very night that David Fergusson had arrived to stay! Things seemed to be changing at Windy Hill – and Jenny wasn't certain that she was completely happy about it.

Later, when she, Matt and David, had demolished the last of Mrs Grace's cheesy pasta, she left David watching television in the sitting-room with Jess and Orla and went upstairs to find her brother. A thin line of light was showing from under his bedroom door. Jenny went straight in.

'Do come in,' Matt said mockingly. 'And thanks for knocking.'

'Sorry,' Jenny said, and sat down on the end of the bed, frowning.

'What's up?' Matt asked, stacking a pile of his college books into a bag.

'Dad's never been out for *dinner* with Mrs Grace before,' Jenny stated.

'I think I was right,' he said, nodding his head. 'Romance is definitely on the cards for those two.'

'I've been thinking about it,' Jenny said. 'I don't feel . . . right . . . about having another . . . mother

. . . living here at Windy Hill. I know Mum isn't actually here, Matt, but, even so, she might not like it if someone takes her place in the family.'

'I know what you mean,' Matt said kindly. 'I wasn't sure how I felt about it at first, but Mrs Grace wouldn't be a mum, would she? She'd be a stepmother.'

'What's the difference?' Jenny asked. 'It still seems as if our mum is being replaced, somehow.'

'Think of it this way,' Matt suggested. 'Mum wouldn't want Dad to be lonely, and alone, for the rest of his life, would she?'

'He's not alone!' Jenny said tearfully. Her face was hot. 'He's got me – and you!'

'And Mrs Grace,' Matt finished. He slipped an arm round his sister's shoulders. 'She's been great, to us – all of us. But I know how you feel. It doesn't seem very long ago that Mum was still here, and now . . .'

But Jenny couldn't listen to another word. Her world seemed to be tilting. Everything she had been sure of was changing. Suddenly it seemed too much. She covered her face with her hands and began to cry.

'We're still a family,' Matt soothed. 'There'll always be Dad, and me and you . . . and Mum, somewhere, watching over us . . .'

'And Jess,' Jenny added, through her tears.

'And Jess,' Matt agreed. 'Mrs Grace is a . . . bonus! She's an added extra! The cherry on top of the cake.'

In spite of herself, Jenny giggled. 'You're right,' she said. 'Mrs Grace is every bit as good as a mum, without actually being Mum.'

'Let's give her a chance, Jen,' Matt urged. 'Anyway, you've got more important things to worry about at the moment than something that might never happen.'

'Yes,' Jenny wiped her eyes on her sleeve. 'Carrie.'

'Carrie,' Matt repeated. 'There's a lot to do, remember?'

'Thanks Matt. I'll get some sleep now, and tomorrow I'll really get organised!'

# 6

It had been the busiest two weeks Jenny could remember. When she woke up on the morning of the sponsored walk, she went over all the details of the day ahead, one last time.

Sponsorship forms had been given out in handfuls, and Jenny was certain there would be a good turnout for the walk. The village hall had been decked out in metres of bright bunting and balloons. Food, prepared by friends and members of Carrie's family, had been arriving secretly over the last couple of days and filled the big chest freezer in the garage at Windy Hill. A traditional band had been booked for the party, too.

Mrs Grace, with Mrs Turner, Mrs MacLay and Sarah, had worked tirelessly, making sure the hired glasses were polished and that the beautiful cake for Carrie was iced to perfection. They had gone about it all so carefully that, in spite of all the unavoidable hustle and bustle, Carrie knew nothing about the evening celebration to come.

It had been David's job to cycle around Graston, sticking up posters wherever he could. 'Nearly everyone in the village knows my face now,' he had told Jenny, arriving back at Windy Hill one evening after a poster-sticking session. 'It's been a great way to make friends.'

Jenny was satisfied that they had all done their best to make it a successful occasion. Even Jess had played his part. Her constant companion as always, the collie had kept Jenny's spirits up when tiredness overwhelmed her. Her only aching worry was Carrie herself, who hadn't been at all well during the last week. The amount of drugs she had been receiving for her illness had been increased, to prepare her body for her transplant, and it had left her feeling weaker and sicker than before.

'Twenty tablets a day,' Carrie had made a ghastly face as she reported this to Jenny. 'You can have it in a liquid medicine, but it tastes too disgusting to drink.'

'Can't you crush the tablets up into something sickly sweet to drown out the taste?' Jenny had asked.

'I've tried it.' Carrie had smiled weakly.

Jenny hoped that Carrie would be well enough to see the walkers set off from Graston post office, even if she wasn't able to walk any distance herself. Jenny wanted her to be there, at least, at the start. The sight of all those people, striding out with Carrie's cause as their inspiration, would boost her spirits, Jenny felt sure. Jess would be sporting a bunch of brightly coloured ribbons – bought for him by Vicky, Matt's girlfriend. All that remained to be done was to give Jess's coat a thorough brushing, so that it would gleam in the sun as he trotted along.

Jenny put on her dressing-gown and went down into the kitchen to groom the collie. To her surprise, Jess wasn't there. His basket was empty. The open kitchen door creaked as it moved in a gentle, early morning breeze. She went to the door and looked out. It was unlike Jess to go off early with her father or Matt. There was no sign of Mrs Grace, either.

The house felt strangely empty without her usual morning greeting.

'Jess!' Jenny called. 'Here, boy! Mrs Grace?'

Ellen Grace's voice came back immediately. 'Over here, Jenny. We're behind the barn.'

Puzzled, Jenny began to hurry across the dewy grass in her bare feet. 'What's happened?' she called out.

'Don't worry . . .' said Mrs Grace, then: 'Wait, Jess, stay still . . . good boy!'

Jenny's heart leaped up into her throat. Was something wrong with Jess? She rushed round the corner of the barn. Mrs Grace was crouching over Jess, who was lying on his side. He looked forlornly up at Jenny as she gasped, 'Oh! What's the matter with him?'

'Nothing at all,' Ellen Grace said reassuringly. 'He wanted to be let out very early this morning and I was making some tea when I heard him give a mighty yelp. He's got a nasty splinter of wood in his paw, poor thing.'

'Oh, Jess!' Jenny knelt down and peered at the collie's paw. The shard of wood had pierced the skin of the pad deeply. Mrs Grace held up Jess's foot, wielding a pair of eyebrow tweezers as deftly as a dentist. She gripped, twisted and pulled – and finally

216

the splinter came out. Jess yelped again as a blob of bright red blood welled up.

'There!' said the housekeeper triumphantly, stroking Jess. 'Poor wee boy!' She took a small lacy handkerchief from her pocket and dabbed tenderly at the collie's bleeding foot, then dropped a kiss on the top of his head.

'Will he be able to walk?' Jenny asked, stroking him.

'He'll be fine,' Mrs Grace said, standing back to let Jess up. The collie got to his feet and took a few paces, holding up his front left paw as he did so. 'But I'll go in and find some antiseptic ointment to put

on the wound to stop it getting infected.'

As Mrs Grace turned to go, Jenny noticed that the knees of her trousers were soiled with mud, and that there was blood on her sleeve. Jess was looking up at the housekeeper with warm, gold-brown eyes, his tail swaying slowly. Carefully, he tried out the injured foot by putting it onto the ground and taking a step. Then he wagged his tail harder.

*He's going to be all right to do the walk!* Jenny thought happily. On a sudden impulse, she reached up and gave Ellen Grace a hug.

The squeeze was affectionately returned. 'What's that for?' Mrs Grace chuckled, looking into Jenny's face.

'I just want to say . . . that I'm *really* glad you live with us and that . . . I hope you'll stay,' Jenny blurted.

Ellen Grace patted the top of Jenny's fair head. 'I might,' she smiled. 'You know, I just might.'


Clusters of people were standing about outside the post office when Jenny arrived with her dad, Mrs Grace, David, Matt and the two dogs. She recognised several of the teachers from school, and the faces of a few of the others were familiar too.

'There's Mrs Linden from the doctor's rooms,' said Mrs Grace, 'and Mr Cole from the bakery.'

'Gosh,' said Jenny, 'Look! Even our headmaster is here.'

As the crowd of walkers began to swell, Jenny saw that a few members of the local police were milling about, smiling and nodding, and keeping an eye out for the safety of younger children. They were putting up a cordon of red tape to keep the cars away. Fiona arrived, with her entire family, and lots of Jenny's classmates. Jess kept close to Jenny's side, though Orla was straining on her lead to reach him. Paul MacLay carried Toby under one arm, and the little Border terrier was shivering all over with excitement.

Jenny looked about, eager to see Carrie. There was no sign of Mr or Mrs Turner, and Jenny's hopes were beginning to sink.

'She'll make it – you'll see,' Matt said, giving Jenny's arm a little squeeze.

'Nearly time to start. Oh, but where's Carrie?!' Fiona was standing on tiptoe, trying to see over the heads of the crowd.

Jenny shrugged. 'Hasn't come – but she might. She only said she would see how she felt, Fi, remember?'

'Shh!' David hissed. 'Look, Mr Hearn is going to say something!'

Mr Hearn, the headmaster of Greybridge, had climbed up onto a small wooden box so he could be seen. 'Ladies and gentlemen, boys and girls,' he boomed. 'Thank you all for coming today to attempt this walk, for an excellent cause. The weather is fine, the planned route is a beautiful one, so please enjoy yourselves and take care. You may begin . . . NOW!'

People immediately started to surge forward, jostling Jenny. She stood still, craning her neck, staring about and willing Carrie to be there, but there was no sign of any of the Turners. She was bitterly disappointed.

'Come on!' David urged her. 'You'll get left behind.' Jenny hurried to catch him up, and began to walk in line with her father, Mrs Grace and Matt. Jess, his beautiful ribbons dancing in the breeze, pranced along eagerly and Jenny was relieved to see that his injured foot was giving him no trouble.

'I'm sorry you're disappointed,' Mrs Grace said, slipping her arm through Jenny's. 'You know Carrie would have been here if she possibly could have.'

'It would have made her so happy to see all these people, from all over Graston and Cliffbay, and all the teachers, too, and . . .' she trailed off.

'I know,' Mrs Grace said soothingly. 'But Carrie will hear about it from you, and Fiona and David. You can describe this wonderful turn-out to her. It will be as good as if she herself had been here.'

Jenny wasn't convinced. But she pushed aside her misery and looked about her. Already the walkers were beginning to peel off the outer layers of their clothing. Jumpers were being stuffed into backpacks and tied round waists. There was a cool freshness to the morning, but the spring sun was starting to climb, and the strenuous pace of the walking was making people warm.

'Jenny!' Sarah Taylor was pushing her way through the throng of people striding along.

'Hello, Sarah!' Jenny said. 'I wondered where you were.'

'A bit late, I'm afraid,' Sarah said apologetically. 'There are so many people here! Isn't it great?'

'Yes,' Jenny admitted. 'But no Carrie.'

Sarah's face clouded over. 'What a shame,' she said. 'I had really hoped . . .'

'Me too,' Jenny said grimly.

They walked on, following the road as it began to wind around the headland and dip away down towards Cliffbay. David kept pace with Jenny, and Orla trotted along, side by side, with Jess. Jenny smiled at him, thinking how well they had got along at Windy Hill together after the sharp words that had been spoken the first day.

'Ouch!' David said. 'I think I've got a stone in my

trainer.' He stepped to the side to allow the stream of walkers to go past him and Jenny hung back, waiting while he untied his shoelace. Jess licked the side of his face as he crouched there, nearly causing him to topple over.

'Ugh! Silly boy!' David laughed.

*I totally trust David now*, Jenny thought, watching the collie's display of affection. *There's nothing strange about him at all – except his father!* 'Jess really likes you,' she said, pleased, as she gazed around her at the many determined faces. Then she felt her heart suddenly squeeze up tight in her chest. 'David! Look!' she cried.

David stood up and looked over to where Jenny was pointing. The crowd behind them had parted, to make way for someone who was forging a speedy path through its midst. Jess barked joyfully, his tail wagging hard.

'It can't be . . .' Jenny said, clutching onto David's sleeve. 'But . . . it is! It's Carrie!' she shouted at the top of her voice. 'Dad, Matt, Sarah, Fiona . . . everyone! Carrie's here! On her roller-skates!'

The others turned round and stopped in their tracks as the painfully thin figure with the little woollen beret sped towards them, a gleeful grin on her face. A cheer went up from the crowd which gradually parted to allow Carrie through.

Jenny saw the look of determination on her friend's face. Mr Turner, on one side of his daughter, and Mrs Turner, on the other, were supporting her under each arm, and jogging along to keep pace with the rolling wheels.

'Jenny!' Carrie yelled. 'I'm here. I made it!'

Jess dashed forward, prancing and leaping in welcome. Fraser Miles began to clap Carrie, and the applause was taken up slowly by the crowd. Within seconds, it erupted down the length and breadth of the group of walkers and became a roar of approval.

Carrie flushed with embarrassment, but looked delighted. Running forward to hug her, Jenny remembered not to squeeze her too tight. 'You *did* make it! I'm so glad,' she shouted above the sound of clapping and cheering. 'And what a good idea!' She pointed at the roller-skates.

'Are you going all the way, young lady?' Fraser Miles asked in a teasing tone. Jenny noticed that Mrs Turner was out of breath and looked pale with tiredness. 'If so, I'd be delighted to escort you.' He bowed playfully.

Carrie turned to her mum, who smiled at Mr Miles. 'That OK, Mum?'

'I suppose I could do with stopping for a rest,' she

said. 'It was quite a dash from the post office to catch you up. So, Carrie, if you're sure?'

'I'm sure,' said Carrie, her eyes shining. She held out her hand to Fraser Miles.

'I'll go on the other side, if you like, Mr Turner?' Matt stepped up, grinning.

'Suits me. Thanks, Matt,' Mr Turner puffed. 'I warn you, it's hard work.'

Carrie, supported by Mr Miles and Matt, looked around, smiling. 'Right,' she said. 'What are we waiting for? Let's go, shall we?'

Jenny began to jog along beside her friend. She glanced down at Jess's glossy head, and as the collie looked up at her, she could have sworn he was smiling.

# 7

'Here they come!' Matt shouted, his nose to the window of the village hall. Saturday evening had arrived at last, and Jenny, her calf muscles stiff from her ten kilometre walk, sprang to Matt's side and peered out.

First, she looked for Jess. His sleek shape was silhouetted against the darkening sky, his nose raised to the dusk air, as he sat in the back of the farm pick-up. He had enjoyed the sponsored walk, but Jenny guessed he was quite happy to be resting now, out there in the cool evening.

Jenny scanned the carpark for the Turners. 'Carrie's in the car! She's made it – again!' she said happily. She had been worried that Carrie would have felt exhausted after her marathon roller-skate, and would have stayed at home to rest.

Mrs Turner's orange mini, with the sunflower painted on the roof, pulled onto the gravel outside. The buzz of chattering and laughing dried up, and people began to duck down to hide behind chairs and tables. Members of the band had tucked themselves away behind a red velvet curtain, drawn across a small wooden stage, and Jenny saw one of them peep out and give the thumbs-up sign to a friend.

'Right,' said Matt, who was still at the window, monitoring what was going on outside. 'Carrie is getting out of the car . . . frowning hard . . . probably asking her parents why they've brought her here! Mr Turner's hand is on the door, and here she comes . . . now!'

Carrie's puzzled face appeared in the doorway, flanked by her parents. There was a terrific cheer from the crowd – which made her jump – as people began to appear from all corners of the big room.

'Surprise!'

Carrie's mouth fell open and her hand flew to cover it, as friends hurried forward to hug her and draw her into the room. She stood looking around, her big green eyes blinking slowly. A sunny smile appeared on her face, as she took in all the familiar faces, the table groaning with a spread of food, the streamers, balloons and the band. As the musicians began to play, she caught Jenny's eye. 'Did you do this?' she asked wonderingly, as Jenny came over.

'Me, and Sarah and David and Fiona and, oh, *loads* of us. We thought you could do with a bit of fun.' Jenny said. She was filled with relief and excitement. She tucked her arm through Carrie's. 'I'm so glad you're here!' she grinned.

'But I'm still wearing my sweaty old trainers and leggings!' Carrie groaned, patting her beret into place. 'And look at you!'

Jenny looked down at her own party dress and shrugged. 'If we'd asked you to change your clothes after the walk, it would have given away the secret,' she said. 'Anyway, how are you feeling after having roller-skated ten kilometres today?'

'Not too bad, though my ankles are a bit sore from the boots,' Carrie said. 'And I think I need to sit down.'

The moment she found a chair, friends crowded

round to congratulate Carrie for having completed the sponsored walk. Mr Miles appeared with a drink, and Fiona brought over a plate of small triangular sandwiches.

'But you *must* be hungry after that walk!' she said, when Carrie refused the offer of food.

'Nope,' Carrie said, watching as people began to dance. 'I just want to sit and look. I can't believe my eyes! How come I didn't find out about this?'

Jenny giggled. 'Clever planning,' she said. She was pleased with the result of her hard work. Everyone had come, even a few of the teachers from school – Mrs Teale and Mr Wallis, and Mr Hearn, the headmaster, with his wife. The dull little hall looked bright and welcoming – and even the music wasn't too loud, as Mrs Grace had feared it would be.

She looked over to see Matt inspecting a pile of sponsorship forms. Mrs Grace was helping him by tapping numbers into a pocket calculator, while Fraser Miles and Mr Turner were pouring drinks. Sarah was deep in conversation with a grey-haired woman Jenny knew to be Mrs Thom, who ran the hospice where Sarah's sister Katie had stayed.

'Look,' she pointed her out to Carrie. 'We're going to give the money raised to the lady talking with Sarah, over there.'

'Do we know how much was raised yet?' Mrs Turner asked, coming over with a bowl of crisps.

'No,' said Jenny, 'but Matt and Mrs Grace are adding it up now. I'll bet it's a lot. The path to Cliffbay was jam-packed with people.'

'Where's Jess?' Carrie asked suddenly, looking up at Jenny.

'Outside, in the back of the pick-up truck,' Jenny said. 'Dad didn't think it was a good idea to have him in the hall right at the start of the party. But he's waited long enough, now. I'll go and get him.'

Jenny crossed the hall and opened the door to the carpark. The music and the laughter followed her out into the chilly, deepening blue of dusk. Jess, still sporting his multicoloured ribbons, was sitting up in the back of the open pick-up, alert for any sign of Jenny. He stood up, wagging his tail, when he saw her. But there was someone sitting beside him in the van.

'David?' Jenny was alarmed. David's dark head was bent, his knees drawn up. 'Is everything OK?'

'I thought he might be lonely,' David said. 'We've been watching the stars come out, haven't we, Jess?' He ran the palm of his hand down the collie's back.

'Well, that's . . . nice of you!' Jenny was touched. 'I've come to take Jess inside now. Everyone's arrived.

You know, you really should have brought Orla.'

'No,' David shook his head. 'Orla isn't like Jess. She wouldn't be able to behave herself at a party the way he can. Anyway, she's tired after that walk. You know,' he added dreamily, 'I think Orla really likes staying at Windy Hill, with Jess, and everything.'

'We like having her too – and *you*, of course,' Jenny said warmly.

It was true, Jenny reflected. It had been much more fun having David around than she thought it would. He had grown more relaxed as the time went on, and had shown himself to be a willing helper, both on the farm and round the house – impressing Mrs Grace no end last Sunday morning by making a pile of pancakes for breakfast!

'Come on,' Jenny said, 'Let's go back in, now, or Carrie will be wondering what's happened to us. And, thanks for looking out for Jess,' she added.

'That's all right,' David said, jumping down from the van. He brushed the bits of straw and the dust from the back of his trousers with his hands. Jess waited, cocking his head at Jenny.

'Yes, come on, Jess,' she instructed and he leaped down, shook himself all over, then began to trot happily in the direction of the hall.

*David has become my friend*, Jenny realised, as she

followed. *I don't know very much about him — except that, like me, he loves his dog and, like me, he misses his mother, but I know that I've made a special friend.*

Carrie was still in the chair where Jenny had left her. Her cheeks were flushed and her eyes bright and happy. She was clapping in time to the music as the dancers whirled around her.

Walking in front of Jenny, Jess threaded his way through the throng to Carrie's side and put his nose in her lap, looking up at her and swishing his long, plumy tail. Smoothing his head, she slipped him a cheesy biscuit as a treat. The collie licked the last

crumbs from his muzzle, then turned and walked away from Carrie, looking back at her over his shoulder. He stopped, and barked sharply, once.

'Jess!' Jenny hissed. But the collie seemed determined. He came back to Carrie, looked up at her face, then turned and walked away a second time, stopping to look back at her and bark once more.

'He wants you to go with him,' Jenny explained. 'Do you feel well enough to follow?'

As Carrie got slowly out of the chair, Jess gently took hold of the sleeve of her sweatshirt with his teeth and, walking backwards, tugged her to the edge of the circle of dancers. Carrie began to giggle helplessly. She half turned to look back at Jenny, and shrugged, as if to say: 'What's he *doing*?' But having reached the dance floor, Jess dropped Carrie's sleeve and trotted back to Jenny.

Carrie's waist was immediately encircled by Mrs McLay on one side, and Sarah on the other. As she was swept up into the ring of dancers and whirled away, Jenny heard her laugh pealing through the room.

'You're *so* special!' Jenny told Jess, laughing and hugging the collie.

'That dog!' Fraser Miles shook his head wonderingly. Then he asked: 'Is Carrie having a good time?' He bent down to talk in Jenny's ear as she sat looking at Carrie.

'Yes, I think she is, Dad,' Jenny said happily.

'And you, Jenny? Are you enjoying the party?' he asked, putting a hand on her shoulder.

'I am.' Jenny smiled.

'Do you want to dance with your old dad?' Mr Miles asked.

'No thanks,' Jenny said 'But I know someone who might. Mrs Grace!'

'Ah, well, now, I think she's a bit busy for . . .' he began, looking disconcerted.

Jenny interrupted. 'No, she isn't, Dad. She'd *love* to dance. Go on, ask her, please! Or I'll get Jess to take you to her,' she threatened, teasingly.

Mr Miles looked suddenly determined. 'All right then, I will!' He handed his glass to his daughter, and surged away through the crowd to Ellen Grace's side. Jenny saw her hurriedly take the last bite of a sandwich, as Fraser Miles led her to the dance floor.

'Your dad is *dancing* with Mrs Grace!' Fiona pointed out.

Jenny nodded, smiling. 'And about time, too,' she said.

Ellen Grace was gazing up at Fraser as she danced,

her eyes wide, a soft, rather secretive, smile on her face. She looked different Jenny thought, though she wasn't sure why. Again, she had the feeling that something had changed – for ever.

A small shiver went through Jenny. Jess edged a little closer to her side and her fingers found the soft tufts of fur on his chest.

She could not remember seeing her father as happy for ages – since her mum was alive, in fact. She sat back on her wooden chair with a sigh of pleasure.

Carrie was still dancing when Mr Turner brought the hall to sudden stillness by rapping on the table. He asked for the attention of the guests, then raised his voice to be heard. 'Carrie's mother and I want to thank you all for making this a day – and a night – to remember. You all deserve our gratitude, but we would like to say a special thank you to Sarah Taylor, whose courage has given our Carrie real hope for a healthy, and happier, future.'

Mr Turner's voice quavered as he lifted a huge, cellophane-wrapped bouquet of flowers and handed it to Sarah. Colour flamed into her face as she hurried forward to cries of: 'Well done Sarah!' and 'Good luck for the operation!' and 'We'll be thinking of you both.' Then, Sarah beckoned to Mrs

Thom, who came forward to accept the money that had been collected from the walk.

'Oh!' said Mrs Thom, as she looked at the amount on the cheque. 'This is amazing – much more than I expected! Thank you all, so very much.'

When the music started up again, Carrie was persuaded by her father to try a lively Scottish reel and Jenny danced with Matt, and then her father. She kept an eye out for Jess, who wandered slowly among the guests, enjoying the strokes and attention he got, and the tasty nibbles that were slipped his way.

Then, suddenly, it had gone midnight, and Jenny was struggling to keep her eyelids open.

Carrie's face was pale, the shadows like bruises under her eyes. Mrs Turner gave Jenny a hug as they left and Carrie said: 'I'll do the same for you, one day, Jen!' and grinned at her sleepily.

Jenny couldn't wait to go home to bed. It had been a wonderful day, one that she would never forget, but the effort of the last two weeks had finally caught up with her. She was exhausted!

Back at Windy Hill, Ellen Grace began to cover the leftover food and wash up the hired glasses. 'I'd rather do it now than have to face it in the morning,' she said gently, when Fraser Miles suggested that it was far too late at night for kitchen chores. 'You go on up to your beds — all of you.'

'If you're sure, Ellen.' Jenny's dad climbed the stairs gratefully.

'I can't stand on my legs another minute,' David confessed, yawning.

'Goodnight!' Ellen chuckled. 'Sleep tight.'

Jenny untied Jess's ribbons and he curled up in his basket, yawning. Then she followed Matt upstairs.

'Jenny! Matt!' Mr Miles called from his bedroom. 'Come in here for a moment, will you?'

Matt looked at Jenny and raised his eyebrows. The bedroom door was ajar, and Mr Miles was pacing under the window.

'What's up, Dad?' Matt asked, sitting on the edge of the bed.

Jenny sat beside him, rubbing her eyes. 'I'm so sleepy, Dad . . . I don't think . . .'

'This won't take a minute,' Jenny's father spoke hurriedly. He looked flustered and uncomfortable. 'I just wanted to know how . . . you would feel . . . if I asked Ellen to marry me?'

Jenny's heavy eyelids flew wide open and she gasped. An unexpected feeling of joy surged through her and she leaped off the bed and ran to hug her father. 'Yes!' she said. 'Oh, yes! It feels . . . *right*. It *is* right. Yes!'

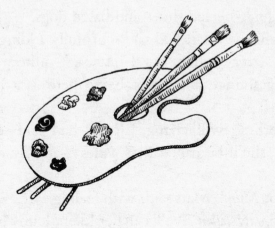

# 8

Jenny slept deeply and woke up late, to the smell of bacon frying. Her first thought was about her father's announcement the night before. Part of her felt sad – wishing things didn't have to happen so fast. But then she thought about Ellen Grace – her warm blue eyes, and the way she loved Jess and Windy Hill – and realised how lucky a family they were to have found her.

'After all,' she had reasoned, as she sat on Matt's bed late the previous night, 'Dad might have chosen someone completely unsuitable – someone who wore high-heeled shoes and hated dogs.'

'Unlikely!' Matt had said scornfully, adding: 'I like her . . . very much, but I just can't quite get over feeling strange about her being here as a kind of *mother*.'

'Nothing will change,' Jenny had said sensibly. 'Only, she'll be called Mrs Miles – and *we* can call her . . .'

'Not *Mum*!' Matt said, with feeling.

'No, silly. *Ellen*. We'll call her Ellen,' Jenny had said decisively, and smiled.

Now, she stretched contentedly as she lay in her bed. Her legs ached from yesterday's strenuous walk but her spirits were high. She would suggest to David that they walk Jess and Orla along the path to Cliffbay. She wished it were possible for Carrie to come along, but after the celebration the day before, Jenny doubted that Carrie would have any remaining energy for a long walk.

When Jenny went down to the kitchen, her fair head tousled from sleep and her feet bare, Mrs Grace was humming to herself. Jenny went straight over and put her arms round Ellen's waist. 'Dad told us – last night. I'm really pleased,' she said simply, squeezing tight. 'You *are* going to say yes, aren't you?'

'I already have!' Mrs Grace laughed. 'Of course!'

'This means you're going to stay at Windy Hill for ever, doesn't it?' Jenny urged.

'I hope so, Jenny,' Mrs Grace smiled. 'And I'm very pleased that you're pleased.'

'Can Matt and I call you Ellen now?' Jenny asked, stooping to say good morning to Jess, who had brought her a slipper. Orla was having a long drink from the big stone bowl under kitchen counter. 'It would be odd to say Mrs Miles.'

'Yes, it does sound odd. Ellen will be fine,' she replied.

'Are you going to have a proper wedding – a huge reception and all that?' Jenny wanted to know.

'Well, not *too* big,' Ellen smiled. 'For one thing, big weddings cost an awful lot of money. And my family are all too far away to come to Scotland and celebrate with us at short notice. Your father and I don't want to wait. We are hoping for a simple ceremony, as soon as possible. There's no point in dragging it out,' she finished. 'Do you agree?'

Jenny nodded. 'I agree. But it's sad that your family won't be with you.'

'Well . . .' Ellen looked thoughtful. 'Perhaps, later in the year, Fraser and I will go and visit them in Canada. That would be fun.'

'And me too?' Jenny teased.

Ellen laughed and ruffled Jenny's hair. 'We'll see. Is David still asleep?'

'I haven't seen him this morning,' Jenny replied. 'So he must be snoozing.'

'Your dad has asked for a cooked break—' Mrs Grace broke off as the phone rang.

'I'll get it!' Jenny said, sprinting into the hall. 'Hello?'

'It's me, Jen,' Carrie's voice sounded faint, as though she was phoning from a long way away.

'Carrie! I was just thinking about you and hoping you might feel like a walk with Jess and . . .'

'I'm going in to hospital – now,' she said flatly.

'Now? You mean, today?' Jenny was confused.

Ellen Grace had come into the hall, wiping her hands on a dish towel. 'What is it?' she whispered, alarmed by the look on Jenny's face.

'I just phoned to say goodbye,' Carrie said.

'But . . . why?' Jenny asked. 'Why do you have to go so suddenly?'

'I've come out in some little blood blisters, under my skin, which isn't a good sign. So I've got to go right away. Will you come and visit me?'

Jenny felt a wave of fear rising up from her feet and her mouth went dry. Mrs Grace put out a hand and Jenny clutched it.

'Yes, of course,' she said brightly. 'I'll be there. I'll bring some sweets . . .'

'The ambulance is here. I've got to go now. Bye, Jen.' The line went dead.

Jenny replaced the receiver and let go of Mrs Grace's hand. Jess was at her side in a trice, sitting as close to her as he could, pushing his nose into her palm.

'Tell me, Jenny!' Mrs Grace urged. 'What's happened?'

'An ambulance!' Jenny repeated, as if in a trance. 'Carrie's being taken to hospital.'

Ellen Grace wound her arms round Jenny and held her close. Then she guided her towards the big pine table and sat her down into a chair. She poured some hot tea from the big brown pot and stirred in two heaped spoonfuls of sugar.

'Take a sip,' she urged Jenny.

'Oh, Mrs Grace!' Jenny wailed, putting her head in her hands. 'Will I ever see Carrie again?'

'Of course you will,' Ellen Grace was firm. 'She's just having her operation a little sooner the planned, that's all. And didn't you just say that you'd visit her in the hospital?'

Jenny sipped at her hot tea, holding tightly to Mrs Grace's hand. Jess put his head into her lap, which

Jenny found comforting, as ever. She took a deep breath. She would have to try hard not to be afraid for Carrie, but to believe, as she always had, that she was going to get well.

'Brave girl!' said Ellen Grace gently, as Jenny managed a watery smile.

When Matt and Fraser Miles had gone off into the fields, and David had gone upstairs to do his homework, Jenny decided to head off up to Darktarn Keep. It was the one place where she could be alone with her thoughts, her own special place to be when there were things she wanted to come to terms with.

Jess's tail thumped steadily against the floor of the kitchen, watching as she fastened Orla's lead onto her collar. She pulled on a fleece and her boots, while Orla yapped steadily in excitement. Then, the kitchen door open, Orla raced out into the yard after Jess, dragging Jenny along behind her.

As soon as she reached the track that ran up the hill, Jenny let Orla off her lead. The dogs bounded on ahead, up the steep rise that led to the stone keep on its crest. A sharp wind rose from a choppy, grey sea far below, but Jenny knew that when she reached the protective shelter of Darktarn's thick and ancient stone walls, she would be snug in the spring sunshine.

It was hard to look down on the cluster of colourful houses in Cliffbay and know that Carrie wasn't there, where she should be. Somewhere over in Greybridge, her friend was lying on a starched white hospital sheet, in a room smelling of disinfectant, and she, Jenny, hadn't even been there to give her a goodbye hug. It wasn't the way she had imagined it at all.

'Blisters?' Mr Miles had said at breakfast time, befuddled from a late sleep and concerned by his daughter's pale and anxious face. 'Doesn't sound very serious to me, Jen.' He and Matt, and David too, had comforted and reassured her, but Jenny's fear lay like a cold and heavy stone in the pit of her tummy – and it refused to budge.

Jess bounded up to the place where Jenny was sitting, her back to the wall, in a pool of soft sunshine. He curled up beside her, lifting his head to look at the gulls that circled lazily above the cliff top on wide, white wings. Together they watched Orla, as she wandered about on the hillside, seeking out and following the scent of fox and rabbit.

'Oh, Jess,' Jenny said quietly. 'What will I do if Carrie dies?' Jess licked Jenny's hand and looked up at her with his intense, caramel-coloured eyes. Then, he stood up and wagged his tail. 'You're right,' she said, smiling at him. 'I'm being far too gloomy. I must try not to think about it. *Especially* when there is a wedding to plan!'

Even the thought of Ellen Grace was somehow comforting. 'I do love her, Jess,' she told him. 'Not in the same way that I loved Mum, but it's love nevertheless. I'm sure of it now. And Mum would be pleased to know there was someone taking care of us at Windy Hill. Don't you think? What am I going to get them as a present, I wonder?'

Jess put his paw into her lap and Jenny was idly examining the little black pad for signs of the wound made by the splinter, when she felt the collie stiffen. Someone was walking slowly up the hill. Jess's ears were alert and he watched intently as the figure approached. Then his ears went down and he streaked away towards it, his tail streaming out behind him.

Jenny soon recognised Mrs Turner. She was carrying an easel and had her painting things in a leather case over her shoulder. Jenny had seen these tools before and was encouraged by the sight of them. If Mrs Turner was here to paint, it must mean there was good news about Carrie. She jumped up and ran to meet her.

'Mrs Turner!' Jenny called. Carrie's mum turned, frowning, and Jenny saw immediately that she had been crying. Her red eyes were ringed with the dark smudges of sleeplessness. Jenny's heart felt as though it had jumped into her throat. 'How's Carrie?'

'Hello, Jenny,' Mrs Turner said quietly. She began to set up her easel. Away in the distance, Orla yapped and pounced on something, but Jess stayed beside Jenny. 'There's no news, just yet,' she said.

'But . . . the hospital . . . what happened?' Jenny pleaded. Her voice was almost a whisper.

'Carrie's condition suddenly got worse,' she explained. 'She's getting tiny blood blisters under her skin which means that her blood isn't clotting properly. The doctors say that's bad sign because the bone marrow is breaking down very quickly, and Carrie is without an effective immune system.'

Jenny slowly shook her head, then looked out towards the sea. She didn't want Mrs Turner to see her cry. 'But Sarah Taylor is going to help . . .'

'Yes,' Mrs Turner brushed her red hair away from her face and straightened her shoulders. She took a deep breath. 'Yes, I'm sure that will give Carrie the chance she needs to get better.'

'When will she be able to come home?' Jenny asked.

'We don't know yet,' Mrs Turner replied. She unrolled a large canvas and set it up on the easel.

'I'm going back to the hospital later. In the meantime, painting will help me to relax.'

'Yes,' Jenny agreed.

'There isn't really much I can do at the moment and Carrie's father and I both feel that our worrying and fussing will only make Carrie feel upset. Her dad's at home cooking a meal – it's his way of relaxing.' She squeezed out a blob of green paint.

Jenny realised that she was looking at a picture that was almost complete. It showed the rugged, wild-flower strewn fields stretching down to the cliffs below Graston, and beyond, to a glassy grey sea. The red rooftops of Windy Hill had been painted in the foreground, standing out in sharp contrast to the hazy gold background of setting sun and sky. It was a lovely picture and, for a moment, Jenny wondered if she might ask Mrs Turner to paint her one just like it, as a gift for Mrs Grace and her father. Then she dismissed the idea as being foolish. Mrs Turner had more important things to think about.

'Are you walking Orla for David?' Mrs Turner asked.

'Yes. David's doing his homework,' Jenny explained. 'Orla loves coming with me and Jess. But I haven't really been walking. I've been sitting in the keep and thinking.'

# THE GIFT

'About Carrie?' Mrs Turner was daubing colour into a tiny gull's wing on her painting.

'Yes, and also about my dad – and Mrs Grace.'

'Yes?' Mrs Turner smiled at Jenny. 'And what *were* you thinking about them?' she prompted, a sparkle in her eye.

'Well,' Jenny began, 'Did you know they're getting married?'

'I suspected they might!' Carrie's mum laughed and for a moment her face was the way Jenny remembered it being before Carrie got sick. 'How wonderful. Are you pleased?'

'Yes,' Jenny nodded, certain of it now. She paused. 'I was wondering what I'd give them as a present. I haven't got a lot of pocket money left and . . .'

'But . . . you must have this *painting*!' Mrs Turner said, putting her hands on Jenny's shoulders and reading her thoughts.

'Oh Mrs Turner! Would you let me buy it?' Jenny was thrilled.

'Buy it! Nonsense, Jenny. You can have it to give to them – with my love!' she said.

'Really? It would be perfect for them. Dad has a very old aerial photograph of the farm, but nothing like this. They'll love it.' Jenny's eyes were shining.

'I expect there are a lot of plans to be made, now.'

Mrs Turner went back to her easel.

'Yes,' Jenny replied. 'It's hard for me to think about a wedding when Carrie . . .'

'Oh, but you must,' Mrs Turner said resolutely. 'Concentrate on your father's happiness – be as involved as you can. It will help the time to pass.' Mrs Turner's troubled eyes filled with tears.

'Thanks so much for the painting. It's really great,' Jenny said quietly.

'We'll keep it our secret, until it's finished. Then I'll wrap it for you,' she said.

Jenny nodded, smiling. 'I'd better get back,' she said.

'Bye, Jenny.' Mrs Turner was already painting again. But suddenly she turned to get up and give Jenny a hug. 'You're a good friend to Carrie,' she murmured in her ear. 'The best.'

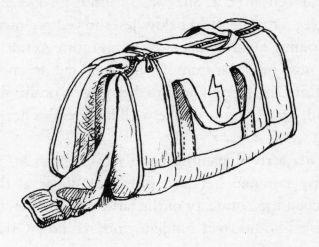

## 9

On the way back down the track to Windy Hill, Jenny tried hard not to think about Carrie but of the coming wedding instead. Mrs Turner was right; there was little point in dwelling on the sad and frightening possibilities of her friend's sickness. She tried to picture the dress Ellen might choose to wear on her special day, and wondered whether there would be a party, and how thrilled her dad would be with Carrie's mum's painting.

Jenny called to Orla. The collie had spotted a rabbit

and raced after it. She was sprinting in sweeping circles across the field below. Jess showed no interest in joining her. He kept close to his mistress's side, his icy nose never far from her hand, his tail drooping.

'I'm OK,' Jenny told him, her fingers on his silky head. 'Don't you worry, Jess. I'll be fine. I'm not the one who's sick.'

Orla arrived, panting heavily from her run, and Jenny fastened her lead onto her collar as they reached the boundary of the farm. Fraser Miles had warned both David and Jenny not to allow Orla to roam anywhere near his sheep, and it was a precaution Jenny had taken to heart.

When she reached the farmyard, she recognised Mr Fergusson's car on the gravel forecourt. The front door of the farmhouse opened and David stepped out, his sports bag in his hand. Jenny could tell it had been packed in a hurry, because the zip hadn't properly closed and she could see the trailing sleeve of a grey school jumper.

'Dad's home,' David said, as Jenny approached. 'Thanks for walking Orla.' Jess and Orla greeted David with wagging tails.

'Are you leaving?' she asked.

'Yeh. He just arrived back. Mrs Grace told me Carrie's been taken to hospital.' David's dark eyebrows were high on his forehead.

Jenny nodded. 'Poor Carrie. She suddenly got worse.'

'Hello, Jenny,' said Mr Fergusson, stepping out of the house with Mr Miles. Jenny's father was in his wellington boots. Nell and Jake milled around his legs, obviously eager to get back to work.

'Hello, Mr Fergusson.'

'Thanks for having my boy,' he smiled.

Jenny wondered again why this man seemed so mysterious; why hadn't he telephoned to say he was on his way back? And why hadn't he been able to tell them how long he would be gone in the first place?

'Yes, thanks,' David nodded at Mr Miles. 'Thanks for letting me stay, Mr Miles.'

'It was nice to have you around,' said Jenny's dad.

Mr Fergusson threw David's bag into the back of the car and Orla jumped in after it. Jess went to the car and looked up. Orla's head appeared over the sill of the back window and the collie's touched noses, briefly.

'Ah,' said Jenny. 'They're saying goodbye.'

'See you at school tomorrow,' David said, getting in.

'Yes. Bye.'

As David's father drove away, Jenny felt a small

pang of regret. She was going to miss having David around.

'*Ellen!*' said Jenny, trying the name out as she came into the kitchen.

Mrs Grace turned, and gave Jenny a happy smile. 'Oh, that *does* sound . . . friendly!' She laughed, and put her arm round Jenny's shoulders. 'It makes me feel that I'm really part of the family!'

'Good,' said Jenny, smiling inwardly about the wonderful secret of Mrs Turner's painting. 'I saw Mrs Turner up near Darktarn Keep. She had been crying,' Jenny reported, her face suddenly serious.

'Did she explain what had caused Carrie to be taken in to hospital like that?' Ellen asked.

'Something about how the cells that clot Carrie's blood weren't working properly any more,' Jenny said, not really wanting to think about it. She changed the subject. 'Mrs Grace . . . Ellen, are you going to wear a white dress for the wedding?'

'Good heavens, no!' Ellen laughed. 'I'm too old for all that. No, something rather glamorous, but dignified, I think. Will you help me choose something?'

'Yes, please!' Jenny eyes lit up.

'And perhaps you'd like to have something special to wear yourself?' Ellen asked.

'Wow, yes!' It had been ages since Jenny had been shopping for clothes.

'Your father and I would like it to be a small wedding. We don't want a big fuss. But there is lots to be done, just the same. Do you want to help me to plan it?' Ellen Grace asked.

Jess barked, and Jenny laughed. 'He approves!' she said. 'And so do I! Yes, when do we start – and where?'

'We'll start with a list of people,' Ellen said. 'Have you got a pen?'

'I'll just fill Jess's water bowl,' Jenny said, 'and then I'll be with you.' It wasn't very long ago, Jenny reflected, that she was making out a list for a different sort of party. Still, it was good to be busy. It was just what she needed.


After lunch, Matt announced that he would have to make an early start back to college. 'There's a party on tonight in my residence,' he said. 'I don't want to miss it.'

'You deserve it,' Fraser Miles grinned at his son. 'You've worked hard this weekend. Thanks, Matt.'

Jenny trailed after Matt as he hurried around his bedroom, packing. 'Are you feeling happier? About Dad and Mrs Grace, I mean?' she asked.

'I . . . think so,' Matt said thoughtfully. 'Ellen is lovely, isn't she? And you are right, Jen. Dad could have chosen to marry someone like that awful Marion woman!'

At the mention of her name, Jenny gave a shudder. 'Ugh! Don't remind me.'

'Jenny!' Ellen Grace's voice came floating up the stairs. 'Fiona's here. She's going to the hospital to visit Carrie. Do you want to go along?'

Jenny gasped. 'Yes!' she shouted. 'I'm coming!' She raced along the passage and took the stairs two at a time.

'Goodbye, Jenny!' Matt's voice was playfully sarcastic.

'Oh, sorry, Matt,' Jenny paused at the bottom of the stairs and yelled. 'Bye – see you next weekend.' Jess had been lying on the floor under the table, and now he got up and came over to Jenny, wagging his tail happily. She planted a kiss on the soft place between the collie's eyes. 'No, no walk just now. Stay there, boy. I won't be long.'

'Give Carrie our love,' Ellen Grace's hands were clasped at her chest.

'I'm so glad I can *see* her!' Jenny breathed, lacing up her trainers in a hurry. 'I didn't think I would. Not for ages. But I haven't got any *sweets*!'

'Don't worry about that. And don't expect too much, will you?' Ellen Grace looked anxious.

'I won't,' Jenny said. 'See you later.' And she sped out of the door just as Fiona leaned forward to toot the horn impatiently on her mother's car.

In the children's ward at Greybridge Hospital, Carrie had her own small room. On a coatstand in the corner, hung a series of snowy-white gowns which reminded Jenny of a ghost costume she'd once worn at Hallowe'en. There was a blue chalk-line marked on the floor around Carrie's bed, which she had to stay behind. Carrie lay inside a special little see-through tent, which had been filled with air that was being kept carefully germ-free.

Jenny stared at her friend. She looked so small and helpless on the other side of the plastic. Her face was several shades paler than when Jenny had last seen her, whirling about in a wild Scottish reel in her father's arms. A rash of tiny blood blisters marked her neck and her hands.

'I'm an alien,' said Carrie, lifting her pyjamas to show them a thin, soft tube emerging from a tiny hole in her tummy. She made a face, and Jenny found herself giggling, though it wasn't funny at all. Carrie's tummy had been painted with a bright orange liquid to keep it sterile and it looked rather painful.

'It doesn't hurt,' she added, as Fiona's hands flew to cover her mouth in horror. 'They put all the medicine in through there, and take some of my blood out. And they'll put Sarah's marrow through there for me, too,' Carrie explained matter-of-factly. 'It's far better than having lots of injections!'

'Yes,' Jenny agreed. There seemed little point in asking Carrie how she was feeling. Jenny could guess that her friend was being brave, but watching her, Jenny felt her heart thud loudly in her chest.

'You didn't bring Jess?' Carrie joked.

'Not allowed,' Jenny grinned. 'He wanted to come, though.'

'What's the food like?' Fiona wanted to know. Jenny could tell she was uneasy.

'Quite good,' was Carrie's response. She shifted the cloth cap she was wearing on her head. The remaining wisps of her red hair were just visible. 'I'm not very hungry, though.'

'Are you scared?' Fiona asked, gazing around the room at all the monitoring equipment. 'Of the operation, I mean?'

'Nope,' said Carrie dismissively. 'I'll be asleep, and when I wake up, it'll all be over.'

The heavy white door of the hospital room swung

open and Sarah Taylor peeped round it. Mrs Turner and a doctor were with her. Behind them, Mrs McLay was sipping a hot drink from a plastic cup.

'Hello!' Sarah smiled, coming in. She looked at Jenny and Fiona. 'Gosh, the whole gang's here!' She was wearing a green hospital gown and her hair had been scooped up inside a paper cap. There was a sticking–plaster on her arm.

Jenny and Fiona said hello, together.

'All right, Carrie?' asked the doctor, peering in on her. Carrie nodded.

'I'm just along the corridor from you, Carrie,' Sarah said.

'Sarah's going to have her bone marrow removed this afternoon,' the doctor announced. 'The operation will last about an hour, then she'll go into the recovery room. Then it'll be your turn.' He smiled warmly at Carrie, who blinked at him.

'It'll be over before you know it, Carrie lass,' Anna McLay said reassuringly.

'How do they get it out? The marrow?' Fiona asked Sarah.

'They collect it from the bones of the pelvis – which is this bit here,' Sarah pointed to the area around her hips. 'They put in a special needle and draw out the marrow – only about one litre. I can go home tomorrow, can't I, Doctor?' Sarah asked.

'You sure can,' he said cheerfully.

Fiona was grimacing. 'Ooh, it sounds painful!'

'A little bit,' said the doctor. 'But she'll be back at that wildlife hospital of hers in a few days.'

'What time will Carrie have her operation, Doctor Willis?' Mrs Turner asked in a small voice.

'About five o clock,' he replied.

Jenny felt as though she didn't want to hear any more about it. She wanted it to be over and for Carrie to be well again. She tried to concentrate on a picture of Carrie running along the path above Cliffbay, the wind whipping her tangled red hair away from her laughing face. It made her feel better. 'When will you be home again?' she asked, looking at Carrie, but directing the question at the doctor.

'That will depend on her white blood cell count,' the doctor explained. 'When it's back up to a healthy number of cells, which are fighting fit, she can go home. It shouldn't take more than about ten days to two weeks.'

'Oh,' said Jenny, and remembered to smile brightly at Carrie.

'May I have a word, Mrs Turner?' the doctor asked. Carrie's mum followed him out of the room.

Carrie yawned, and turned her head away on the

pillow. She looked so sad that Jenny's heart turned over.

'I think it's time we were off,' said Mrs MacLay quietly. 'Fiona? Jenny?'

'Yes,' Jenny said. She wished she could slip her hand into Carrie's sterile tent and squeeze her fingers, or crawl right under it and give her a hug. 'Good luck, Carrie,' she said simply.

'Bye, Carrie,' Fiona echoed.

'Say hello to Jess for me,' Carrie smiled at Jenny. She lifted her fingers in a limp little wave.

'Goodbye.' Jenny was glad to get out of the room. The tears that had been threatening since the start of their visit began to spill silently down her cheeks.

'It was *horrible!*' Jenny told Ellen Grace. She paced about the kitchen back at Windy Hill, unable to settle. Mrs Grace clasped a mug of tea and watched her sadly. In his basket Jess's ears were pricked, his head to one side, as he followed Jenny with eyes full of concern.

'Seeing her lying there, looking so . . . white and blotchy and sick. It was horrible,' she said again. Her tears had dried up, and in their place had come a fierce anger at the unfairness of it all.

'Well,' Ellen Grace spoke soothingly. 'It's all

happened sooner than we expected. But this is the first step to Carrie's recovery, Jenny. Try to think of it that way. The next time you see her, she may be just like the old, fiery redhead we know and love.'

Jenny stopped striding about, and drew up a chair beside Ellen. She put her chin in her hands. 'How am I going to stop thinking about it?' she asked. 'Until she's better?'

'For a start, we've got a wedding to plan,' Ellen Grace smiled. 'And there's that new dress you wanted . . .'

Jenny sat up and gave herself a little shake. 'Yes,' she

said. 'That's a nice thought. A new dress . . .'

'I've got a friend in Graston who is a wonderfully clever dressmaker,' Mrs Grace said. 'If you like, we could pop along and see her this evening . . . get some ideas?'

'I'd like that,' Jenny smiled. 'That will take my mind off Carrie.'

Jess wandered over to Jenny, looking forlorn. She could tell by his face and the expression in his eyes that he knew something was up. Jenny hadn't paid him the usual amount of attention. She realised now, with a stab of guilt – that she hadn't given his coat a good brushing for days.

Jenny slipped off her chair and sat down on the floor beside the collie. Jess rolled over onto his back, his tail wagging. His bright button eyes blinked happily at her. 'I want to give Jess a cuddle,' she told Ellen, 'and then I'll be ready to go!'

# 10

The morning of the wedding, two weeks later, dawned a murky grey. Light rain and a playful breeze quickly turned into a downpour, with wind that buffeted around the farmhouse and made the windows shake.

In her bedroom, Jenny was putting on the dress made for her by Ellen Grace's friend. She was examining herself in the mirror, watching the jade green of her silk skirt twirl about as she moved. The dress was beautiful, very simple in design, with a matching blue silk jacket. It had been carefully chosen to complement Ellen's. Jenny never usually gave a thought to her clothes – and she certainly wouldn't have chosen a fussy, full dress for the wedding, but even she was pleased with the way she looked.

At the thought of the ceremony to come, the butterflies in her tummy began to flutter. Sheena Miles, Jenny's mother, smiled serenely at her from the photograph frame on her desk, and she went over and planted a little kiss on it.

She hadn't thought of her dad as being lonely before. After all, he had his blackfaces and his beloved Windy Hill, and a daughter who loved him . . . but the look on his face, ever since Ellen Grace had accepted the pretty, antique pearl ring he had given her, told a different story.

Jenny went over to the window and looked out over the rain-soaked fields of the farm. She willed the rain to stop and the sun to come out, for Ellen and her father's walk down the aisle of the church. A sunny day seemed right, somehow. Lifting the frill of her bedcover, she peered under the bed. Mrs Turner's painting was there, lying flat, wrapped in a single cotton sheet and tied with string like a parcel. Carrie's mum had added more detail to the canvas, putting in the shearing shed that stood at right angles to the house, the stable block and the lambing barn. 'To make it more personal,' she had said. The painting was the perfect gift.

Jenny brushed her hair, and twisted it into a neat little knot on the top of her head, the way Ellen had shown her. She looked again at the picture of her mother, then opened her bedroom door.

'Well!' breathed Matt, when she appeared in the kitchen. 'Who would have thought they could make a *lady* out of you!' He grinned at his sister as Jess hurried over, wagging his tail.

'I hope we can make a best man out of *you*,' she retorted, teasingly, patting the collie. 'Look at the state of you!' Matt's hair was standing up in peaks, and his face and clothes were dirty.

'I'll have you know I was up half the night with one of our ewes,' Matt said, rubbing his eyes. 'Nasty case of foot rot. Anyway I've got time to shower and spruce myself up.'

'I hope so,' Jenny smiled. 'How's the ewe now?'

'Better. Dozing peacefully last time I checked. Nell wouldn't leave her though. She's lying up there in the barn with her.'

'How sweet,' said Jenny. 'Do you like my dress?' She spun around, showing it off.

'I haven't ever seen you look so good,' Matt said seriously.

'Are you happy – about Dad and Ellen, I mean?' Jenny checked again.

'Dad's is over the moon, isn't he? Then it must be right.' Matt yawned and stretched. 'Well, I'd better go and get ready.'

'Oh, Matt, before you go, can I have a peep at the rings?'

'All right.' He stood up. 'They're over here, in this dresser drawer . . . no . . . wait a minute!' Matt frowned and put his hands on his hips.

Jenny had to stand on tiptoe to see inside the small top drawer of the dresser. It was empty. 'Oh! Matt,' she said in dismay. 'You haven't lost them!'

'Now, don't panic. I'm sure I've put them somewhere sensible. Let's think . . .'

'Yesterday morning – you picked them up for Dad from the jeweller in Greybridge. Did you leave them in the car?'

'I couldn't have! But I'll go and check.' Matt dashed to the kitchen door and flung it open. 'Ugh!' he shouted, as a shower of rain blew into his face.

'You're not going for a walk in this weather are you, Matt?' Ellen Grace stepped into the room. Matt had vanished round the side of the house. 'Jenny . . .

270

where *is* your brother go— Oh! Jenny, you look perfect, love.'

'Thanks.' Jenny looked down at the dress she wore.

The kitchen door slammed shut and Matt reappeared, looking more dishevelled than ever. 'I can't understand it!' he said, perplexed. 'I'm usually so practical . . .'

'So careless, more like!' Jenny said crossly.

'What's happened?' Ellen asked.

'Matt's lost the rings.' Jenny said flatly.

'I've misplaced them, that's all,' Matt said.

'Oh!' Ellen's face fell. She looked around the kitchen, rather helplessly. 'But where . . . oh! what on *earth* is Jess up to?'

The collie was in the small utility room to the side of the kitchen. Through the open door they could see him burrowing frantically in the laundry basket. He had managed to overturn it and, with his scrabbling paws, was dragging out the items of dirty clothing waiting to be washed.

'Jess!' Matt bellowed, his irritation rising.

'Wait,' said Jenny. 'Jess never does anything without a good reason. Did you, by any chance, put the rings into a pocket? Jeans? Trousers? Jacket?'

Jess had singled out a pair of corduroy trousers. He grabbed hold of the fabric with his teeth and began to shake them, as Jenny had seen hunting dogs do with wild animals.

Matt's face broke into a smile. 'Yes! You're right, Jess! Well done, boy!' He patted the collie's side and took the trousers from him. Slipping his hand into the pocket, he pulled out a small, navy-blue box. 'Here they are!' Matt was triumphant, while Jenny ruffled Jess's ears.

'Good boy!' Jenny turned to her brother. 'You'd better go and get washed and changed!' Matt saluted her mockingly, and hurried off up the stairs, as Jenny remembered she still hadn't had a look at the rings.

'Jess!' laughed Ellen. 'You're a hero.'

There was a knock at the door. Jenny ran to open it.

Mrs Turner was standing dripping in the porch, holding a small bouquet of flowers. 'Oh! Don't you look lovely, Jenny!' she smiled.

Jenny smiled back at her, then stepped aside quickly to let her in as she hid the flowers behind her back.

'I know you said you thought carrying a bouquet might be overdoing it,' Mrs Turner said to Ellen Grace, 'but I thought something small and pretty might be suitable.'

Ellen Grace drew in her breath as Mrs Turner held

out a bunch of delicate lilac and white flowers, tied with a wide white satin ribbon. 'They're lovely! Thank you so much.'

'They'll look perfect with your dress too!' Jenny said, admiring Mrs Turner's artistic touch. Then she added: 'How's Carrie?'

'She was much brighter when I saw her last night,' Mrs Turner said. 'The transplant seems to have been a success. Of course, she's desperate to get out of the hospital and is giving everyone there a hard time. But it won't be long now, because her white blood count is rising steadily.'

'What good news,' said Ellen, putting the stems of her flowers into a jug of water.

Jenny was disappointed. She had badly wanted Carrie to see the ceremony. She had been in hospital a full two weeks and Jenny had expected her friend to be better by now. She bent to smooth Jess's head so Mrs Turner wouldn't notice her disappointment.

The collie's tail went from side to side. Jenny knew that he could sense the excitement in the room. Now, his ears pricked up and he ran to the back door and barked happily. There was a loud knocking.

'It's like Edinburgh station in here this morning,' laughed Ellen. 'At rush hour!'

'David!' said Jenny, as she opened the door. 'Come in . . .'

But David had already pushed past her and into the kitchen. He appeared not to notice her dress. Jenny saw Ellen Grace glance down at his feet, which were mud-covered. The rain dripped off him, forming a small puddle on the kitchen floor. Droplets of rain were scattered across his dark hair and sparkled there like jewels.

'Hello, David,' Ellen and Mrs Turner said together.

'I know it's the day of your wedding and everything but I had to come! There's some news . . . you see, I think, that is, *we* think . . .' David was speaking so fast he couldn't get the words out. Jenny had never seen him so excited.

'Hang on,' Jenny laughed. 'Take it slowly! We? We who?'

'My dad and I,' David said, checking himself. He took a deep breath. 'We think that Jess is the father!'

'What?' Jenny asked, frowning. She was instantly protective and her hand went out to the collie. 'What do you mean?'

'Orla is going to be a mum!' David finished, his eyes shining. 'You see, we noticed she was putting on weight. She seemed so hungry; so Dad said we should take her to the vet. Mr Palmer said there's nothing wrong with her at all, only, she's going to have puppies!'

'Oh, Ellen! Can it be true?' Jenny thought she was going to burst with excitement.

'I don't see why not. After all, Jess and Orla were together here at Windy Hill for quite a while.' Ellen Grace was smiling.

Jenny let out a little shriek of excitment. 'We're going to be . . . parents!' she shouted and David burst into laughter.

'What *do* you mean?' Matt asked. He was combing his wet hair with one hand as he walked, and brushing the lapel of his dark suit with the other. Jess began to bark and dance about. 'Has everyone gone completely mad?'

'I'll leave you now,' Mrs Turner chuckled, 'and see you later at the church.'

'Oops, sorry about the mess,' David said, looking down at the floor.

'I don't mind. It'll mop up,' Ellen Grace sighed. 'As long as nobody goes into the front room where the reception will be. It's been polished and prepared to perfection!'

'Matt!' Jenny tugged the sleeve of his suit. 'Jess is going to be a father! Orla's going to have puppies!'

'Hey, that's great,' Matt grinned.

Jenny turned to David, her face serious. 'David,' she breathed, 'you won't want to keep all of the pups, will you? I mean, you'll want to find homes for some, won't you?'

'I don't know if my dad will let me keep any of them,' David shook his head.

'Carrie would love one!' Jenny decided impulsively. 'And so would I! Can I? Have one for Carrie and one for me, I mean?'

'I don't see why not,' David said. 'We'll have to see how many are born, though.'

'Well, that's wonderful news, David,' Mrs Grace said. 'Thank you for coming to tell us. I must go and get changed now, or Fraser will be at the altar wondering if I've changed my mind!'

Matt looked at his watch. 'I'm off to collect Dad at Dunraven now,' he said. He walked over and gave Ellen a kiss on her cheek. 'We'll see you in church, Ellen.'

To Jenny's relief, the cloud began to break up just before they left Windy Hill for the church. When the convoy of cars reached St Thomas's, the fourteenth-century chapel on the outskirts of Graston, the spring sun was beaming down on its ancient slate roof.

Steam was rising from the grass in spirals like smoke. The wind had blasted the flimsy blossom from a cherry tree in the churchyard, and the petals lay along the stone path as though someone had scattered fragrant, pink confetti.

Jenny patted her hair into place and took a deep breath. Everything was ready, and it was going to be a wonderful day. She thought of the party to come back to Windy Hill. The dining-room table had been draped with a snowy cloth; and she knew that her father had borrowed a silver bucket to chill a special bottle of champagne. Matt had helped her to sneak Mrs Turner's painting down to the sitting-room, and it was now propped against the sofa, a surprise, waiting to be unwrapped. Jenny could hardly wait to see her father and Ellen's faces when they first saw it. She smiled to herself as Matt parked the car. The only thing spoiling her complete happiness today was that Carrie wasn't with her.

'You look absolutely wonderful,' she whispered to Ellen, as she got out of the car.

Mrs Grace wore a suit of the palest oyster grey and a frothy, cream-coloured hat. 'Thank you,' she smiled. 'I feel wonderful – except I'm afraid this hat looks a little bit like a meringue!'

Jenny spotted Fiona with her parents, Anna and

Callum McLay, standing in a group of people outside the church. There was Paul, and Mr Turner and Tom Palmer and his wife, and several of the farmers in the district whom her father knew, and Mr Fergusson with David. Jenny recognised many of the faces from having seen them in the village hall, at Carrie's surprise party. Just then, Father Finn arrived, and the crowd followed him into the chapel.

Jess stood proudly beside Jenny. She believed that he knew that it was a very special occasion and she trusted that he would be on his best behaviour. The collie's head was high, his tail was still, all of his boundless energy curbed for this important occasion.

'Mum would have loved you,' Jenny whispered, and reminded herself to bring up the subject of keeping one of Jess's puppies with her father after the ceremony.

She walked with Jess, behind Ellen, into the dim, cool interior, as the organ music rang out and the guests inside got to their feet.

As Jenny went slowly down the aisle towards her father and brother, her eyes swivelled from side to side, hoping, by some miracle, that Carrie would be there on this special day. Sarah Taylor smiled at her and Mr Turner grinned and waved. Jenny couldn't see Mrs Turner anywhere in the church and she wondered if she had decided to visit Carrie in hospital instead.

Fraser Miles, wearing a crisp, charcoal-grey suit, glanced behind him to smile encouragingly at Ellen as she came to join him at the altar. Jenny noticed her brother nudge him gently with his elbow and wink. She and Ellen reached them, and Father Finn's deep voice began to ring out, echoing around the tiny church as he began the ceremony.

Jenny saw Ellen glance up at her father. Her face was radiant; she blinked back tears of joy. She held Mrs Turner's bouquet in one hand, the satin ribbon trailing down the front of her elegant dress, and with the other she nervously clutched one of Fraser Miles's big hands.

Father Finn paused to open his Bible – and there was a shuffling disturbance from the back of the church. Jenny felt Jess's tail began to twitch, then he wagged it hard against her. Jenny put a restraining hand on his head and looked behind her.

The old wooden door had been pushed open, and someone at the back had jumped up to hold it there. Mrs Turner, her scarlet hat askew, was steering a small wheelchair into the chapel. Wearing a baseball cap for the occasion, Carrie smiled out at the sea of faces staring back at her.

'Sorry we're late,' she said, her voice echoing and loud in the sudden silence.

Jenny gasped with delight and only just stopped herself from rushing to the back of the church to fling her arms around her friend. Carrie, so small and pale in her chair, grinned at the crowd, bravely acknowledging their smiles of greeting.

Father Finn nodded, then went calmly back to his Bible, simply saying, 'A warm welcome to our courageous Carrie.'

Jenny listened solemnly, as her father and Mrs Grace became man and wife. Matt produced the rings at the right moment and Jess stood obediently all the way through the service. Once or twice, Jenny turned and caught Carrie's eye and smiled, and her heart gave a little jump with happiness.

She had a new mother; Jess was going to be a father of a whole litter of gorgeous pups – and it looked as though Carrie was going to beat her illness after all. Jenny wondered if she had ever felt happier.

'I wanted to surprise you,' Carrie said, when they were gathered outside the church after the service.

'I'm so glad you came,' said Jenny.

'We only just made it,' Mrs Turner explained. 'The doctor wasn't happy at all about Carrie leaving the hospital. But she made his life a misery until he agreed!'

'You mean . . .' Jenny said, 'that you have to go *back*? You're not finished with that place?'

'Not yet,' Carrie shook her head, and looked at her hands in her lap. 'Soon, maybe.'

'Oh.' Jenny struggled to mask her disappointment. 'I'll come and visit you,' she said cheerfully.

'Yes, of course you will,' said Carrie's mum briskly. 'Now, we really must be getting you back to Greybridge, Carrie, love.'

Fraser Miles and Ellen, Sarah, Fiona and Matt, crowded around Carrie's wheelchair to say their farewells. Jenny slipped her hand into Carrie's and gave it a squeeze. It was then that Jess nosed his way through to Carrie. Gently, he laid his head in her lap. He looked up at her, his chin on her knee.

'Ah, Jess,' Carrie murmured, stroking his head.

Jenny bent down and spoke softly in Carrie's ear. 'Guess what? Jess is going to be a dad! Orla is going to have puppies!'

Carrie's eyes were shining as she looked up at Jenny. 'Really? A whole lot of miniature Jesses running around. What a lovely thought!'

'David says he doesn't think his father will let him keep the puppies and so . . .'

'Goodbye, everyone, and thanks,' Mrs Turner interrupted. She sounded rather anxious, as she began to push Carrie's wheelchair.

Jenny stepped back. 'Bye. Thanks for coming.'

Fraser Miles offered his arm to his new bride as they went into the farmhouse at Windy Hill. Jenny hurried behind in them, so she could be there when they spotted the painting.

Ellen went into the sitting-room to make sure everything was ready for the party. 'What's this, Fraser?' she asked, pointing.

'It's my present, to you,' Jenny spoke up. 'I was hoping you would have time to open it before the guests get here.'

'Oh, Jenny!' Ellen was touched. 'How did you manage to keep *this* a secret? She and Jenny's father tugged at the string and the sheet fell away from the large rectangular canvas and sighed to the floor in a heap.

For a moment, nobody spoke. Then Ellen Miles covered her mouth with her fingers and tears sprang to her eyes. 'A painting! A painting of Windy Hill – I can't think of anything I would want more. Mrs Turner?' she asked Jenny.

Jenny nodded proudly.

'She's so talented – she's captured it all so well.' Ellen was glowing.

Fraser Miles put his arms round Jenny and hugged her. 'How many years have I dreamed of hanging a painting like this in this house? You're a marvel, my lass! Thank you.'

'Yes, thank you, Jenny,' Ellen said, dabbing at her eyes with a tissue.

Jenny was lost in a dreamy kind of happiness, admiring the beautiful painting, when the telephone rang.

'Get that, Jen, will you?' Matt yelled from the

kitchen. 'My hands are full of glasses and there are guests coming up the driveway.'

'Hello? Jenny Miles speaking.'

'It's me,' said Carrie.

'Carrie! Are you at Cliff House?' Jenny asked, confused.

'No, silly. I'm phoning from the hospital. It's about the puppies. Mum says you can put my name down for one of them, for when they're born, OK?'

'Wow! That's fantastic. You're going to be a pet owner, like me. We can go for long walks with the dogs together and . . .'

'I've got to go now,' Carrie interrupted. 'Don't forget, will you? I want a boy puppy, just like Jess.' The phone went dead.

Jenny replaced the receiver.

Jess, who was sitting beside Jenny, barked. She sat down on the floor and put her arms round his neck. Jess rested his head on her shoulder.

'You know,' said Jenny to the collie, 'I've got an awful lot to look forward to.'

# THE
# PROMISE

*The Promise*

**Special thanks to Ingrid Hoare**

Text copyright © 2000 Working Partners Ltd
Created by Working Partners Ltd, 1 Albion Place, London W6 0QT
Illustrations copyright © 2000 Sheila Ratcliffe
Jess the Border Collie is a trademark of
Working Partners Limited

First published as a single volume in Great Britain in 2000
by Hodder Children's Books

# 1

'Hello Jenny!' said Mrs Turner with a welcoming smile.

Jenny Miles felt herself relax as she steadied her bike against the whitewashed wall of the house. It was a good sign that Carrie's mum was her usual cheerful self. These days, Jenny never knew quite what to expect when visiting Cliff House, but the expression on the face of her best friend's mother was always a reliable clue. Only last week, Mrs Turner had opened the door with a blotchy, tear-stained face

– and predictably, Jenny had found that Carrie was terribly unwell.

'Hello, Mrs Turner,' she replied brightly, shrugging off the backpack she wore. 'How's Carrie feeling today?'

Jess, Jenny's Border collie, sat down on the paved path outside the door, his tail swishing vigorously from side to side.

'Chatty,' Carrie's mum replied, 'and hungry, which is good. It's so *lovely* to have her home from the hospital! Come in and say hello. And you, Jess!'

Jess responded immediately, bounding into the house in search of Carrie. He always accompanied Jenny when she went to see the Turners. Jenny could sense that Jess missed Carrie and the rambling walks the three of them shared, as much as she did. Carrie's illness – leukaemia, a type of cancer of the blood – meant that walking an energetic dog was out of the question.

'Is that you, Jen?' came a voice, and Jenny followed it into the sitting-room. Jess had run ahead and already had his front paws up on the sofa. He was trying to lick Carrie's face and she was giggling helplessly. 'Get off!' she squeaked, pushing weakly at his chest.

'Down boy!' said Jenny, laughing, too. The collie's

snowy white socks immediately dropped to the floor and he hung his head, his ears flat.

'Oh, he's lovely,' said Carrie, rubbing his ears. She was sitting on the sofa next to a table on which a large and complicated-looking jigsaw puzzle was spread out. Taking a proper look at her friend, Jenny noticed the peculiar colour of Carrie's skin. It was a bruised yellow, and the colour had spread into the whites of her eyes. Jenny tried not to stare, not wanting to make Carrie to feel in the least bit uncomfortable.

'What have you got there?' Carrie asked, pointing at the backpack.

'This?' Jenny lifted it. 'Lots of things for you. Chocolates, comics and that magazine you like . . .'

'You're spoiling her, as usual!' Mrs Turner had come into the room. She went over to push back a curtain and open a window. The summer sunshine streamed in, making the cosy little room even brighter. Carrie's mum was an artist, and her love of colour was reflected everywhere in the house. This room had a flowery wallpaper with a background the colour of honey. It made Jenny feel as if she was sitting in the middle of a sunny meadow. Up until recently, Cliff House, had always been a happy and lively place to visit.

'I deserve spoiling!' said Carrie, rummaging in the bag for the chocolates. 'Hmm . . . thanks, Jen.'

Jess's ears pricked up and he edged a bit closer. His nose twitched at the sugary smell.

Jenny laughed. 'No, Jess, they're not for you.'

'How are the two love birds?' Carrie asked mischievously, her cheek bulging with a chocolate-covered toffee. She offered one to Jenny, who shook her head.

'They're fine,' Jenny grinned. She knew that her friend was talking about her father and Ellen, his new wife. Even though Ellen had been the long-term, live-in housekeeper at Windy Hill, the sheep farm where Jenny lived with her dad, their sudden decision to marry had taken everyone by surprise.

'They're planning a visit to Canada, to see some of Ellen's family,' Jenny said. 'It'll be a kind of late honeymoon, I suppose.'

'That will be good – for both of them,' Mrs Turner put in, popping back into the room with two glasses of Coke. 'Your father could certainly do with a break.'

Jenny's father, Fraser Miles, farmed a huge herd of blackface sheep across land that had been given to him by his parents-in-law. When Jenny's mother, Sheena, had been killed in a riding accident, he had been more determined than ever not to give in to his shock and grief, but to repay her family's trust in him by turning the farm into a thriving business. He had worked hard, and it had paid off.

'What's it like, having Mrs Grace for a stepmother?' Carrie asked.

'Oh, not much different, except that I call her Ellen now. It's *almost* – but not quite – the same as having Mum around. Ellen was already part of the family, really.'

Jenny didn't want to seem disloyal to her mother. It had taken her, and her nineteen-year-old brother Matt, a period of adjustment to come to terms with the thought that Ellen Grace would be sharing her father's life permanently, but now they were both pleased.

'And guess what?' Jenny added, 'Ellen has left all the photographs of Mum around the house, just exactly where they were.'

'That's so nice,' Carrie smiled. 'Most people would have put them away somewhere. I suppose it's because they were such good friends. I think your mum would approve!'

Mrs Turner put her head round the door. 'I'm going out to do a bit of weeding in the garden,' she said. 'Shall I let Jess out? He can have a wander around.'

'Good idea,' Jenny said. She gave Jess's glossy black back a pat and then he trotted after Carrie's mum.

Carrie had swung her legs up onto the sofa and was resting her head against a cushion.

When she looked again at the peculiar, ghostly glow of her friend's skin, Jenny couldn't help being reminded of a Hallowe'en mask she'd once seen. 'How are you?' she asked hesitantly. Carrie inspected her fingers, then began to chew carefully along the edge of a nail. Jenny waited. Something inside her made her dread the answer.

'The bone marrow transplant hasn't worked,' Carrie stated bluntly. 'And now I've got a problem with my liver – which is why I've turned this horrible mustard colour.' She sounded calm and seemed resigned to the situation.

'But . . .' Jenny felt lost. 'The marrow from Sarah Taylor's bones is the same as yours. It *must* have worked.' Sitting in the chair opposite the sofa, she felt her heart begin to speed up.

'Well, it hasn't,' Carrie said and helped herself to another chocolate. She shrugged. 'Sometimes, it just doesn't work.'

'Will you go back into hospital – will they have another go?' Jenny asked in a small voice.

'There isn't any point,' Carrie explained. 'The

292

only thing to do now is to try and get by on my medication and the chemotherapy. But, you know, I may not. Get by, I mean.' Carrie was watching Jenny intently, as if waiting for a reaction.

'What?' Jenny said, hating the way her face felt as though it was draining itself of blood. Carrie seemed so unaffected by what she was saying, it was as if she was talking about somebody else's illness. But Jenny knew that her friend was drawing on an incredible inner strength that she had found since her recent bout of leukaemia.

'I know I can say these things to you, because you're my best friend,' Carrie said, speaking quietly and looking Jenny straight in the eye. 'I can't talk to my parents like this. I don't want to upset them.'

Jenny nodded, lost for words, suddenly engulfed by her own sadness.

'I'm not afraid to die. Not *really*,' Carrie said, sighing. 'It can't be as bad as everyone thinks.'

'Stop it!' Jenny jumped up from her chair. 'Carrie, stop! You're not going to die! You're *not*.' She wound her arms round Carrie's thin shoulders and tried to pull her into a hug.

But Carrie gently pushed her away. 'Now, you're not going to go all mushy on me, are you?' she smiled.

Jenny's felt her legs begin to wobble and she sat

down suddenly on the carpet in front of the sofa, resting her elbow on the corner of the table. 'You won't die,' she said again. How would I get by without you?' A tide of anguish and self-pity washed over her, and Jenny's eyes brimmed with hot, stinging tears.

'You've got other friends,' Carrie reasoned. 'There's Fiona, and David.'

'It's not the same,' Jenny mumbled. 'They're not *you*.' The tears were flowing freely down her cheeks now.

'And Jess,' Carrie went on. 'You've got Jess, remember.'

Into Jenny's mind came a picture of Jess, lying in a soft blue blanket in her arms just hours after his struggle to be born. He'd had a damaged leg and Jenny's father had been adamant that there was no room on a working farm for a lame dog. The furry bundle had gazed trustingly up at her with his big bright eyes, and Jenny had seen in them such fierce determination to live that her heart had gone out to him. She managed to persuade her father to change his mind and eventually he'd agreed that Jenny could keep the puppy if she looked after him herself.

'Oh, Jen, don't cry,' Carrie pleaded. 'It will upset my mum.'

Jenny hurriedly wiped her sleeve across her face and sniffed loudly.

'Look, you've got to make me a promise,' Carrie said. 'Are you listening?'

'Yes,' Jenny whispered.

'A promise you can't break? You must promise.' Carrie frowned.

Jenny could see she meant business. She looked into her friend's eyes and nodded sombrely.

Carrie continued, 'If I can't live, then you must live *for* me. OK? I mean I want you to do all the things we did together, just as if I was there with you.' She took a sip of her Coke and still Jenny said nothing. 'Make a pact with me? You'll have a go at things, and have fun? Do you promise?'

Jenny gave herself as little shake. She had been lost in a memory of a day at school when Fiona McLay had been bullying her and Carrie Turner had come to her rescue. Fun-loving and spirited, the flame-haired new girl had surprised Jenny by choosing her as a friend.

Jenny blinked back her tears and swallowed hard. She had to be strong for Carrie. She was determined to battle the terrible sadness and fear that gripped her. She stood up. 'I promise,' she said, smiling.

'Promise what?' said Mr Turner, coming into the

room with carrier bag full of groceries.

'Girls' talk, Dad,' Carrie said dismissively.

'Hello, Jenny!' he said. 'Phew! Graston market is murder on a Saturday morning!'

'Hello, Mr Turner.' Jenny's voice was steady.

'I hear that your Jess is going to be the father of a litter of pups, Jenny,' he said, grinning

'Yes,' she replied. 'Isn't it great? And Carrie's going to have a puppy, isn't she?' Jenny felt that, somehow, becoming the owner of a puppy would mean Carrie *had* to get well. It would at least give her friend something to look forward to and to focus on.

'Yes,' Mr Turner confirmed. 'Carrie can have one of Jess's litter, if all goes well.'

'A boy,' Carrie said. 'I want a boy puppy, just like Jess.'

'Well, we'll have to wait and see,' Mr Turner said and Jenny saw his shoulders slump and a shadow cross his face. 'Right, I'll just go and put these things away in the kitchen,' he said. Then he added; 'Oh, Carrie lass, I found you that book you wanted.'

'Thanks, Dad!' Carrie said, smiling and standing up. She wobbled alarmingly and put out a hand to steady herself on the arm of the sofa. Then she repositioned the little woollen beret that she had worn ever since her wonderful, wild red hair had fallen out due to the chemotherapy, and stepped round the table. 'Come with me into the kitchen,' she said to Jenny. 'This is a great book that I've wanted for ages! It's full of—'

But Carrie never got any further. She suddenly doubled over, and then slid sideways onto the carpet, rolling onto her back as she landed.

Jenny gasped and covered her mouth with her hands. 'Carrie?' she whispered. Then, she opened her mouth and shouted as loudly as she could. 'Mr Turner! Mrs Turner! Come quickly!'

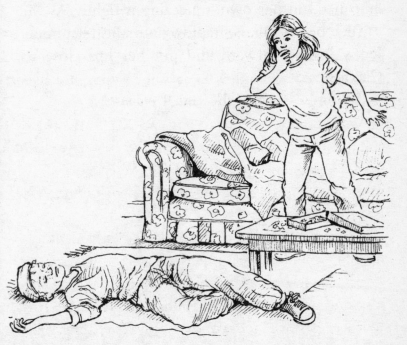

Within seconds, both Carrie's parents had rushed into the sitting room. Jenny watched helplessly, with tears already streaming down her face, as Mrs Turner fumbled to feel her daughter's pulse and Mr Turner stroked Carrie's forehead, murmuring her name repeatedly, his voice strained with shock.

'Phone the hospital, Thomas,' Mrs Turner said urgently. 'Get Doctor Wallis – and tell him it's an emergency. I'll get her medication.'

Jenny was suddenly alone in the room with Carrie. Impulsively, she knelt beside her friend and took her limp hand in her own, squeezing it tightly. As Mr Turner began talking rapidly into the telephone, Jenny leaned forward and put her lips close to Carrie's ear.

'I promise, Carrie,' she said. 'I *promise*.'

## 2

Early the following morning, Jenny was woken by Jess. His warm breath on her cheek startled her and she opened her eyes to see him looking down at her, a troubled expression in his gentle eyes.

Jenny found that she had fallen asleep on the big, wide sofa in the sitting-room at Windy Hill. She was still fully dressed, but someone had thrown a quilt over her, and her shoes lay neatly, side by side on the rug. Jess's pink tongue darted out, licking the back of her hand.

'Hello,' Jenny said softly and tickled his chest. Her eyes felt swollen and sore and her throat ached. She remembered curling up here beside Ellen after supper the previous evening and giving vent to her misery over Carrie. She had cried and cried, until Ellen had given her a mug of hot milk and honey that had soothed her into a dreamless sleep.

'We decided not to move you. You looked so peaceful.' Jenny turned her head to see Ellen in the doorway, and Jess's tail thumped out a welcome on the floor. 'You've woken your mistress, Jess,' Ellen scolded.

Jenny smiled and stroked the collie. Short of getting up onto the sofa, he had manoeuvred himself as close to Jenny as he could get. 'It doesn't matter,' she said. 'What time is it?'

Ellen looked at her watch. 'Just gone eight-thirty,' she said 'Your father and Matt have gone off to mend the barn roof. How are you feeling?'

'OK.' Jenny rubbed her eyes. 'But my eyes hurt.'

'I'm not surprised, love.' Ellen smiled kindly. 'I rang the Turners, after you'd gone to sleep,' she went on. 'Mr Turner said the doctor had visited Carrie and she was asleep as well.'

Jenny sat up and pushed her tangled fair hair away

from her face. 'What was the matter with her? Why did she fall down like that?'

'Something to do with an infection that's started in her liver,' Ellen shook her head sadly. 'They'll let us know as soon as she's well enough to have you over to visit. In the meantime,' she smiled, 'what about a bit of breakfast?'

'Hmm, I'm not very hungry,' said Jenny, who felt an emptiness gnawing in the pit of her stomach that wasn't hunger. Then she remembered her promise to Carrie. She didn't expect Carrie would be feeling very hungry this morning, either. But if she had been well enough, Carrie's choice would have been a heap of creamy scrambled eggs piled high on a piece of soggy toast. 'Actually, Ellen,' she said, 'I *am* hungry! Can I have scrambled eggs on toast?'

Ellen arched her eyebrows in surprise. 'Really? Is that what you feel like? It's unlike you to have such an appetite in the morning!' She chuckled. 'I'll put the kettle on too. Come through when you're ready.'

Jenny got off the sofa and stretched. 'OK. Now, Jess, I'll have a wash and change, then I'll take you for a long walk.' At the mention of the word 'walk', Jess's plumy tail began to wag furiously.

Jenny squared her shoulders. A promise was a

promise. She was going to be as good as her word.

Jenny finished her mug of tea at the kitchen table and kept Ellen company whilst she washed up the breakfast things.

'There's a car coming up the drive,' Ellen said, plunging the small saucepan coated with sticky scrambled egg into the washing-up bowl. 'It's Anna McLay . . . and Fiona! How nice.' She hurried to open the back door and the late June sunlight streamed across the flagstone porch.

'Have you time for a cup of coffee, Ellen? Hello, Jenny!' Mrs McLay called.

Jenny went out to the top step. She had brushed her hair into a ponytail and changed into clean jeans and a T-shirt. Her tummy felt huge with the big breakfast she had eaten. 'Hello, Mrs McLay.' She smiled. 'Hi, Fi.'

Fiona hurried over and leaped up the steps, looking serious. 'How's Carrie? I rang her house last night and her mum said she wasn't very well again.' She stooped to put her arms round Jess's neck. But Jess was looking expectantly up at Jenny.

'I was just going to take Jess for a walk. Do you want to come with me and then we can talk as we go along?' Jenny suggested.

'OK,' Fiona said. 'Is it all right if I go out with Jess and Jenny for a bit, Mum?'

Mrs McLay was sitting at the big pine table in the kitchen, whilst Ellen spooned coffee granules into two mugs. 'OK, but don't be too long, Fiona. We're on our way into Greybridge for a weekly shop,' she explained to Ellen.

Fiona followed Jenny out of the door. Jess bounded ahead as they headed up a steeply sloping rise towards the land that ran along the crest of Windy Hill, the hill from which the farm took its name.

Black-faced sheep grazed contentedly along the horizon and, away in the distance, Jenny could see an expanse of blue sea, the same colour as the sky. 'Poor Carrie!' she said, linking her arm through Fiona's. 'I went over to see her yesterday and she was sitting up doing a jigsaw puzzle. But, when she stood up, she collapsed!'

'Did she faint?' Fiona said, frowning worriedly.

'Not a faint, exactly. She just fell over. She's got an infection in her liver, or something, which is making her weak.' Jenny shook her head, feeling yesterday's sadness creep over her again.

They had reached a little track that wound along the fenced land given over to the grazing sheep. One or two of the bolder animals raised their faces and

sniffed the air, trying to sense if they were in any danger from Jess; others scampered away and some bolted in panic.

The girls walked on until they came to a section of field earmarked for the ewes and their recently-born lambs. They sat down to watch as the still awkward animals tottered about on their thin, wobbly legs, bleating loudly. Jess dropped down, panting from his run. He was not a working dog, but his instinct was good, and he knew how to behave among sheep.

'Carrie looked . . . awful!' Jenny confided. 'She was all yellow and thin. Oh, Fi, what are we going to do if Carrie *dies*?' Jenny covered her face in her hands.

Fiona put her arm round Jenny's shoulders. 'She won't,' she said firmly. 'There must be something the doctors can do at the hospital to make her better.'

Jenny gave a great, shuddering sigh and Jess came a bit closer. He whimpered and Jenny stroked him.

'He always seems to know when you're sad,' Fiona said wonderingly.

Jenny nodded. She felt wretched and she knew the collie could sense it.

'I know I haven't always been a good friend to you,' Fiona went on. 'Especially at first. I was quite nasty at times. I suppose I was a bit jealous of you having Carrie and Jess, and everything . . .'

Jenny looked at Fiona. 'Go on,' she urged.

'Well, I'm really sorry about that now. And, I just wanted to say that if Carrie . . . you know . . . ever . . .' She broke off.

'Dies,' Jenny finished, in a whisper.

'Yes, dies . . . then I'll try to be as good a friend to you as she has been. OK?'

'Thanks, Fi.' Jenny turned and gave Fiona a hug. They sat together like that for a minute, not talking.

Jenny felt comforted. She pulled away. 'We'd better go back down, or your mum will be wondering where you are.'

The two girls stood up, brushing the grass from their jeans.

'Right,' said Fiona.

'Fi?' Jenny said. Her friend turned. 'Thanks,' Jenny said simply.

When Mrs McLay and Fiona had gone, Ellen remembered to give Jenny a message. 'Oh!' she said, 'I forgot to say that David Fergusson rang when you were out with the dog. He wants you to meet him to go walking with Jess and Orla, after football practice this afternoon.'

'I don't know . . .' Jenny was hesitant as she filled Jess's water bowl. She felt too miserable to want to do anything much.

Ellen came over and smoothed Jenny's cheek. 'Go on, Jenny. It'll do you good to get out, and I'm sure it would take your mind off Carrie.'

Jenny looked over at Jess. He had curled up in his basket and was looking straight at her, his head to one side. It made Jenny giggle. 'Well, we don't have to ask Jess what *he* thinks of the idea!' she said. 'OK. I'll cycle over to the pitch and meet him there later.'

Jenny went upstairs to tidy her room. She put aside a few bits and pieces to take over to Carrie when next she visited her: a book she'd read that she knew Carrie would enjoy, and a few comics and some bubble bath she'd had for her birthday but not used. Then, whilst eating a sandwich that Ellen had brought her upstairs for lunch, she answered a letter she had had from Ellen's nephew, Ian, in Canada, and told him all about his aunt's wedding.

Later that afternoon, as Jenny cycled out of the gates to Windy Hill, she tried not to allow her thoughts to dwell on Carrie. Jess loped along at her heel, his tongue already lolling and the tips of his ears rising and falling with each stride. It had clouded over, a bank of grey cotton wool coming in from over the sea, accompanied by a light wind.

When Jenny reached the football ground, some half a mile beyond Dunraven, the farm where the McLays lived, the game was just ending. Jenny looked at the dirt-smeared clothes and bleeding knees of the players. She shook her head. She couldn't understand the appeal of football, though David would have argued passionately in favour of the sport.

She spotted her friend, his dark, curly hair damp from his exertion, and waved. Jess put his nose in Jenny's hand, and she looked down and followed the collie's gaze. Orla, David's Border collie, was lying in the shade of a tree, waiting for her master. Even at the distance they were, Jenny could see Orla's tail swishing from side to side along the closely cropped grass at the side of the pitch.

Jess sprang forward to greet Orla as Jenny wheeled her bike up to the tree and propped it against a low-lying branch. 'Hello, girl,' she said softly and dropped down beside her to give her a stroke. Orla tugged at her lead, which was looped round the trunk, trying to reach Jess. 'I'll untie you,' Jenny told her, 'but I'd better not let you go. If you go tearing onto the pitch looking for David I'll be in real trouble.'

When the coach blew the final whistle, David jogged up to where Jenny was sitting, a dog on either side of her. 'Phew! What a game! We won,' he said triumphantly.

'I saw,' said Jenny. 'Ugh, you're all filthy and smelly.'

'Well, I don't have to change to walk the *dogs*, do I?' David laughed.

'I suppose not,' Jenny wrinkled her nose. 'Just keep your distance from me!' she teased.

'Right. Have you locked your bike?' Jenny nodded. 'Good. You can leave it here and we'll get it on the way back,' David suggested.

Jenny got to her feet and both collies jumped up and began to prance about excitedly. 'Let's walk that way, away from the pitch. There are too many cars swarming around collecting the other players,' she said.

They walked towards the sea, to where the fishing village of Cliffbay nestled under the cliffs. Jenny's thoughts turned back to Carrie, lying in her bed somewhere down there, and marvelled again at her amazing courage. She was just about to tell David the news about Carrie when a car appeared, driving slowly across the grass, straight towards them.

'What's he doing?' David said, squinting at the driver. 'Why can't he use the road like everyone else?'

The man behind the wheel was frowning and Jenny saw his passenger laugh. 'Let's go over to the shelter of the trees,' she suggested, feeling a bit nervous about the approaching vehicle.

They began to jog, but the car, a blue Volkswagen, followed a short distance behind. Jess, Jenny noticed, had begun to growl in a menacing way. The hackles on the back of his neck were standing up. Orla seemed afraid rather than angry. She was slinking along, her belly low and her ears flat.

They reached the cover of the coppice and peered out at the car. It had pulled up and now the men were getting out. Jess began to growl even more loudly and Jenny put a hand on his head. 'Jess!' she hissed. She looked over at the football pitch. The crowd had dispersed, all the players having been picked up. There was no one was about.

'What *do* they want?' David asked Jenny. 'Perhaps they are foreign . . . and lost. I'll go and find out—'

But at that moment, the men began to run straight towards them. Jenny clutched at David, her stomach lurching with fear. 'No!'

Jess barked fiercely, snapping his teeth in a way that scared Jenny. She couldn't remember ever seeing him behaving so aggressively.

David took a step backwards, and staggered. The

determined, leering faces of the men were bearing down on them. 'Run, Jenny,' he said. 'Run!'

# 3

Jenny's legs were paralysed with shock. Her brain told her that this could not be happening. It felt like a nightmare. Was it a joke? Had they been caught up in some kind of a play, being acted out on the green? Or was it a dream?

Her fingers curled into Jess's leather collar; his front feet were off the ground as he strained against her hold, his lips drawn back in a snarl. She heard David tell her to run, but Jess wouldn't move either. Jenny was frightened of letting him go – he might get hurt and she wanted him close beside her.

'Jenny!' David yelled. '*Move*, will you!'

Reluctantly, Jenny let go of the Jess's collar and he sprang forward, barking furiously. She turned and ran, following David as he ducked and dived under the low-hanging branches of the trees. She could hear his breath rasping as he ran. Her heart seemed to have slipped up into her throat. It thudded loudly in her ears.

It took only a moment before one of the men caught up with David. Jenny saw him reach out and seize her friend's upper arm, then, with a little jerk, David collided with the man's big body and fell against his legs.

Behind her, the other man was trying to fend off Jess. He had his leg outstretched, his big boot threatening to kick the collie in the chest. Orla was circling the man, snarling.

Jenny stopped, gripped by terror. 'Jess!' she screamed. The collie was holding his own, but a large cloth sack had been thrown over David's head. Jenny took shelter behind a tree, and peeped out. It had become clear that it wasn't her that the men wanted – it was her friend. David kicked out. She could see his muddy football boots flailing. His yells were muffled as he struggled inside the brown sack.

Pressed against the bark of the tree, Jenny gripped the trunk. Jess, with Orla close at his shoulder, had followed the other man to his car and had only just missed having his nose slammed in the driver's door. The blue car came jolting over the grass as David was pushed, stumbling towards it.

Not a word had been exchanged during the attack, but now, as Jenny watched her friend being shoved head-first into the back seat, the man who had caught him laughed. The driver revved the engine, and the car spun round and took off in the direction it had come.

'Jess! Here!' Jenny shouted, but the collie, usually so obedient, appeared not to hear her. His eyes were fixed on the back wheels of the car, and he began to chase it. Orla took her lead from Jess, looping around to join him as they bore down on their escaping quarry.

Realising she had to do something, Jenny hurried out from behind her tree and began to run after the car. Her legs felt like jelly and she was weak with fear. 'Stop!' she shouted. 'Jess! Come here! Oh, please . . . stop.' She could see Jess's speed hadn't faltered; he was keeping up well, while Orla, excited by the chase, was running alongside the driver's door.

Then, as the car slowed to negotiate a deep rut in

the ground, Orla drew level with the front of the car and sprinted round ahead of it. Just then the driver accelerated. Jenny heard a sharp yelp as the car struck her.

'Oh, no!' Jenny gasped. 'Orla! Orla!' She gathered speed, racing towards where the collie was lying. Having reached the road, the driver of the car put his foot down. The car tyres gripped the smooth tar and he headed easily out of sight.

Jess gave up his pursuit. He slowed, and came back to Jenny at a trot, his tongue dripping and his eyes wild with his exertion. He fell onto his side on the grass beside Orla, panting hard.

'Oh, Jess!' Jenny was relieved that the collie had returned safely to her. She dropped to her knees. 'Orla, are you hurt?' She ran her fingers gently down Orla's silky sides, feeling for a wound. She expected to feel the warm stickiness of blood, but found none. The collie lifted her head, and looked at Jenny with a bewildered expression in her eyes. Jenny smoothed her heaving sides, as Orla winced and whined.

'Oh, you *are* hurt. Poor girl!' Jess eased himself next to Orla. Jenny put a hand out to him. 'Good boy,' she said. 'You tried to protect us. You tried to help.' Then Jenny had a sudden thought. The puppies! She put her hand softly on Orla's belly. What if they had been

# THE PROMISE

damaged by the blow of the car?

Jenny jumped up and looked around for someone who might help her. The green was deserted. Jess got up, his tail wagging slowly, and Orla struggled to get to her feet. The effort was too much for her. She yelped again and lay back. 'You stay here, Orla,' Jenny told her anxiously. She made a quick decision. She would leave Jess with Orla and cycle home for help.

Jenny took a deep breath to try and calm herself. Now was not the time to think about where the men had taken David, or what they might do to him. It was like an unfolding nightmare but, Jenny reasoned, there was nothing she could do immediately to help David – not until she got back to Windy Hill. And if she hurried, she might save the lives of Orla's puppies.

'Stay, Jess,' Jenny commanded. 'Wait there with Orla. I'll go home and bring Dad or Matt. Stay!' Jess cocked his head at his mistress, his tail still. Then he sat down, close to where Orla was lying. 'Good boy.' And Jenny started to run towards the tree where she had left her bike.

She willed herself to stay calm and wheeled the bike out of the coppice, steering it around the jutting roots of the trees. Her eye was caught by something smooth, shiny and yellow-brown in colour, lying among the bracken. Jenny snatched it up and turned it over quickly in her hand. It was a wallet, made of reptile skin. There was no time to inspect its contents, so she stuffed it into the pocket of her jeans, jumped on the bike, and pedalled as fast as she could for Windy Hill.

Matt was out in the cobbled yard, grooming his horse, Mercury, when Jenny skidded to a halt just inside the gates of the farm. It had begun to rain, a light, misty sort of drizzle that had settled on Jenny's eyelashes and made it difficult for her to see. She left her bike on the ground and began to run towards the house.

'Matt!' she shouted. 'Quick . . . I need help.'

Her brother looked up, surprised. 'What is it?' he said. He was tall in his riding-boots and, with his dark hair, looked very like their father, Fraser Miles. He held the grooming brush in one hand, and was gaping at his sister in obvious confusion.

'David's been taken away by two men and Orla got hit by their car. I think her puppies are hurt . . .' Jenny babbled, tugging at Matt's sleeve.

Matt blinked and was about to speak when Jenny, infuriated by his slowness, interrupted. 'Oh, Matt!' she shouted. 'Don't just *stand* there! Do something!'

She dashed off into the house, yelling: 'Dad! Ellen!'

For once, Fraser Miles was not up in one of the farm's distant fields. He was in the kitchen, pulling a nail out of his boot with a pair of pliers. Jenny could have kissed him she was so glad to see him. Her chest was aching with the effort of her running and her terrified heart still pounded in her ears.

'Dad!' she sobbed, and her father dropped the boot he was holding and came quickly to her side.

'What, Jenny? What is it? Is it Carrie?' Fraser held his daughter against his chest, stroking her hair with the palm of his hand.

'Two men forced David into a car down on the green and drove off with him. Orla was hit by the car as they drove away – I think she's . . . hurt!' Jenny said, explaining it as clearly as she could.

Ellen appeared from the utility room next to the kitchen, a frown on her face and an incredulous look in her eyes. Then Matt rushed in from the yard. Jenny was made to sit down and tell the story from the beginning, ending with her decision to leave Jess and Orla on the green.

'But this is . . . very hard to believe,' Fraser Miles said slowly, shaking his head.

'I'm not making it up – any of it,' Jenny said crossly. She stood up. 'I want to go back to the dogs, Dad.'

Ellen put her hand over Jenny's. 'We don't think you're making it up. Not at all.' She smiled encouragingly. 'And Jess will be fine there, for a while. You know how obedient and intelligent he is.'

'This just seems incredible . . . Who would have thought it?' Matt said. 'Right here in sleepy old Graston – a kidnapping!'

'Fiona always said there was something strange about David and his father. She thought they were criminals. Remember when Mr Fergusson called David *Douglas* once?' Jenny remembered, in a small voice. 'Poor David – he must be really frightened. I wonder if those men will hurt him?'

'Yes, well, better not to dwell on that right now.' Mr Miles said. 'I think we had better ring the police.' He went to use the telephone in the hall. Ellen slipped an arm round Jenny and squeezed her shoulder.

Jenny looked up at her pleadingly. 'But . . . Orla! We must get Mr Palmer to look at her, Ellen. She's hurt!'

'But there isn't any sign of a wound, you say?' Matt asked.

'No, but . . .'

'Shh!' Ellen hushed them while her husband began to speak to the police.

'Yes, Fergusson, that's right,' he was saying. 'Simon – and the son is David. About an hour ago – out on Parson's Green, the football pitch. The car? Hang on a minute, please.' He looked at Jenny and raised his eyebrows inquiringly.

'Blue,' she said. 'Um . . . a hunched-over little car – the one that looks like an insect.'

'Volkswagen beetle,' Mr Miles said into the telephone. 'Blue. No, we didn't get the registration, sadly.'

Jenny felt a pang of regret. She had been in a such a flurry of fear she hadn't even thought to look at the registration number of the car. Now she hadn't a clue to give to the police, except perhaps a vague description of what the men had looked like.

'Thank you, officer. We'll be waiting.' Fraser Miles replaced the receiver and came back into the kitchen. 'They're going to come up to Windy Hill. They'll want to take a statement from you, Jenny lass.'

'How long will they be, Dad? I've got to get back to the dogs – and get Orla to the vet. I can't hang about . . .' Jenny was agitated. She couldn't help thinking that the men might come back to get their revenge on Jess for trying to attack them. She knew that Jess wouldn't leave Orla. He had been told to stay – and stay he would, no matter what.

'They'll get here as soon as they can, but they haven't got anyone available to come out to us right this minute. Matt, can you drive your sister back down to the green? Ellen, will you help? Take a blanket for the dog. I'll ring Tom Palmer and tell him you'll call in at the veterinary surgery.' Jenny's father was brisk. A worried frown creased his forehead.

'Yes, of course,' Ellen said, snatching up a jumper from the back of a kitchen chair. 'I'll get some water for the dogs, and a bowl . . .' She hurried about the kitchen, filling a plastic squash bottle with cold water and screwing on the cap.

Jenny thrust her hands impatiently into her jeans pocket. She was desperate to get back to Jess and Orla. Just then, her hand came into contact with something smooth and cold. 'Oh, I found this, Dad . . .' She pulled it out. 'Near the place where those men took David.' Jenny put the wallet on the kitchen table.

'A wallet!' Fraser Miles opened it. 'Well, this should give us something to go on, if, that is, it belongs to the kidnappers. Go on, you three go and get the dogs. Hurry now, and I'll be waiting here with the police, when you get back.'

Jenny took the outside stairs at a single leap. 'Hold

on, Orla,' she said under her breath. 'I'm coming.'
*And please,* she prayed to herself, *don't let those puppies
be harmed!*

# 4

The rain was falling steadily as Matt steered the pick-up in the direction of Cliffbay. Jenny sat in the front between her brother and Ellen, peering eagerly out of the window for a glimpse of the two collies.

'We should have brought a towel,' Ellen said, 'The dogs will be soaked in this weather.'

'There's plenty of rags and things in the back, under the old tarpaulin,' Matt said. 'We can use those.'

Jenny was silent. She still couldn't believe that David had been grabbed, right before her eyes, by two normal-looking men, and in broad daylight. Perhaps, she reflected, they meant to demand a ransom from Mr Fergusson in return for his son's life – but, no, that just seemed too fantastic to even think about.

'I wonder if Mr Fergusson is rich?' she asked out loud.

Ellen looked puzzled. 'I shouldn't think so. Not especially. Why?'

'I was just wondering if those men had taken David in order to get some money out of Mr Fergusson,' Jenny said.

'There are plenty of wealthy farmers around these parts who'd make better pickings than the Fergussons,' Matt reasoned. 'This kidnapping just doesn't make sense.'

'That's what I think.' Jenny was puzzled.

They had reached the football pitch and Matt slowed the pick-up. As it lurched up onto the grass verge he braked. From there the ground sloped away, before levelling out, then rising again to the crest where the coppice stood, shrouded in a misty cloak of rain.

Jenny gave a shout. 'They dogs are still there! Oh, thank goodness. Quick, Matt,' she urged. 'Try and get a bit closer, will you?'

'I don't want us to get stuck in the mud,' Matt muttered, as he slowly accelerated. 'That would be disastrous.'

Jess turned his head as they approached, and recognising the pick-up stood up and wagged his tail hard.

'Jess!' Jenny climbed over Ellen's legs and jumped out. Jess barked happily, but he didn't leave Orla's side. She had raised her head, her ears pricked. In spite of the coolness of the driving rain, the injured collie was panting.

Ignoring the water that dripped from her hair onto her cheeks, Jenny hugged Jess, congratulating him again and again for having obeyed her instructions so faithfully. The collie's thick coat was wet through and he shook himself vigorously, sending a shower of droplets into her face.

The other two clambered out of the pick-up and hurried over. Matt knelt next to Orla and began to examine her. He moved his hands cautiously over the dog, probing as gently as he could.

'She's not getting up, Matt,' Jenny said anxiously. 'Look, she can't move!'

'Well, I'm not a vet,' Matt said, dashing the rain out his eyes with the back of his hand. 'But I'd say she's broken a rib or two, from the feel of things.'

'Oh, gosh! The pups?' Jenny asked. 'Will they—?'

'I don't know, Jen,' Matt said kindly. 'Let's lift her into the truck and get her to Tom Palmer straight away.'

Ellen's dark hair was plastered to her scalp. She crouched on the muddy ground beside the collie, stroking and soothing her. 'There, you're a good girl. You're going to be just fine.'

Jenny was really grateful that Ellen had come along. She was so level-headed and kind.

Between them, Matt and Ellen managed to slide a blanket under Orla's body, making a sling to carry her to the pick-up. Jenny tried to keep Orla calm, but she struggled and whimpered, evidently fearful of the swinging motion of the makeshift hammock.

When Orla settled in the back of the truck, Jess jumped in, and Jenny made herself comfortable next to them, pulling the tarpaulin over herself and the two dogs. She picked through a pile of rags and decided against using them as towels. They were oil-smeared and smelly.

'Jen, come and sit in the front with us,' Matt urged.

Jenny's head popped out from under the tent she had made for warmth. 'No, I'll stay with the dogs. Drive as quickly as you can, Matt, please!'

★   ★   ★

The waiting-room in Tom Palmer's veterinary surgery was crowded with pet owners and their animals, but Orla was hurried straight through to the surgery examination room where Mr Palmer and his nurse lifted her gently onto the table.

'Your dad rang me, Jenny,' Mr Palmer began, 'so I have an idea what this is all about.'

Jenny nodded, and slipped her hand into Ellen's as Orla began to whimper. She had every reason to trust Tom Palmer – he had performed the operation on Jess that had straightened his damaged leg. She watched as he checked Orla's gums and the rims of her eyes.

'Well, she's a nice healthy pink, so she's not bleeding internally – that's a good sign,' he smiled. Then he listened to Orla's heart and lungs with a stethoscope. 'And no sign of any damage to the organs, either.'

Orla cowered on the smooth surface of the table, her head low and her tail tucked tightly between her legs. The room smelled strongly of disinfectant and other animals. She looked imploringly at Jenny.

When Mr Palmer moved his hands over her ribcage, she yelped sharply. 'Fractured ribs, I expect,' he said. 'Poor girl.'

'What about her puppies, Mr Palmer,' Jenny

breathed. 'Will they be all right?'

'I should think so, Jenny, but I'm afraid there is no way of knowing at this stage. We'll have to wait until she's ready to have them, in, say, about a week's time?'

Ellen nodded. 'That's about right,' she said.

'I'll give her something for the pain.' Mr Palmer prepared his syringe, then went on, 'My advice is that she is kept as quiet as possible. It might prove difficult for her to give birth with a couple of broken ribs – she may need a Caesarean operation when the time comes. But we'll wait and see.'

'Thanks, Mr Palmer,' Jenny said.

'Let's move her gently back to the pick-up, now,' he said. 'Left alone, those ribs will sort themselves out.'

'Matt will help . . . he's out in the truck, with Jess,' Jenny said. 'I'll go and get him.'

Orla seemed relieved to be back in the truck. She lay on her good side on the blanket, and twitched her tail gratefully when Jenny climbed in beside her. Rainwater had pooled in places in the open back of the pick-up, and as Matt drove away from the veterinary surgery it began to slosh about.

'Ugh!' said Jenny to Jess, who was pressed up against her. 'This is awful.' She was shivering in her damp clothing, and couldn't remember when she had last eaten. She closed her eyes, her arm supporting Orla, pushing out of her mind all the worry about the unborn puppies and David, and thought instead about a steaming mug of creamy hot chocolate.

When they reached the track leading to the farm, Jenny looked out from under the tarpaulin, expecting to see a police car. She held on to Orla, trying to shield her from the lurching of the pick-up as Matt negotiated the muddy and rutted road to the house. There was no sign that the police had come to Windy Hill – not even a lone policeman's bicycle was in evidence.

'They haven't come!' Jenny said indignantly, as Ellen got out of the cab and came round to the back. 'And David is in real *danger*!'

'I'm sure they'll be here soon,' Ellen said reassuringly. 'Let's go inside and ask your father . . . there might be news.'

Warmth from the big range in the farmhouse kitchen lifted Jenny's spirits. She kicked off her soaking shoes, and Ellen did the same.

'Make way!' called Matt, as he carefully eased himself through the door with Orla in his arms. 'She's heavy – and those ribs will be tender.'

'Put her down next to the Aga,' Ellen suggested.

Matt lay Orla on a blanket Jenny had placed there. The collie was looking very sorry for herself. Jess went over and inspected her, sniffing at her coat curiously, and particularly at the spot on the back of her neck where she had had her injection. Then, he went and drank from his water bowl.

'Dad!' Jenny called.

'Fraser – we're back,' Ellen was at the bottom of the stairs. But there was no answering shout from the top floor of the house.

Matt had flopped into a chair and was using his

handkerchief to wipe his wet face. 'He can't have gone out, surely? Wasn't he going to wait in for the police?'

'That's what he said,' Ellen looked puzzled.

Jenny, whose head was filled with the strange confusion of the last few hours, suddenly gasped. 'Oh! Ellen! You don't think the men have come back and . . .' But the slamming of the back door stopped her and she turned to see her father kicking off his wellington boots in the kitchen porch.

'Dad!' She ran to him. 'Any news?'

'Ah, you're back, lass. The dog all right?' Fraser, too, was wet through, and slightly out of breath.

'She's broken a couple of ribs, poor girl,' Matt said.

'Mr Palmer doesn't know if the puppies have been hurt,' Jenny added. 'He says we'll have to wait and see. Did you ring Mr Fergusson?'

'I tried – no reply, I'm afraid.' Fraser put an arm round Ellen, then sat down. 'I had to go out. Callum McLay came over to say that our ram had got out of the top field.' Jenny's dad shook his head and sighed. 'What a job I had trying to catch him!'

'Oh, Fraser!' Ellen was dismayed. 'Not again!'

'Yes. The hikers have weakened the wall by climbing it, I think. And someone had removed the flat top stone and put it into the field to use as a handy picnic table! So the ram had an easy escape route.'

'How did Mr McLay spot Sam?' Matt asked.

'That cheeky ram came over onto Callum's land – looking for the ewes, I expect!' Fraser Miles chuckled.

'Sam is safely back behind the wall now, I take it?' Ellen smiled.

'He is, thankfully,' Mr Miles yawned. 'Any chance of a good, strong cup of tea, Ellen?'

'Or a cup of hot chocolate?' Jenny put in hopefully.

'Why don't you and Matt go and change your clothes Jenny, and I'll do the same. Then, we'll turn our thoughts to something to eat and drink, all right?'

'Good idea,' said Matt and Jenny together.

Jenny was first down into the kitchen and took the chance to spend a little time with Jess. He was curled up in his basket, snoozing, but wagged his tail when she came over.

'Hello, boy,' she said softly. 'What a day it's been!' She sat down on the floor beside him. Orla was fast asleep and didn't stir.

Jess lifted a paw and put it on Jenny's arm. He looked at her steadily, his brown eyes fixed on hers while she stoked his ears and the top of his head, then she took his paw in her hand. 'Good dog,' she told him. 'Clever boy.'

She noticed a smudge of blood on her bare forearm. Quickly, she turned Jess's foot and looked at the pad. The leathery skin was scored by gravel-filled cuts, one of which was still bleeding.

'Oh, Jess! You're hurt!' Jenny cried, and examined each foot in turn. The back feet were less affected, but Jenny guessed that the lacerations under the front feet had been caused by the collie's frantic dash along the tarred road after the speeding car that had taken David away.

Jenny brought over a twisted strip of raw hide for Jess to chew. He accepted it with a gentle mouth. While he was busy, she cleaned out the cuts by soaking each of his feet in a bowl of warm water. The gravel floated free and the water turned pink and brown.

'What are you up to?' Ellen was peering over Jenny's shoulder into the muddy, bloody bowl.

'I'm cleaning his feet. I hadn't realised he had been hurt when he sprinted along the road after David,' she replied.

'You're doing a great job there, Jenny,' Ellen said approvingly. 'I'll give you a little antiseptic ointment when you're finished, if you like.' She put the kettle on and took out a loaf of brown bread.

'The police are here, Ellen,' Matt announced, coming down the stairs. 'I saw the car from my bedroom window.'

'Oh, good.' Jenny was relieved. 'About time! Those horrible men are probably in Cornwall by now!'

# 5

Matt showed the police officers into the sitting-room. From the kitchen, Jenny could hear him making the introductions and her father politely thanking them for coming.

'I'll tidy up in here,' Ellen said, as she surveyed the puddles on the floor. 'You go and tell the police what you know. I'll join you in a minute or two.'

'Thanks, Ellen.' Jenny stroked Jess. 'You stay there, boy, and rest!' The collie climbed into his basket, turned in a circle and settled with a big sigh. Jenny stood up and took a deep, calming breath, feeling her tummy rumble at the same time. The sky outside was now a brooding dark grey and rain pattered relentlessly against the windows. She longed for good news, something to eat – and for the terrible events of the day to be over.

'Hello,' she said shyly, from the sitting-room doorway. A tall, young officer stood with his back to the small fireplace, which was filled with a basket of dried flowers. He had his cap tucked under his arm and he was examining the wallet she had found near the coppice on the green.

He looked up and smiled. 'Hello, there. You must be Jenny Miles?'

'Yes,' Jenny replied.

The second officer, an older man with a white moustache, was sitting beside Matt on the sofa.

'It sounds as though you've had a frightening day, Jenny,' he commented.

'Less frightening for me than for my friend . . . David,' she said. She perched on the arm of the big chair her father was sitting in and he took her hand in his.

'You've been a brave lass, Jen,' he said quietly.

'Yes,' the young policeman agreed, nodding. 'I'm PC Tim Lucas, by the way, and my colleague is PC

Alex Reece. Your father has filled us in briefly on what happened out on Parson's Green this afternoon. Are you able to tell us what these men looked like, Jenny?' He spoke gently, and Jenny found herself feeling less nervous.

'Well, they were very . . . ordinary looking,' she said. 'I didn't really get a chance to look *very* carefully, because we were trying to run away . . . and then I hid behind a tree.' Jenny looked up as Ellen slipped quietly into the room.

'This is my wife, Ellen,' Fraser Miles said. Ellen smiled and sat down.

'Go on, Jenny,' PC Lucas said.

'Um . . . one was quite tall, with sort of long, dark hair – straight hair . . .' Jenny was struggling. There didn't seem to be any distinguishing feature that she could describe. Then she had a sudden recollection of something she had seen while David was struggling inside the hessian sack. A flash of gold. 'That's it!' she said. 'An *earring* – quite a big, dangling loop. The man who pushed David into the sack was wearing it.'

PC Reece's pencil had been poised above a small notepad and now he began to write. 'Well done,' he said. 'That's the sort of information we need.'

'Do you have any idea where they could possibly

have taken David?' Jenny asked, adding: 'Will you be able to rescue him?'

'We have got a pretty good idea who these men are.' PC Lucas had turned to face Mr Miles. 'They're two members of a large syndicate of international criminals who mastermind the smuggling of skins and endangered animals into this country.'

'Really!' Matt's eyebrows had shot up. 'Big time stuff, then?'

'Yes.' PC Reece nodded grimly. 'A nasty bunch, indeed.'

'But why take David?' Ellen put in, puzzled. 'What's he got to do with endangered animal skins?'

'It's an attempt, we believe, to get to his father, Mr Simon Fergusson,' the officer explained.

'What's he done – David's father, I mean?' Jenny asked, her voice barely above a whisper. If Mr Fergusson *was* a criminal, then Fiona's – and her own – early suspicions would have been correct. If his father had to go to jail then David, whose mother had also died, would be left all alone. Jenny was already deciding that David would live with them, at Windy Hill, when PC Lucas spoke up.

'Mr Fergusson is innocent,' he said. Jenny let go of the breath she had been holding. The officer went on: 'He's been under police protection for several months now.'

PC Reece took up the story: 'When Mr Fergusson lived in England, with his late wife and son, he was employed as an inspector for the RSPCA. It was he who stumbled across the work of this gang and reported it. Their ringleader was arrested, as a result, and was jailed,' he explained.

'So, now the rest of the gang are after Mr Fergusson?' Matt suggested.

PC Lucas nodded slowly. 'It seems they have successfully traced him to Graston – and have taken his son as an attempt to get to him.'

Matt whistled. 'This is like something you'd see on telly!'

'Why do they *want* Mr Fergusson?' Jenny asked, puzzled. 'What are they going to do with him?'

'They want to . . . stop him,' PC Reece said gently. 'You see, there is a big trial coming up in court in England. They don't want Mr Fergusson's evidence to be heard. He knows too much. What he has to say could bring in the whole of the gang, many of whom are in South America.'

Jenny looked across at her father. He was rubbing his eyes, as if in disbelief. 'How on earth could we have got mixed up with this . . . madness?' he asked, looking at Ellen and shaking his head.

'What are you going to do now?' Jenny prompted, looking from one police officer to the other. 'Do you *know* where they've taken David?'

'No,' PC Lucas said. 'Not yet. We'll take a few more details from you, Jenny, then, with the information we have from the wallet you handed in, we'll soon have several officers out on the trail. Don't you worry.' He winked at her and smiled, but Jenny didn't feel very reassured. Hours had passed since David had been taken from the green – anything could have happened to him.

'Will they . . . hurt David?' she asked.

'Not likely!' PC Reece blustered. 'If they're trying to lure his father to where they're taken the boy, then David is worth keeping in good health, don't you think?'

Jenny nodded. *Poor David*, she thought for the second time that day. *He must be absolutely terrified*.

PC Lucas loomed over her, his notebook in his hand. 'Now, Jenny,' he said, 'I want you to tell me everything that happened this afternoon. Starting from the very beginning. All right, lass?'

When the police had finally gone, Jenny checked that Orla was sleeping peacefully, then sank wearily onto a kitchen chair. She put her chin in her hands. 'Phew! They asked so many questions!'

'They have to be sure of the details,' Matt said, helping Ellen carry the plates to the table.

'I suppose so.' Jenny yawned and looked out of the window. The low-hanging cloud had lifted and, as the sun slid slowly into the west, the sky turned a pretty apricot pink. Night was approaching – Jenny felt a little shiver of fear as she thought about David, out there, somewhere, alone.

'I've just tried Simon Fergusson again,' Mr Miles said, coming into the kitchen. 'No reply from the bungalow. I wonder where he's got to?'

'Well, the police are trying to contact him too,' Ellen reasoned. 'He's bound to turn up sooner or later.'

Jenny took a large helping of sliced cold meat and salad, some new potatoes and brown bread. 'Well I'm *starving*!' she said apologetically, when Matt raised his eyebrows at her.

'I'll make you that hot chocolate later, Jenny, I promise,' Ellen said.

'I hope Sam hasn't gone romancing the neighbourhood ewes again.' Fraser Miles grimaced as he speared a small, buttery potato. 'You'd think that wretched ram would be satisfied with the large number of ewes he has at his disposal here at Windy—'

Mr Miles was interrupted by a loud knocking on the back door. He pushed back his chair and hurried to answer it.

'Oh, *now* what?' Ellen said, looking perplexed.

Jenny saw David's dad step into the back porch. He was a head taller than her father, and strongly built, but, somehow, to Jenny, he looked as though he had shrunk since she had last seen him. His shoulders drooped, his head hung sadly and the expression on his face was extremely grim as he followed Fraser Miles into the kitchen.

'Hello,' Mr Fergusson said. 'Oh, I'm sorry to interrupt your meal – but I've just had a call from the police.'

At the sound of his voice, Orla raised her head and Jenny watched her wag her tail in welcome. The injured collie made no attempt to get up, but Jess wandered over sleepily to greet Mr Fergusson.

'I see you've got Orla here – thanks,' Mr Fergusson said.

Ellen stood up, pushing her plate away from her. 'We're so sorry about David. You must be very worried. Can I get you something? A drink?'

'No, thanks.' Mr Fergusson's skin was ashen. 'I really came to explain a few things—' he broke off. Lines of worry furrowed his brow. 'You've heard nothing further, have you?'

'I'm afraid not,' Ellen spoke for all of them. 'But the police have been here and they seem very certain that they'll be able to find these men.'

Fraser Miles pulled a chair up to the table and gestured for Mr Fergusson to sit down. He sank wearily into it.

'I blame myself, Fraser,' he said bitterly. 'I should have told the boy the whole truth. I should have seen to it that he was better protected. I failed him.'

'No,' Ellen said gently. 'You had no reason to think that this gang were going to trace you here to Scotland, Simon.'

'Also,' Matt put in, 'you *have* been under the protection of the police. You must have felt that you and David were safe.'

'So the police have filled you in on the background?' Mr Fergusson sighed. 'Perhaps I should have made David more aware of the situation – instead of just telling him half-truths. Then all this might have been avoided.'

'Do you mean,' Jenny asked, her eyes wide, 'that David doesn't *know* about why you're really living here in Graston – and about the gang of criminals and everything?'

'He knows to a certain extent.' Mr Fergusson sighed, again, more heavily. 'But I thought the less he knew, the better. He had enough to cope with after the death of his mother. I simply told him that, for reasons to do with home but which I couldn't explain yet, we had to move and we would have to change our names – and that the less we talked about the past the safer we would be.'

Jenny watched with pity as he wearily rubbed his eyes. 'Teale's our name, actually,' he went on. 'I'm Robert Teale and David is really Douglas, you see . . .' he trailed off, and sighed again, shaking his head. 'The police advised a change of identity because this particular gang operates on such a wide scale.'

'Poor boy,' Ellen said sympathetically. 'What a time it's been for him . . . for you both!'

'Yes,' Mr Fergusson agreed, adding, 'I suppose David just accepted the name-changes and the move because he was so upset at the time – he probably just thought of it as some sort of bewildering time when everything in his life was changing. He trusted me to know best. I feel awful now that I didn't explain everything to him. I thought I was doing the right thing.'

*So that would explain the note I found a few weeks ago, pinned to the Fergussons' front door and addressed to Douglas,* Jenny thought to herself She felt, in some small way, relieved. David's reluctance to tell her the reason for his father's unexplained absences from Graston made sense to her now. It wasn't that he didn't consider her trustworthy – but that he was confused and frustrated himself. 'Will you go back to using your real names now?' she asked.

'Best not, yet, I think, Jenny,' David's father replied. 'We'll stick to the names we're known by here until this whole nasty business is properly cleared up.'

'Seems sensible,' Fraser Miles put in.

'David's a bright boy,' Mr Fergusson went on. 'He must have worked most of it out for himself. He's kept his word and not talked about his life in England, before we moved here. But he hasn't asked me any questions.'

'It makes sense now,' Jenny nodded, 'why David has been so quiet and secretive.'

'What exactly is this syndicate of criminals up to, Mr Fergusson?' Matt asked.

'Capturing and slaughtering animals for their skins, for export,' he replied. 'Mostly the skins of endangered animals – caymans, snow leopards, cheetahs, those sort of animals. I used to work for the RSPCA, you see. One day there was a report that a German shepherd dog had trapped itself in a disused yard in south London and I went in after it. The dog was frightened and ran from me, finally squeezing through a small gap into a derelict building. I broke in – and found the gang's plunder. I went back, with a video recorder, and got my evidence on tape.'

'Good for you!' Jenny said enthusiastically, disgusted that anyone could trade in animal skins. Jess had wandered to her side and put his nose affectionately into her lap. Jenny stroked his head, pleased that he didn't seem to be bothered by the cuts on his feet.

'I quite agree,' Fraser Miles added.

'It's what I believe in – protecting animals – but I never anticipated that it would put David's life in danger. Anyway,' Mr Fergusson shook his head, 'I'd better get back home in case the police need to contact me again.' He stood up. 'I just wanted to fill you in, really. And I'm glad you're all right, Jenny. Thanks for acting so quickly.'

'David would have done the same for me,' Jenny said seriously. 'And don't worry, they'll find David, I'm sure of it.'

'I hope you're right,' Mr Fergusson said. 'Listen, I'll keep in touch. Goodnight now.'

'Goodnight,' Ellen said. 'Take care.'

When Jenny had finished helping Ellen to clear the table and tidy the kitchen, she decided to telephone Carrie. Only a day had passed since she had witnessed her friend's collapse, yet it felt like a week – so much had happened in such a short space of time.

'You don't think it's a bit late to be phoning now?' Ellen wondered, looking at her watch.

'It's not nine o clock, yet,' Jenny said. 'I'm sure it'll be OK. I really want to talk to her and I'm sure she'll be glad of a chat.'

'OK,' Ellen shrugged and smiled.

Picking up the telephone, Jenny about thought how wonderful it would be if Carrie were able to come into school the following day. For a second, she allowed herself to imagine her friend as she once had been . . . her sunny, cheeky face, and the mop of unruly red hair, demanding that Jenny help her with her maths homework *quickly*, before the teacher arrived to start the lesson . . . And then she remembered that David wouldn't be in school the following day either and she felt a knot of fear twist in her stomach.

Pushing the thought to the back of her mind, she dialled Carrie's number. Mrs Turner answered straight away. Her voice sounded strained and anxious. 'Hello?'

'Hello, Mrs Turner. It's Jenny,' she said. 'Is Carrie feeling better now? Is she still up? Can I talk to . . .'

'Carrie's not here, Jenny,' Mrs Turner cut her short. 'She's back in hospital, I'm afraid.'

'Oh.' Jenny's heart turned over, adding to her feeling of anxiety. She couldn't think of anything sensible to say. 'Um . . . sorry I bothered you,' she said, in a small voice.

'Jenny?' Mrs Turner's voice was gentle. 'I'll let you know when you can visit, OK?'

'OK,' Jenny repeated woodenly. 'Thanks. Bye.' She

replaced the receiver and sank to the floor. The lights in the kitchen had been turned out. Jess's paws made a pattering sound as he came across to her and sat down next to her. Jenny wound her arms round his chest and back and buried her face in his fur. He smelled of rain and heather.

'Oh, Jess,' she said sadly, 'I can't bear it. I just can't bear it.'

# 6

Jenny's alarm clock startled her awake at six-thirty the following morning. She had an urge to snuggle up in her blankets and go back to sleep. That way, she would not have to think about Carrie, or David, or the possibility of Orla losing her puppies.

In the middle of a big stretch and simultaneous yawn, her bedroom door was eased open and Fraser Miles put his head round it.

Jenny sat up, surprised. 'Dad! How come you're not out on the farm?'

'I had a little lie-in this morning.' Her father grinned. 'Ellen spoilt me with breakfast in bed – and as Matt is leaving for college at lunch-time he offered to go out and do the work that needs doing.'

Jenny was suspicious. 'But you never miss your early-morning start.'

'I wanted to spend just a few minutes with you,' her father replied, sitting on the bed beside her. 'How are you?'

'How am *I*?' Jenny shrugged and wrinkled her nose. 'Well, I'm . . . healthy. So, I guess that makes me lucky.'

'But,' her father persisted, 'how are you feeling – inside?'

'Oh, up and down. I feel really positive one minute and scared and sad the next,' she said. Jenny smiled encouragingly at her father. He looked concerned and she didn't want to worry him.

'It's a tough time for you,' he stated. 'There's been a lot to cope with.'

'Yes,' Jenny said. 'I'm worried about David, and Orla's puppies, but mostly I'm worried about Carrie. I feel so helpless. She hates hospital . . . she hates the drugs and having no hair and being so sick . . . and I can't do anything to help her,' Jenny finished, frowning.

'You're doing all you can,' Fraser Miles took Jenny's fingers in his big, rough hands and squeezed them. 'You're being strong for Carrie. And that's that's the most important thing a friend could do.'

'Actually, I made her a promise,' Jenny said wistfully. 'I promised her that I would live life for her, and enjoy it for her too. That's what I'm really trying to do. But it's hard. It's hard to be without her, and to be cheerful.'

'I know it is,' Jenny's dad agreed. 'And I want you to know that I'm very proud of you.'

Jenny smiled at him and then became aware of the rhythmic thumping of a tail on wood. Jess's brown eyes looked lovingly at her from the door of the bedroom.

'Jess!' The collie took Jenny's greeting as an invitation and bounded into the room, grabbing a slipper as he did so. He presented it to Jenny by dropping it onto the bed and putting his nose gently into the palm of her hand.

'Now, that dog ought to know better. He is not supposed to be *upstairs* in the house . . .' Fraser Miles began, his tone playfully stern. Jess dropped to his haunches and began to ease himself gingerly under the bed.

Mr Miles threw back his head and laughed. 'All

right, Jess. Maybe just this once.' He winked at Jenny, knowing full well that there had been plenty of times recently when Jess had been sneaked into her bedroom for a cuddle. 'Maybe you can get her out of bed and off to school, can you?'

Jess sat up and his bright eyes seemed to be smiling at Jenny. She smoothed his silky ears and he licked her hand. 'I've always got you, Jess,' she said. 'Thank *goodness* I've got you!'

Jenny sat next to Fiona on the bus to school that morning. The swaying motion of the lumbering vehicle made her sleepy and her head soon began to nod.

'Hey, sleepyhead,' Fiona said, nudging her. 'You're flopping onto my shoulder.'

'Sorry.' Jenny yawned. 'I couldn't sleep last night, not very well, anyway.'

'Thinking about Carrie?' Fiona asked, her eyebrows coming together in a frown.

Jenny nodded. Fiona had also telephoned Cliff House and discovered that Carrie was back in hospital. But Jenny didn't dare let on what else she was worrying about. That morning, as she ate her cereal, her father and Ellen had advised her against talking about what had happened to David.

'Mr Fergusson will inform the headmaster, I expect, Jenny,' Mr Miles had said. 'We don't want everyone talking and making a fuss. It'll only make things worse.' Ellen had agreed with him and warned Jenny that if the newspapers in the district became involved, there would be no peace.

'You'll have news reporters snooping around for days,' she had said, with a shudder. 'They'll hound us for every tiny detail. Best not to say anything – remember it could put David in further danger.'

Jenny had promised, but her heart was heavy as she left for school. Jess had waited at the door after his breakfast for his usual morning walk up to the field before Jenny caught the bus. His tail wagged briskly, expectantly, but she had decided against taking him. The pads of his paws were still tender and when she gently prodded, he pulled his foot away sharply.

Orla had pottered around on the grass in the back garden, stepping hesitantly, like a dog grown suddenly very old. From time to time, she paused to lick the site of her injury, to soothe her obvious discomfort. Jenny had put her hands on the collie's tummy, feeling hopefully for signs of life. It felt warm and full, but beyond that she could feel nothing.

Now, lost in thoughts of Jess's mournful eyes as she

had left him in the kitchen, she spoke impulsively. 'Jess is desperate for a good walk.'

'Why?' Fiona asked. 'Didn't you walk him this weekend?'

Jenny flushed. 'Um . . . not as far as he would have liked, really.'

'Let's go after school today, then, shall we? I'll meet you on the cliff path.'

Jenny's friend was eager, so she nodded, not wanting to explain to Fiona about Jess's sore feet – hoping that the rest he'd had at Windy Hill during the day would mean he would be up to it.

'All right,' she said.

When they reached Greybridge Senior, Jenny heard the boys talking as they got off the bus. 'Good old Fergusson,' said one. 'He's managed to wangle a day off school to get out of doing his science test!'

'Nice one!' said another, and laughed.

Jenny wondered for the hundredth time where David was, and how he was being treated. A science test seemed like a positive comfort in comparison.

Jess was so keen for a walk when Jenny got home from school that she relented immediately. 'You win,' she laughed, as Jess pounced and pranced around her. 'But go easy on those poor old feet!'

'You'll take care, won't you, Jenny?' Ellen was putting some cut flowers from the garden into a vase. 'Stick to open places and the paths you know.'

'I will, Ellen,' she said. 'And, don't worry, I've got Jess to look after me.'

'Yes,' she agreed. 'I don't think I would be happy to let you go without him, so it's just as well his feet are on the mend.'

Jenny took a moment to check on Orla. The collie was dozing on her blanket, lying on her good side. She opened her eyes and blinked at Jenny but made no attempt to lift her head. 'Poor girl,' Jenny kissed her soft head, as Ellen brought over a bowl of milk for the collie.

'I'm trying to build her strength, but she seems to have very little energy,' she said with a frown.

'Do you think we ought to take her back to Mr Palmer?' Jenny asked.

'He advised us to let nature take its course,' Ellen shrugged. 'She'll heal – it'll just take time for the bones to knit.'

'Ellen, we haven't *got* much time, have we? I mean, before the puppies are born?' Jenny asked anxiously.

'Not really, no,' Ellen agreed, stroking Orla's smooth back. 'It won't be long. That is, if our calculations are correct.'

Jenny sighed. 'We just have to hope for the best,' she said, getting up off the floor. 'I'm going out now with Jess to meet Fiona.'

'Bye, love,' said Ellen.' Please take care, won't you?'

But Jess had already persuaded Jenny out of the door. She was racing along behind him, her spirits suddenly lifted by the fresh air and the exertion.

Fiona was waiting at their agreed meeting place. She gave Jenny a hug. 'You look better,' she announced. 'You were miserable at school today!'

Jenny wished she could share her burden of troubles with her friend, but she only smiled. 'I'm fine,' she grinned. 'Come on, let's go!'

Jess trotted ahead, pausing to examine the places that interested him. Fiona tucked her arm through Jenny's. 'I've decided,' she began, 'we're not going to talk about Carrie this afternoon. We're going to try and put her sickness out of our minds and enjoy the afternoon.'

'Right,' Jenny agreed, remembering her promise to Carrie. 'What shall we talk about?'

'Well, my having one of Orla and Jess's puppies, for a start!' said Fiona.

Jenny stopped. 'Really?' Her eyes were wide. 'Did your mum say you could?'

'No.' Fiona made a face. 'She says we've already got a dog and we can't have another. But Toby is Paul's dog. I'd like one of my own – one like Jess,' she finished.

'Maybe you'll persuade her,' Jenny smiled. She couldn't allow herself to worry about Orla's litter being born anything but strong and healthy. The arrival of a perfect puppy was too important to Carrie for fate to cheat her now.

It was nice walking along in the sunshine with Fiona. Jess seemed to be fine and not at all bothered by his damaged feet. They walked with their backs to the sea, sticking to the familiar track that wound its way along the cliff top, which was still tacky with mud from yesterday's rain.

But suddenly, Jenny noticed that Jess was behaving unusually. He had strayed some way from the path and was standing stock-still, one paw lifted, staring into the undergrowth.

'Jess! Here, boy,' Jenny called, walking towards him. The collie looked up, but didn't move. Instead, he began to bark loudly and paw at the ground.

'He's found something he wants to play with,' Fiona decided, following Jenny. Jess had managed to drag something from the tangle of ragwort and stinging nettle. He held it in his mouth and, as Jenny approached, dropped it at her feet.

'A can of Coke – empty!' Fiona said, smiling. 'What a pity, Jess. A cold drink is just what I feel like, too!'

The collie looked intently up at Jenny, barking sharply. He sniffed the dented aluminium can, rolling it over with his nose and smelling the underside of it. Then, while Jenny looked after him in puzzlement, he ran off into the trees, yapping all the while.

'What's up, I wonder?' Jenny turned to ask Fiona. Moments later, Jess tore back towards Jenny, barked insistently, then ran back to the thicket.

'You know him better than I do,' Fiona said, shrugging. 'It can't just be a rabbit, or a stray cat – can it?'

'No,' Jenny felt certain. 'No, for some reason, Jess is trying to get us to follow him.' The dog's nose was glued to the ground, like a hound on the scent of the fox. He was making it clear that he wanted Jenny to pay attention.

'Come on,' Jenny said suddenly. 'Let's go with him.'

'Um . . . do you think we should?' Fiona was hesitant. 'We're not supposed to go off the track we know, are we?'

'But this might be important,' Jenny said firmly. 'Come with me, Fi, please.'

'But . . .' Fiona looked uncertain. She pointed to the trees. 'We don't know where this leads.'

'We're not far from the road that runs along down to Cliffbay,' Jenny reasoned. She put out her hand as Jess approached her again, and took hold of his collar. 'What's the matter, boy?' The collie began to pull with all his strength, tugging Jenny in the direction he wanted her to go.

Jenny remembered her promise to Ellen to be careful and she hesitated. She might be leading Fiona into danger – and Fiona had no idea about David's plight. But Jenny's faith in Jess overruled the warning voice in her head. The collie was as tense as she had ever seen him, and determined to follow and investigate the scent he'd picked up on the Coke can. Jenny could hardly restrain him a moment longer.

'That's it,' Jenny said firmly. '*I'm* going with Jess. Are you coming?'

'Oh, all right,' said Fiona. 'I do trust Jess, but I hope this isn't just a wild-goose chase.'

Jenny shook her head. 'I'm sure it isn't. Go on, Jess. We're coming with you. Go on!'

The collie sprang ahead, pausing briefly to look back over his shoulder and make sure that Jenny was following. Then, nose to the ground, he took off.

# 7

Jess sprinted along through the bracken, leaping effortlessly over the hillocks of brush, and ditches full of stinging nettles. The girls jogged after him, heading away from the path they knew. The ground was rutted and difficult to cross and soon mud coated their trainers, making it difficult to grip the surface.

'Keep up!' Jenny urged Fiona.

'Can't you get him to slow down, Jen?' she grumbled. 'Why do we have to hurry like this?'

Jess darted this way and that, his nose quivering.

Once or twice he stopped, and lifted a paw, looking around as though he was thinking. Then he found a trace of the trail he was on, and he loped away again.

'Jess feels this is urgent!' Jenny explained. She hadn't seen her dog quite so solemn and so intent on anything before. He was on to something, and Jenny silently hoped that, somehow, he was going to lead her to David. After all, she reasoned, Jess had never let her down before.

'I don't know how much further I want to go, really, Jen. I mean, this . . .' Fiona had started to speak when Jenny saw Jess drop like a stone. He crouched there, his belly on the ground and his nose on his paws, panting, just the way Nell and Jake did when they were herding sheep.

'Shh!' She put a warning finger to her lips and glared at Fiona. She could see immediately that her friend was puzzled and a bit hurt. 'Sorry,' she hissed. 'I didn't mean to get cross. I'll explain everything to you in a while, OK? Just stay with me – and don't *talk*!'

Fiona's frown deepened but she followed Jenny's example and dropped to her haunches.

Up ahead of them, just visible through the trees, was a dilapidated shack, a half-ruined croft long since abandoned to the forces of nature. It had been pitched forward by the trunk of a tree growing close to its foundations, tilting it dramatically to one side.

As Jenny peered at the building from behind an overhanging fringe of leaves, she felt her mouth go dry. She gestured to Fiona to stay where she was. Jess hadn't moved. He was busily licking the underside of his front paw. It seemed that his job was done.

*What do I do now?* Jenny thought, feeling fear began to stir in the pit of her stomach. *I was crazy to come here*, she scolded herself. But then, the sound of a muffled shout came clearly to her ears.

'David!' said Jenny, looking at Fiona, her eyes huge.

'David?' whispered Fiona, whose hair had become entangled with the branches of a low-lying bush. 'Here? Have you gone completely mad?'

'It *is* David!' Jenny said triumphantly. 'This must be where the men have hidden him.'

Jess's ears were pricked and his head cocked to one side. He was listening intently. The shout came again, louder this time, tailing off into a weary sounding groan.

'David is at home, feeling poorly,' said Fiona, who was still staring blankly at Jenny. 'That's where *David* is. Um . . . we are talking about David *Fergusson*?'

Jenny crawled over to be closer to Fiona. 'Listen, Fi,' she said, speaking quietly. 'I'm not supposed to tell you any of this. David was kidnapped on Sunday from Parson's Green. The police are looking for him right now...'

'What?' Fiona's jaw dropped. She wrenched herself away from the grasp of the bush. 'Ouch!'

'I know it sounds as though I'm making it up but I'll tell you everything later...' Jenny said.

'Tell me now!' Fiona had seized Jenny's sleeve and was tugging at it.

'*Later!*' pleaded Jenny.

A long, low moaning sound reached them. Goosebumps broke out over Jenny's arms but Jess's tail had began to wag happily. 'You see!' Jenny hissed. 'It is David in there! It must be! Jess recognises his voice. Come on.'

Jenny crawled forward cautiously.

'Shouldn't we tell the police? He may be hurt . . . he'll need a doctor,' Fiona protested behind her.

'Come *on*,' Jenny said firmly. 'Come with me, Fi, *please*.'

Taking her lead from Jess, who had gone forward to the shack, Jenny approached a dusty window. She felt as though her heart was going to burst it was hammering so hard. Using her sleeve, she wiped at the outside of the pane, which was partly covered with ivy, leaving only a small, smeared space to look through. Years of dirt clung to the glass inside, and Jenny found herself peering in on a pile of rotting wood.

'See anything?' whispered Fiona, fearfully.

Jenny shook her head. She walked cautiously round the old croft, stepping over fallen timber as she went. The roof had collapsed in places and the walls were crumbling. But then, when she reached the far side of the building, she discovered a little room standing intact. Jenny guessed it had been a later addition to the place. On a heavy wooden door, a brass padlock was hanging, shining new in the bright sunshine.

Jenny knocked softly. She found herself breathing so hard that her chest was rising and falling, making her hand shake. Jess, beside her, nudged her with his nose and wagged his tail encouragingly.

'David?' she called softly. There was no answering sound.

'Here,' said Fiona, pointing, 'there's a knothole in the wood of the door, look.'

Jenny knelt and put her eye to the smooth, oval opening. She gasped. In spite of the gloom, she could clearly see David, his face towards her and his eyes closed. He was curled on his side on the floor. Jenny's heart somersaulted in her chest and she clutched at

Fiona. 'He's in there! He doesn't look . . . at all well.'

Fiona nudged her aside and put her face to the hole. 'Oh, gosh, Jen . . . he *is* alive, isn't he?'

'We heard him. He must be.' Jenny was desperate. Should she try and break down the door or run home for help? Her hands were clasped anxiously, her fingers twisting, when she saw Jess's ears go up. His body tensed and he looked up at Jenny and whined. Then the collie began to hurry away in the direction they had come, stopping once to look back pointedly at his mistress.

Jenny listened. 'There's a car coming!' she breathed. 'Quick, Fi, follow Jess.'

Putting her faith in Jess's good sense, Jenny grabbed Fiona's hand and followed the collie to where a water-worn ravine had been carved out across the land. A thin trickle of foul-smelling, brackish water flowed towards the sea. It had pooled in places, dammed by twigs and leaves and the odd bit of litter blown there by the wind. As Jess leapt into this gully, Jenny noticed a Coke can, dented like the one they'd seen before, bobbing in the water. Fiona hesitated only a second before she joined Jenny in the ditch.

'Oh, yuck!' she said. Her hands were smeared with mud, which had also travelled from her trainers up the lower half of her jeans. Then, looking at Jenny, she added in a whisper. 'I'm so scared my teeth are chattering.'

Jenny tucked her arm through her friend's and pulled her closer, to where a screen of fern leaves growing along the bank provided a scanty shield.

'Keep down,' she urged. 'We can see what's going on from here.'

Jess began a low, rumbling growl and his fur bristled. There came the slamming of a car door, then a second. Jenny put her hand softly on the back of Jess's neck, trusting that he wouldn't give the game away.

'You drink any more of that, Dylan,' said a voice, 'your teeth will rot.' Jenny raised her head a fraction, and peeped through the fronds. Two men had got out of a car – the same blue Volkswagen in which David had been driven away. One of them – Dylan, Jenny guessed – drained the last of his Coke and lobbed the can towards a tree. The big gold earring he wore jiggled.

'Nah,' he said, grinning. 'I ain't got my own teeth anyway, see, Ken?' To Jenny's disgust, he eased the false teeth away from the roof of his mouth, making them clatter, then laughed at his own joke.

'Yuck,' whispered Fiona again. Jenny glanced at

her and put a finger to her lips. Her friend was as pale as chalk, hunched in the ditch hugging her knees, a streak of mud across one cheek.

'Now,' said Ken, groping in the pocket of his baggy trousers and hauling out a big key, 'Let's see how our scrawny little friend is doing in here.'

'I got him beans,' said Dylan. 'Kids like beans, don't they?'

'Beans? You mean beans in tomato sauce? Didn't you bring him a sausage at least?' asked his friend.

'Nah. That kid's got no appetite anyway. He's too scared. Beans is fine.' As Ken unlocked the door to the shed, Dylan idly examined the label on his tin of beans. 'I remembered to bring the opener, too,' he remarked.

The door swung open smoothly, silently. Jenny stood up to get a better look. The hair at the back of her neck was wet with sweat but she felt cold, with fear as Fiona tried to tug her down again.

'Stand up, boy,' Ken was commanding loudly. 'Get to your feet. You need to eat. Come out.'

It was some moments before Jenny heard a shuffling sound. David emerged into the sunlight, blinking. His hands were tied behind his back and his ankles were roped together. Jess whimpered and cocked his head, not taking his eyes off David for a second.

Fiona squeaked. 'Oh, Jenny . . . *poor* David.'

It was obvious that David had been crying. His face was swollen and his eyes puffy. He limped along, his head drooping. He looked the picture of misery. *How dare these men treat him this way!* Jenny thought furiously. Anger surged through her, making her feel suddenly very hot.

Jess stiffened; he was ready to spring, but Jenny held his collar. 'No, Jess,' she warned.

Dylan opened the beans and thrust a spoon from his pocket into the tin. 'Here, boy,' he grinned. 'I got you a little treat.'

David shook his head. 'Why have you brought me here?' he demanded. 'Why can't I go home?'

Dylan and Ken cackled. 'Because you're our bait,' Dylan told him. 'You're the bait that's gonna catch us our fish, see?'

'Not long to go now either, I reckon.' Ken sniffed. 'We're soon gonna move you to a nicer place, see? A place where you can hear the sea, and the birds calling . . .'

'Are we?' Dylan looked surprised. 'Where's that then?'

'The boss said something about moving him down

374

to that wharf building he was telling us about.' He began to pick his teeth. 'You gonna eat them beans or not, boy?' he added nastily. David shook his head again.

'Don't waste my time!' shouted Dylan, aiming a kick at David's shin.

The open can of beans emptied onto the ground as Dylan's boot collided with David's leg. He gasped and tears began to slide down his cheeks.

Jenny looked at Fiona, horrified, and in that second, Jess slipped from her grasp and bounded out of the gully. 'Oh, no!' Jenny breathed.

Jess's hackles were up and his teeth bared. He growled threateningly as the men spun round in surprise.

'Jess!' sobbed David. 'Oh, Jess!'

'Looks like that mutt we saw yesterday, the one who was with the girl,' Dylan said, backing away.

'Same pesky animal, I reckon,' said Ken. 'The one we *didn't* manage to hit with the car.' He chuckled under his breath.

The two girls peered fearfully from the lip of the ditch. Jenny's heart was pounding in anguish as she watched her beloved dog crouching in front of the two men. The collie looked from one to the other, as though he was trying to size up the most efficient means of attack.

Then Jess made his decision. He raced round behind Dylan, coming in fast and low. Launching himself, he grabbed the fleshy bit of the man's thigh between his teeth and bit down, hard.

Dylan screamed and toppled over backwards. 'Brute!' he yelled. 'Get him, Ken, will ya?' He clutched the back of his leg.

Ken felt in his pocket once more, and this time he pulled out a knife. Jenny saw the glint of the long, sharp blade as it twisted in his hand. She stood up, but Fiona yanked her back down. 'Don't be *stupid*!' she begged Jenny. 'That man has got a *knife*!'

Jenny was breathing hard, her hands covering her mouth in terror.

'Jess . . .' she murmured. 'Oh, be careful.'

'You want a fight do you, doggie?' snarled Ken, as he squared up to the collie. 'Come on then . . . come on, good doggie. You come and get Ken.'

Jess crouched low, growling and prowling around the man like a lion closing in on its chosen prey.

'You know this dog, don't you, boy?' Dylan asked David. 'Do you want to see him die?'

Ken took a step towards Jess and raised his knife. It was poised to strike should the collie come any closer. But Jenny could take it no longer. With one swift leap she was free of Fiona and out of the gully, tearing towards the men, and David.

'Jess! Don't!' she screamed.

'Jenny!' David yelled.

Jess turned his head quickly as she came, and Ken plunged his knife down towards his spine. But the collie sprang aside in time and, with open jaws, went for Ken's arm.

'Aargh! You beast!' he yelled, dropping his weapon. His eyes were fixed on Jess, who was still circling menacingly.

'Ken, it's that girl. The one we saw on the green,' Dylan shouted.

Jenny, her whole body trembling violently, stooped and snatched up the knife, then began to back off. 'The police are on to you!' she shouted, beside herself with rage and fear.

'Now, we don't want no trouble, sweetheart,' Ken said, holding up his uninjured arm. His eyes flickered from the knife in Jenny's hand to the fierce, slavering jaws of Jess.

'Ken,' Dylan said, 'let's move out. This is getting too complicated. We don't want to involve no one else in this. No serious injuries, the boss said. Remember?'

'Call your dog off,' Ken said. 'Call him off, and we'll go.'

'All right,' said Jenny. She was dumbfounded at the effect she and Jess had had on the men. 'Here, Jess!' Could the men mean to free their prisoner?

Jess, still growling, went quickly to Jenny's side. She put a trembling hand on his collar. But to her dismay, she saw Dylan beginning to move David towards the car.

'Leave him!' Jenny shouted. 'Oh, *please*, leave him . . .'

But Ken laughed nastily, as he pushed David into the back seat. 'Not likely, you meddling brat.'

Jenny's legs gave way under her and she sat down with a bump on the ground and burst into tears. She heard Dylan rev the engine, and saw a cloud of dirt rise around the back tyres as the car sped away.

A few silent moments passed then Fiona was by Jenny's side. 'Don't cry, Jen! she pleaded, putting her arms around her. 'You were fantastic – so *brave*. You're not hurt are you?'

Jenny shook her head and gave a small smile as Jess began gently to lick her mud-streaked, tear-stained face. 'Poor David,' Jenny said wearily. 'We must get help.'

'Yes,' Fiona agreed. 'Come on, I'll give you a hand up.'

Jenny got shakily to her feet. 'We've got to get back to Windy Hill quickly, Fiona. We'll have to run.'

She patted Jess, then the two girls set off at a sprint towards the track that would lead them home.

## 8

The girls hardly spoke as they hurried along. The shock of coming across David's makeshift prison, the arrival of the men who held him, and the fight to save Jess, now began to take its toll. Jenny found she was trembling so violently that even her speech came out as a stutter.

'Are you cold?' Fiona asked.

'No! I'm hot.' Jenny shuddered. 'I just can't stop shaking.'

Jess paused once or twice to inspect his sore front

paws, soothing them with a few licks of his tongue. Jenny felt a spasm of guilt as she looked at the torn and bleeding pads. She should never have allowed him to walk so far and work so hard. In spite of it, she was very glad to have had him with her. The men – Dylan and Ken – had seemed genuinely afraid of Jess and he had protected her and Fiona well. She put a loving hand on his smooth head as he trotted along, close beside her.

The sight of the gates to Windy Hill had never seemed so welcoming. Jenny put an arm round Fiona's waist and brought them to a standstill. 'We've made it!' she said, breathless from running. She took a lungful of air and then turned to her friend, 'Fi, listen – I just wanted to say that I'm sorry for getting you mixed up in all of this.'

'*I'm* sorry I wasn't a bit braver,' Fiona replied, biting her lip.

'No, I put us both in danger,' Jenny said, in a small voice, as the truth of what might have happened out in that secluded spot began to dawn on her.

'Well, in the end I think we did the right thing by following Jess.' Fiona smiled weakly, relief in her voice. 'After all, at least we now know what those horrible men look like.'

'And, this time, I've memorised the number plate

of their car,' Jenny said, looking towards Windy Hill.

The high afternoon sun baked down on the red roofs of the farm buildings up ahead. Jenny could see the washing, pegged and fluttering on the line, and the black faces of the sheep as they grazed lazily in the top field. Ellen's carefully tended flowerbeds were a riot of cheerful summer colour. It made a homely and peaceful picture – and it seemed a world away from the desperate scene they had just witnessed.

'Come on, Fi.' Jenny began to run. 'Ellen!' she shouted. 'Dad!'

Ellen appeared on the top step outside the kitchen door, a washing basket under her arm. She shaded her eyes against the sun with a cupped palm. 'What is it, Jenny?' she called pleasantly. But as Jenny drew nearer, her expression changed. She had obviously taken in her stepdaughter's pale face, her shaking hands and her muddy clothes.

Ellen dropped the empty basket on the step and rushed forward to take Jenny in her arms. 'Are you *hurt*?' she asked, looking at Fiona over Jenny's shoulder.

Fiona shook her head slowly and spoke for both of them. 'No, Mrs Miles,' she said. 'We're just scared and tired.'

Jess, came limping up slowly behind the girls, his pink tongue lolling.

'Oh . . . Jess!' Ellen said anxiously. 'What . . .?'

Reluctantly, Jenny pulled away from the comfort of Ellen's arms. 'We have to contact the police,' she said. 'Urgently. And get Dad, too.'

'Oh my *goodness*!' said Ellen. 'What on earth has happened?'

'We found David,' Fiona said, 'but the men came and they've taken him away again. They fought with Jess and Jenny tried . . .'

Ellen held up a hand, her alarm reflected in her eyes. 'On second thoughts, you'd better come inside,' she urged. 'Rest a bit . . . and Jess needs water, by the look of him. It sounds like you'll need to tell the whole story to the police.'

Inspector Moran gratefully accepted the cup of tea Ellen offered him and cleared his throat. 'I must say,' he said, 'you've been very brave, both of you lasses.' He smiled at Jenny and Fiona.

Fraser Miles nodded gravely at his daughter. 'Brave,' he agreed, 'and very foolish.'

'I know,' Jenny said, apologetically. 'We took a chance, Dad.'

'You can say that again,' said her father, grimly.

Jenny felt much calmer, now that she was back at home and they had finished painstakingly describing the events of the afternoon to the police. She and Fiona had had a chance to clean up and Ellen had made them her special hot chocolate to drink. 'Hot, sweet drinks are good for shock,' she had said, as she whipped the milk into a froth.

Jenny was curled up in the big old chair in the sitting-room, looking over Inspector Moran's head at the beautiful picture Carrie's mum had painted of Windy Hill and the surrounding countryside. She had given it to her father and Ellen as a wedding present and it had taken pride of place above the mantel ever since.

'Right,' said the inspector, putting down his cup. 'I won't waste much more of your time. We've got the registration number of the vehicle and, of course, the wallet . . . can you think of anything about either of these men that might, in any way, be unusual? Some, shall we say, distinguishing feature? I know we've been through this before, but now you've had a better look . . .'

'Teeth!' said Fiona, looking at Jenny. 'Remember?'

'Oh, yes,' Jenny made a face as she recalled the unpleasant sight. 'The one called Dylan, the one who drank all that Coke I told you about? Well, he had false teeth. At one point, he took them out!'

The inspector smiled. 'Not a pretty sight, I'll bet!'

'Inspector,' Jenny said, her face suddenly serious. 'Will your officers be able to find this wharf building – the place where they said they were going to take David?'

'My guess is that they were referring to that storage wharf alongside the old whaling station,' Fraser Miles put in.

'Yes. The one just a couple of miles along the coast from Cliffbay,' Inspector Moran said, adding cheerily,

'I've already been on the radio and I feel sure by now my men will have raided the place.'

'Oh *good*!' said Jenny, relieved to think that the police were acting so quickly. Then she sighed. Nobody in the room had put into words what she feared most. Dylan and Ken might have realised that their early conversation about the wharf had been overheard, and decided to take David somewhere altogether different. She dreaded, too, to think what their 'boss' might feel about a meddlesome girl and an aggressive dog that had spoiled their plans so completely.

Inspector Moran stood up and smiled at Ellen. 'A lovely cup of tea,' he said. 'And now, if you don't mind, Mr and Mrs Miles, I'll use your telephone again to speak to the men at the station. Then I'll be off.'

'Of course,' said Ellen, who still looked shaken.

'Oh, and, if you'll take my advice, young lady,' the inspector turned to Jenny, 'it'd be best if you didn't go off anywhere on your own for a few days, just till we round this lot up. OK?' He winked broadly.

'OK,' said Jenny readily. She felt sure that Jess wouldn't want to go out again in a hurry anyway.

'I'll run you home in the truck, Fiona,' Fraser Miles said. 'I'll not have you walking back to Dunraven at dusk, not after a day like today.'

'Thanks,' said Fiona, looking relieved.

While Inspector Moran was making his call, Jenny and Fiona said goodbye.

'You've really been great, Fi,' Jenny said.

'I didn't do enough to help you,' Fiona insisted. 'I was so frightened!'

'But you stuck by me,' Jenny smiled. 'You came along, even when you didn't really think it would be a good idea, and you saw it through.'

'You're so brave, Jenny,' Fiona said, simply. 'I wish I could be like you.' She climbed into the truck beside Mr Miles and waved. 'See you at school tomorrow.'

Jenny waved back. She experienced a warm glow inside. It was a nice feeling to know that Fiona admired her – the way Jenny admired Carrie.

Jenny sat on the kitchen floor between the two dogs, putting an arm round each of them. Orla's tail wagged gently in welcome, but her deep brown eyes lacked their usual glow. Her coat, too, was dull and in need of grooming. Jenny hadn't dared try to brush her, fearing that even the slightest pressure would cause her pain.

She felt again for signs of life, and Orla licked her wrist as she gently probed her tummy. 'I hope, hope,

hope . . .' Jenny whispered. 'Please, Orla, for Carrie. You *must* have a puppy in there. For Carrie.' She dipped her fingers into the bowl of milk and Orla licked them with a warm, dry tongue. *She seems so listless, almost depressed*, Jenny reflected. *She must be missing David.*

Inspecting Jess's feet, she began to feel a bit brighter. The damage was less severe than it had appeared on their return journey from the clearing. Ellen had helped her to bathe his paws while they had waited for Inspector Moran to arrive, and the amount of blood in the bowl had been a shock. Now that they were clean, though, they didn't look nearly as bad.

Jenny kissed Jess's nose. 'You were a star today, my boy,' she said. 'A real hero.'

Ellen came into the kitchen. 'I forgot to tell you, Jenny,' she said. 'Mrs Turner telephoned when you were out today. . .'

'How's Carrie?' Jenny said quickly, her face hopeful.

'Well,' Ellen smiled. 'Carrie has asked her mum to ask you to visit her in hospital – she's feeling much better today.'

'Oh, good!' said Jenny, jumping up. 'That's wonderful news. When can I go?'

'I'm afraid I'm really busy tomorrow,' Ellen said. 'Will the day after be all right?'

'After school? Great!' Jenny was pleased. Then her face suddenly fell. 'She'll want to know all about Orla, and how she's getting on . . . and I'm going to have to *lie* to her. I can't tell her about Orla having been hurt.'

'Best not to,' Ellen agreed. 'Perhaps you could just say that Orla seems fine, and leave it at that.'

'Poor Carrie has been longing to have a dog of her own. I couldn't bear for her to think that Orla might lose her puppies.' Jenny sighed.

Ellen slipped an arm round her and drew her in for a hug. 'I understand how you're feeling, Jenny,' she said softly. Jenny relaxed against Ellen and felt tears prickle behind her eyelids. She blinked them away.

'I'm tired,' she said. 'I think I'd like to go to bed.'

'You do that, love,' Ellen said. 'And try not to think about anything that makes you feel sad. You need a good night's rest.'

Jenny was up in her bedroom, brushing her hair, when she heard a ring on the front doorbell. She glanced at her clock. It was nine o'clock – not the sort of time anyone would pop in for a social visit. It must mean news of one kind or another, she decided. She tightened the cord of her dressing-gown and ran down the stairs in her bare feet.

She recognised the face of the young police officer that had visited Windy Hill previously. 'Hello, Constable Lucas,' she said.

'Have you got some news for us?' Mr Miles prompted, showing PC Lucas into the sitting-room. 'Inspector Moran was here earlier today and he seemed fairly certain that . . .'

'Excellent news,' the young man interrupted, his face beaming. 'Some crack detective work from the young lady here, and her dog, of course, have turned up the result we were hoping for.'

Jenny gasped. 'Really? Have you *found* David?'

'We have indeed – and he's quite safe and well.' PC Tim Lucas bent to stroke Jess, who had wandered away from his basket and come to inspect the visitor.

'Oh! That's *wonderful* news,' Ellen clasped her hands together in relief.

'Yes. Thank heavens for that.' Fraser Miles rubbed his hands through his hair and let out an enormous sigh.

'Fantastic!' Jenny shouted, clapping her hands together and startling Jess. 'And have you arrested the gang?'

'Those of them who had made camp in the old wharf building, yes. The others . . . well, it's just a matter of time. We'll round them up.'

'Where's David now?' Jenny asked eagerly.

'He's at home, with his father. He was very hungry, so I'm told, but otherwise unhurt.' PC Lucas grinned. 'And apparently he's very pleased to have you as a friend, Jenny,' he added.

Jenny laughed. 'I'll bet he's impressed that I turned up *where* I did, *when* I did,' she said.

'Very much so. And, of course, he knows that you gave us the registration number of the vehicle, and the wallet – and an accurate description of his kidnappers, too,' Tim Lucas said.

'Perhaps I should think of joining the force!' Jenny smiled.

'I think the only thing you should be thinking about right now is bed!' said Fraser Miles.

'It's been a long day.' Ellen nodded in agreement.

'OK.' Jenny grinned. A huge wave of relief washed over her. David was safe. He might even be in school tomorrow and he would tell her all about it. 'Goodnight, everyone,' she said, feeling that for the first time in a few nights she really would sleep well.

# 9

When Jenny woke up on Tuesday morning, her spirits were higher than they had been for a long time. The peculiar churning sensation in her stomach, caused by gnawing worry over David's safety, had left her at last. There was her visit to Carrie in hospital to look forward to, as well. Perhaps she would notice a big change for the better in her friend, Jenny reflected hopefully, as she dressed for school. Carrie might even be out of hospital for the start of the summer holidays, which were not far off.

Brushing her teeth, Jenny drifted off into a pleasant daydream in which she and Carrie were out walking Jess and the new puppy along the cliff path. They were heading for the beach, for a picnic, taking the little collie for his first taste of a splash in the sea.

'How lovely!' Jenny sighed dreamily, twisting her hair into a ponytail. 'How perfect it would be. *Will* be,' she chided herself. '*Will* be.'

Fiona gave a shriek of excitement that attracted more than a few curious stares when Jenny reported in a whisper that David had been rescued by the police.

'Why didn't you *ring* me?' she asked, hopping up and down.

'It was too late,' Jenny said, shifting her heavy schoolbag to the other shoulder. 'I was unbelievably tired, too. But it's great, isn't it?'

'Just imagine!' said Fiona, who seemed struck by the brilliance of their joint detective work. 'If we hadn't followed Jess into the wilderness, and he hadn't found that horrible watery ditch thing that we hid in, we might never have heard the men talking about where they were going to take David . . . and . . .'

'And they might still be searching for him now,' Jenny finished triumphantly. 'Good, isn't it?'

'Brilliant,' she agreed. She looked around. 'Is he

at school, do you know? David?'

'I haven't seen him. Ellen said we should leave him alone for a bit, but I might go round after school today and see him.'

'Does he know about Orla's accident?' Fiona asked with a grimace.

Jenny shook her head. 'Not unless his dad has said anything, but I expect he won't want to worry David with *that* kind of news just yet.'

'Are you going to tell him?' Fiona asked.

'Well, I'll have to really, won't I? But I'm not going to say anything to Carrie. She's got enough problems to cope with at the moment,' Jenny said wisely.

'You're going to . . . lie to Carrie?'

'Yes,' Jenny was determined. 'If I have to, I will. There goes the bell. Fi, do you want to come with me to see David later?'

'I can't.' She wrinkled her nose. 'It's Tuesday. I've got a piano lesson. Yuck.'

'Oh, right . . .' Jenny laughed. 'Well, I'll phone you and tell you how he is, OK?'

Fiona went ahead of her into the classroom. 'OK,' she said. 'Don't worry about how late it is, just ring me. And be sure to tell him I think he's very brave.'

Jenny raised an arm in a cheery wave to her father

as she cycled out of gates to Windy Hill. Below her, to the left, she could see Nell and Jake streaking across the field, weaving expertly in and out of a flock of sheep that had strayed to the furthest boundaries of their land. She could hear the shrill of the whistle that gave the dogs their cue to round up the flock and bring them in for dipping.

Gathering speed, she automatically looked round for Jess, then remembered her pledge to force the collie to rest. He had looked at her pleadingly, pawing at the kitchen door and yapping purposefully, but though she was tempted, Jenny hadn't given in. 'The summer holidays are nearly here,' she told him. 'And then there'll be millions of long walks — but not today. Look after Orla, Jess.'

Now, as she rounded the curve in the unmade road and saw the Fergussons' bungalow ahead, her heart skipped a beat. The police constable had said that David hadn't been hurt during his ordeal, but what if he had been in some way traumatised by his kidnapping and didn't want to see her?

Jenny wished she had had the sense to telephone before leaving Windy Hill. She knocked with a little rat-a-tat-tat, which she hoped sounded friendly, and the door was opened almost immediately by David.

Jenny's fears vanished as she saw him smile.

'Wow! It's you,' he grinned. 'My heroine. Come in.'

'Heroine?' said Jenny, wrinkling her nose. 'I'm no heroine. I almost died of fright. It's Jess you want to thank.' She followed him into the sitting-room.

'Where is he?' David asked eagerly, looking past her, expecting Jess to be following.

'Not here,' Jenny shook her head. 'I didn't bring him. His paws were hurt when he tried to chase the car, and the cuts opened up again yesterday. He's at home, resting.'

'And Orla?' David's eyes were shining. 'Dad told me she was staying at your place, so, thanks for that. How's she getting on?'

'This is nice,' Jenny looked around, changing the subject. The front room was very tiny, but boasted a big bay window which provided a panoramic view of the pale blue sea. 'It's like being in a ship!' Jenny exclaimed. She turned to David. 'How are you?'

'I'm fine – a bit tired. I guess it's from the shock – I thought my last hours had come out there in that smelly old shack. It was horrible.' He flopped onto the sofa, and Jenny sat down opposite him.

'I can imagine,' she said sympathetically.

'I couldn't believe my eyes when Jess, and you, came flying out of the bush . . . it was *great!*' David smiled. 'I owe you one, Jen.' There was a bruise on his temple and a cut on his lip, but other than that he looked the same as he always had.

'Fiona says to tell you that she thinks you were very brave,' Jenny reported.

'Did you tell her everything? David asked. 'I'm sure everyone at school must be talking about it.'

'No,' Jenny said. 'Nobody knows anything about it. They all thought you were sick – except Fiona, because she was with me.'

'What?' David looked puzzled. 'Really? At the shack?'

'Yep.' Jenny grinned. 'We were out walking Jess when he picked up the scent of the men and became determined that Fiona and I should follow him! So we did.'

'Fiona was hiding, watching everything?'

Jenny nodded. 'I would have stayed hidden, too, if Jess hadn't taken it into his head to try and rescue you by attacking what's-his-name . . . Dylan. And when I saw the knife in that man Ken's hand!' Outrage still surged through Jenny when she pictured Ken's fist gripping the glinting blade, poised above the spine of her beloved dog. 'David,' she said suddenly, 'didn't you *know*? About your father, I mean?'

'I had guessed some of it,' he replied, shrugging. 'It was all a bit weird when we had to leave England in such a hurry to come here. All Dad would say was that I was not allowed to talk about my life in any detail, to anyone. He was so secretive, and . . . nervous, but I understand now that he thought he'd be putting me in danger by telling me what was really going on. To be honest, I was too upset about Mum to care much at the time.'

Jenny nodded, knowing just how that felt.

'And I might have told someone, if I'd known. It's hard *not* to, isn't it?' David asked.

'Yes, hard to keep such a big secret,' Jenny agreed. She paused, then asked, 'What shall I call you now by the way – David or Douglas?'

He shrugged. 'To be honest I'm used to being called David now. Everyone around here knows me as that. I prefer it to Douglas anyway.'

'Oh, good. It would have been difficult to start calling you a different name.' Jenny grinned. 'Will you be moving back to England now that this is all over?'

'I don't think so,' David grinned. 'We like it here – in spite of everything – and my dad has been offered a proper job, too.'

'Oh, that's good. Where?'

'Well, you know he loves wildlife? All animals, actually – that's why he worked for the RSPCA in England. He's going to work as a wildlife conservationist right here on the Scottish Borders.' David looked pleased.

'Remember how we first met?' Jenny mused. 'The day that Jess discovered that oil-covered puffin and your father took us out to rescue the birds on Puffin Island?'

'I can't believe all the things that have happened already since we've known each other.' David laughed.

'There'll be more to come, I'm sure,' said Jenny.

'Starting with the arrival of a litter of Orla and Jess's pups!' David said excitedly.

'Um . . . David,' Jenny began. She coughed and pushed her hair away from her face. 'I haven't got very good news about Orla, I'm afraid.'

David sat up straight, his face suddenly serious. 'What?' he said. 'What do you mean?'

'Didn't you realise that she was struck by the car as it sped away from the green on Sunday?' Jenny said softly.

David stood up, his hands flew to cover his mouth.

'She's fine!' Jenny said quickly, alarmed at how pale he'd gone. 'Honestly, she's doing quite well . . . resting.

It broke two of her ribs, that's all.'

'I heard Jess and Orla barking after they'd pushed me into the back of the car. But my head was in that sack, and Dylan was practically sitting on me . . . I never *felt* anything . . .'

'They hit her sideways, as she tried to cross in front of the car,' Jenny explained. 'It was . . . horrible!'

'Dad didn't say a word! I should have gone to her the moment I was out of there!' David shook his head. 'That's so typical!' He was suddenly angry. 'He never tells me—' He broke off, as the ringing of the telephone cut into his thoughts. He strode away to answer it, asking her as he went, 'But what about the *puppies*, Jenny?'

Jenny didn't get a chance to answer.

'Mrs Miles!' she heard David say. 'Yes, she's here with me. Really? Oh! . . . that's fantastic. She's going to be all right, isn't she? Yes, yes, we'll come over immediately. Thanks. Goodbye.'

'Orla?' Jenny's heart had begun to pound as she sprang to her feet. 'The puppies . . .?'

'Yes! Ellen called Mr Palmer out to Windy Hill. Orla is having her puppies *now*!'

David cycled furiously fast, leaning forward into the wind as though he was trying to win a race, and

Jenny was hard-pressed to keep up with him.

'Slow down!' she pleaded. 'Mr Palmer's there to help her. She'll be fine.'

But David flew on towards Windy Hill, his curly hair pressed against his scalp by his speed, his knuckles white on the handlebars.

Jenny was out of breath when they finally pulled up outside the back door. She hurried to dismount and open the door and David pushed ahead, calling, 'Mrs Miles? We're here – have we missed anything?'

Ellen looked grave as she came to meet them in the porch. 'No,' she said, and gave a big sigh. 'The poor lass is having a wee bit of a battle . . .'

Jenny and Ellen exchanged glances as David stepped into the kitchen. Mr Palmer was kneeling on the floor beside the collie, listening intently, with his stethoscope poised over her heart. Orla raised her head and, at the sight of her master, began to wag her tail weakly.

'Orla!' breathed David and dropped to his haunches. He put out a hand, hesitantly, and smoothed her soft head. The collie looked steadily at David, her sad eyes never leaving his face.

'Mr Palmer . . .?' David whispered.

'David, lad . . .' replied the vet briskly. 'You're not to go getting your hopes up now, do you hear me?

402

I'm going to do all I can for her, but, if she can't manage it, I'm going to have to take her in to the surgery.'

'But . . . are the puppies all right, Mr Palmer?' Jenny hardly dared to ask the question.

'So far, lass, I think I can feel movement, which is a good sign,' he assured her.

Jenny reached out for Ellen's hand. 'Where's Dad?' she whispered.

'I sent him to find the whelping box he used for Nell. I'm certain he told me it was stored away in one of the sheds.' She squeezed Jenny's fingers and answered the question that she knew would come next. 'I've put Jess in the sitting-room,' she smiled. 'He was behaving very much like an expectant father – pacing around and getting in everyone's way.'

'According to my dates,' Mr Palmer was saying, 'Orla is slightly early having her litter. The normal gestation period is sixty-three days in a dog, but she's only gone sixty; that's fine, but the pups might be a bit on the weak side.'

Jenny watched as Mr Palmer began to clip away the long white hair on Orla's lower body, cleaning and tidying the area to prepare for the arrival of the puppies.

Orla was becoming increasingly nervous. She

tried to get up and yelped in pain as she did so. She flopped back down again and began to pant heavily.

'Oh, poor girl,' murmured David, his eyes like saucers.

'I'll give her something for the pain, now,' Tom Palmer said. 'I would think her whelping is imminent,' he added. 'Her temperature is below 37.8 centigrade.'

'Is that serious?' David asked.

'Normal, laddie,' Mr Palmer assured him. 'Quite normal.'

And suddenly Orla began to strain. As she did so, she whimpered, her head whipping round to lick at her wounded ribs.

'Oh, poor girl,' David said again.

Jenny had her fingers crossed tightly behind her back. *Please*, she begged silently. *Oh, please let the puppies be all right.*

Time passed slowly as Orla heaved and strained, with no result. After fifty minutes, Tom Palmer shook his head. 'I'm not going to let her go any longer than an hour,' he announced. 'If she can't deliver soon, I'll sedate her and take her in.'

Jenny glanced at David. He was biting his lower lip, his eyes fixed helplessly on his dog. Mr Palmer began to prepare to sedate the collie. 'It will have to be a Caesarean operation. It will make things easier for her,' he decided, looking up at David. 'I think the pain is stopping her from contracting successfully and—'

'Mr Palmer! Look!' Jenny shouted. Orla had shuddered and, in that second, a tiny membranous sac slipped away from her body and onto the blanket.

'Aha!' said the vet happily. 'Here we go, then! Good girl. Now, stand back everybody – well back – that's it. Let her have some peace.' Orla began to remove the soft sac with a gentle tongue and then clean her puppy.

Jenny and Ellen, with David between them, huddled on the other side of the room while Mr Palmer stood behind Orla, keeping a close eye on proceedings. The puppies tumbled free of her, trailing their little umbilical cords. Orla sniffed interestedly at each tiny bundle, nosing it over and licking hesitantly. She seemed surprised, and to have temporarily forgotten about the pain in her side.

Jenny clutched David's sleeve during what seemed like an agony of waiting to know whether the puppies were going to be healthy enough to survive. When Mr Palmer had counted four puppies he announced that he suspected that was the lot.

'Are they all alive?' Ellen asked, putting into words

the question that was making Jenny's heart race.

'I'll just check . . .' Mr Palmer examined each pup in turn. They had started to breathe, snuffling and making small mewling sounds that made Jenny want to rush forward and gather them protectively into her arms. But she held back, knowing that it was right that David be the first to enjoy Orla's litter.

'How marvellous! They all seem quite well, if on the small side,' Mr Palmer said. 'This one's a girl,' he said, as he examined the underside of the minute puppy. 'Ah, another girl . . . and yet another girl!'

As relieved as she was that the puppies had been

born alive and unscathed by Orla's accident, Jenny felt a small stab of disappointment. Carrie had so badly wanted a boy puppy.

Mr Palmer picked up the last of the litter and carefully turned it over.

'And the last one is . . . yes, it's a wee boy!'

'Oh, thank goodness!' said Jenny. 'Oh, how lucky! How lovely! I can't believe it.' She threw her arms round Ellen, who hugged her back.

'That's Carrie's pup,' Jenny said. 'That's Charlie – Carrie's gorgeous little Charlie.'

# 10

Jenny hadn't realised how long she had sat watching Orla with her puppies until Ellen switched on the lights in the kitchen and began to set the table for supper. Reluctantly, she left the four tiny, determined little Border collies that suckled so eagerly from their proud mum, and went to help her.

'They're perfect,' she sighed. 'Aren't they, Ellen?'

'Wonderful,' she smiled. 'Who would have thought Orla could have produced four such healthy pups after the terrible knock she had?'

Jenny looked over at Jess. He lay on his tummy, his tail straight out behind him, looking at the crawling creatures in the whelping box with undisguised fascination. He had been kept apart from Orla, on the orders of Tom Palmer, but had been allowed to view the feeding and cleaning of his offspring from a safe distance.

'You never know,' the vet had warned. 'It sometimes happens that the bitch will attack the male after giving birth. She might see him as a threat to the lives of her puppies.'

Jenny felt she knew differently, but didn't argue. For the time being, Jess seemed content just to look, and every time one of the pups made a tiny squealing sound, his ears pricked up and he cocked his head. Jenny had slipped an old cushion into the wooden box in which Orla lay, and the collie rested against it drowsily, looking up at Jess from time to time.

'Clever boy,' Jenny soothed him. 'You're a dad, now.'

She took the cutlery Ellen handed her. 'I wish . . .' she began, and then felt she was being a bit selfish and stopped.

'What do you wish?' Ellen prompted.

'I know I've got Jess and everything,' she said, 'but I'd *love* to be able to keep a puppy.'

'Here we go again!' Ellen laughed. 'Your dad told

me how determined you were to keep Jess after his birth!'

'But these are Jess's *children*!' Jenny insisted. 'It seems such a shame . . .'

'Well, Mr Fergusson has already found homes for one or two of the females, hasn't he?' Ellen asked, as she put a jug of water of the table. 'And Carrie is going to have the boy.'

'Charlie,' Jenny said, and smiled, adding, 'I suppose you're right.'

'I'm going to ring Mrs Turner to ask her the best time to visit the hospital tomorrow. I'll give her the good news about . . . Charlie, shall I?'

'Oh, yes,' said Jenny happily. 'She'll be so pleased.'

'Supper ready?' asked Fraser Miles, padding into the kitchen in his socks. 'I'm starving.' He glanced over to where Orla lay. 'What a fine whelping box,' he complimented himself.

'It is, Dad,' Jenny smiled. 'Thanks for finding it, and cleaning it out and everything. Orla's very happy in there.'

'Supper won't be long,' Ellen said. 'I've got a phone call to make.'

'How long's she staying? The mother dog, I mean?' Mr Miles asked, opening up the evening newspaper and beginning to browse through it.

'Orla, Dad,' Jenny said. 'Her name's Orla. And she can't be moved until her ribs are mended. As you can see, she's rather busy at the moment!'

Jenny laughed as she saw one of the puppies roll over onto its back, all four, snow-white feet in the air. She loved the milky smell of them, and their screwed up little faces, and the snuffling noises they made.

'Well!' said Ellen, coming back into the kitchen from the hall. 'Carrie's mum has suggested we take Charlie to the hospital for a visit to his owner-to-be!'

'Charlie who?' said Jenny's dad, glancing up.

Jenny gave an exasperated sigh. 'Charlie is the name of the puppy *Carrie*'s going to have, Dad,' she said. She turned back to Ellen. 'I think that's a great idea! Could we? Would we be allowed?'

'It seems Mrs Turner has had permission from the oncologist, and Carrie's ward sister, too. A special little room has been set aside for the visit.'

'Oh, wow!' Jenny clapped her hands with excitement.

'It will mean it will have to be a brief visit, Jenny,' Ellen cautioned. 'The puppy won't want to be separated from Orla for very long.'

'OK,' she said.

'David Fergusson gone home yet?' Mr Miles looked idly round the kitchen. 'I thought he was never going to be able to leave.'

'Poor David,' said Jenny. 'He has to go home and I get to spend time with the puppies. It doesn't seem fair.'

'Is he going to be allowed to keep one?' Mr Miles asked.

Jenny shrugged. 'I don't think so.' Suddenly, she looked at her watch. 'Oh, is it too late to phone Fiona? I promised I would – and in all the excitement, I forgot.'

Ellen smiled. 'Go on, then,' she said. 'I'll put the food on the table.'

Imagining Carrie's reaction to her new puppy, Jenny was distracted throughout the school day. She was in a fever of anticipation to get to the hospital and see her friend's face light up in a smile of delight as she cradled Charlie in her arms.

She sat with David and Fiona at break, describing to them every detail of each of the puppies, making Fiona groan with longing. 'I want one!' she cried. 'When can I come and see them?'

'Not today,' Jenny replied. 'I'm taking Charlie to Greybridge Hospital after school.'

For Jenny, the day couldn't end soon enough. She ran up the hill from the bus stop and burst in on Ellen, who was doing the ironing. 'I'm here,' she sang, flinging her schoolbag into a corner. 'I'm ready.'

Ellen chuckled. 'So I see. Right . . . do you want to change?'

'No. Let's just *go!*' Jenny put her arms round Jess and gave him a cuddle, as Ellen found the keys to the pick-up. 'How are your feet?' She peered at the underside of each of the collie's front paws. 'Good. Much better. We'll soon be able to go for a walk.'

'Wrap Charlie in this blanket,' Ellen advised. 'And hold him close to your heart so he can feel it beating. That'll give him comfort.'

Gingerly, Jenny reached out and lifted the tiny puppy. His paws splayed out and he squeaked in protest. Then, feeling the surrounding warmth of the soft blanket, he gave a little sigh and settled back to sleep.

'Orla's just fed them,' Ellen commented. 'So our timing is perfect. He won't be hungry for a while.'

Charlie seemed unconcerned by the jolting of the farm truck. He dozed peacefully in Jenny's arms all the way into Greybridge and she found it almost impossible not to disturb him by kissing his silky head.

★ ★ ★

At the hospital, Jenny and Ellen were greeted by the ward sister, who was expecting them. 'Mrs Turner has just left.' She smiled. 'She usually takes the chance to go home if visitors are coming for Carrie. It gives her a break.' She looked down into the bundle in Jenny's arms. 'Oh! The wee darling! This must be Charlie.'

Walking down the long, sanitary corridors, listening to the tapping of the sister's heels on the linoleum floor, Jenny felt as though she was carrying the most precious gift in the world. Charlie, she felt certain, was going to give her friend a reason to live; the drive to fight the terrible sickness she had battled for so long. The dozing puppy, who had cheated what might have been a cruel fate himself, had no idea how important he was.

'Here we are,' said the sister, dropping her voice to a whisper. 'We're breaking hospital rules letting the dog in here, but we're making an exception in this case.' She winked at Jenny.

The door swung open on a small room furnished like a sitting-room. There was a sofa and two big chairs and television on a table in the corner. Carrie was sitting upright, an expectant smile on her face, her hands clasped excitedly in front of her. 'Oh!

Have you brought him, Jen?' she asked.

Jenny went slowly towards Carrie and lowered her arms. 'Here he is,' she said. 'Here's your Charlie.'

Jenny felt she could almost see Carrie's heart turn over as she held the puppy against her chest. Charlie wriggled, and snuffled at Carrie's neck. He laid his warm button nose against her skin and nudged her, then Jenny saw him open his tiny mouth and begin to search for milk.

Carrie laughed, and her face came alive with the

thrill of it. The puppy's pink tongue was warm and as light as a butterfly's wing as he rooted about. Then, finding no sustenance, he gave a small belch and turned round in the blanket to present a full, fat, little tummy for Carrie's inspection.

'He's the most wonderful puppy I've ever seen,' Carrie declared. 'He's just like Jess! Look, four white feet.' She stroked him with a finger.

Jenny took a moment to look at Carrie. They were alone – Ellen and the sister hadn't yet come in. Her friend was wearing a pair of loose pyjamas and a beret that Jenny hadn't seen before. She had lost yet more weight, and the ghostly yellow tinge to her skin was still present. Disappointed, Jenny looked at Carrie's happy face, and she heard her rasping, laboured breath as she gazed adoringly at Charlie.

She began to tell Carrie about the whelping. There were things that had to be left out – Orla's injury, and how she had come to be struck by the car in the first place. Jenny felt this was an especially happy few minutes for Carrie. It would be spoiled by all the horrible details of the last, frightening few days.

'When you're well again,' she said, 'we'll teach Charlie the things that Jess knows. We'll have picnics on the beach in the summer and—'

Carrie was shaking her head, a gentle smile still on

her face. 'I don't know about that,' she said. 'I'm not sure if I'm *going* to come out of here, actually . . .

Jenny pleaded. 'Don't, Carrie . . .'

'I'm so tired,' Carrie went on, rubbing her finger rhythmically over Charlie's tummy. 'I just want it to be over, Jen, you know?' She held Jenny with clear, steady eyes.

'Over?' Jenny whispered. Her legs felt hollow and her mouth had gone dry.

'Remember the promise?' Carrie wagged a playful finger. 'If I don't make it – and all that – will you keep Charlie for me? You mustn't let him go to anyone else. You must love him as you've loved Jess – and teach him to be as wonderful as Jess is. Will you?'

The blood had begun to drain from Jenny's face and her heart to thud fearfully in her chest. She felt a terrible urge to run from the room, to blot out what Carrie was saying. But she had made a promise. To live life as Carrie would have lived it – gratefully, at a furious pace – and with great courage. She swallowed hard and smiled. 'I remember,' she said solemnly. 'And, of *course* I will!'

Charlie snuggled deeper against Carrie and gave a little sigh of contentment. She lifted him gently and kissed his head. 'Charlie,' she said softly. 'What a beautiful boy you are.' And her face lit up with the happiest smile Jenny had ever seen.

It seemed they had shared only a few minutes when the ward sister's head appeared round the door of the room. 'All right?' she asked, smiling.

'Fine,' Jenny replied steadily.

'I'm afraid you'll have to go now, Jenny lass. I want to get Carrie back to the ward and take her blood pressure.'

'Oh, so soon?'

The sister nodded.

Jenny sat beside Carrie and looked at her, willing her features to mirror the courage she could see in her friend's calm face.

'See you,' she said.

'See you,' Carrie grinned. 'And, Jen? Thanks.'

Wordlessly, Jenny lifted Charlie in his blanket. 'I wish he could stay,' she managed.

'Yes.' Carrie stood up, swayed a little and sat down with a bump.

'Oops! I've got you!' said the sister, grasping her under the arm.

'Bye, Carrie.' Jenny put her arms round Carrie's frail shoulders. Then, quickly, she turned and hurried out of the room.

She fled down the corridor, running from the terrible thought that she might never see her friend again. She found she was searching for Ellen.

'I'm here.' Ellen was beside the hot drinks dispenser. 'I've been waiting.' She put a comforting arm round Jenny, who was very pale. Ellen took the sleeping puppy from her and looked into Jenny's face.

'You didn't let Carrie see you cry, did you?' she asked gently.

'No,' Jenny whispered. 'Why didn't you stay?'

'I wanted you to have time together, just the two of you,' Ellen explained. 'I felt it was important.'

'Is Carrie going to . . .' Jenny couldn't finish the sentence.

'It's not looking too hopeful at the moment, Jenny,' Ellen spoke honestly.

'I saw it in her eyes,' Jenny said simply. 'It was a goodbye – a *for ever* goodbye.'

Jenny climbed the knoll to Darktarn Keep and sat with her back to the ancient wall, looking out over the sea. The stones pressed against her back, imparting the warmth of the sun, sinking now, and leaving a fiery path across the water.

She had walked very slowly, keeping pace with Jess. He stepped lightly. carefully, but was eager to be out and by her side. He seemed to sense her desolation and sat very close, his nose nudging and nuzzling her to offer comfort.

'I can't believe it,' Jenny spoke aloud. 'I can't believe she's not going to get well. It *can't* be true.'

But, in her heart, Jenny knew that it was true. Something she had seen in Carrie's face had convinced her of that. She knew, too, that Carrie was not afraid, and that, in her usual bold-spirited way, she had asked Jenny to visit the hospital in order to say goodbye. Her friend had let go of her struggle.

'And *I've* got to let her go, Jess,' Jenny said softly. 'And be true to the promise. I'm not going to let her down. It's the least I can do.'

For a long time she sat there, listening to the calling of the gulls as they wheeled high above the cliffs. In the quiet, she could hear the waves washing up the beach and the bleating of the sheep across the fields of Windy Hill. The sky turned pink and gold and Jenny, looking up, wondered if there *was* a place up there where people could rest in peace and comfort. It looked so beautiful, she felt sure that there was.

She felt lucky to have had Carrie as a friend. Through her friendship, she had felt herself become strong and whole.

'Come on, Jess,' Jenny stood up. 'Let's go home.'

Picking her way down the side of the hill, she saw

her father and Ellen come out into the yard below. Standing side by side, they watched her.

'Hello, lass,' Fraser Miles said gently, when Jenny reached the bottom.

'Dad?' Jenny looked from one face to the other. Ellen was holding her father's hand so tightly she could see the whites of her knuckles.

'She's gone, Jen,' he said. 'Carrie died an hour ago.'

'Yes,' Jenny nodded. 'I know.' She gave a great, shuddering gasp. 'But she's happier now.'

Ellen looked surprised, but drew Jenny into a hug and began to cry softly.

'I'm thinking about the way she smiled when she held Charlie . . . I'll always remember that smile,' her words were muffled against Ellen's shoulder. 'It was such a *happy* smile!'

'Um, about Charlie . . .' her father began.

Jenny pulled away from Ellen, blinking back her own tears. 'Yes?' she said eagerly.

'Would you like to keep him? Mr Miles asked.

'Oh, yes! I would, Dad,' Jenny smiled. '*Very* much.'

'That's settled then,' he said. 'He'll need training – I'll not have another idle mutt like Jess wasting farm time and . . .'

'Dad!' Jenny was outraged, and then she saw that her father was laughing.

'Only joking, lass,' he said, gathering Jenny up into his arms. She snuggled against the rough wool of his jumper and laid her head there for a second. She thought she was going to cry – cry and cry until her heart snapped in two – but Carrie's smile came up clear and bright in her mind once again.

'Jess! she cried. 'We're going to keep Charlie! Come on, let's go and tell him.'

And she broke free of her father and raced towards the kitchen, her faithful Border collie at her heels.

*Another Hodder Children's book*

**PUP AT THE PALACE**
**Animal Ark Holiday 10**

*Lucy Daniels*

*Mandy Hopes loves animals more than anything else. She knows quite a lot about them too: both her parents are vets and Mandy helps out in their surgery, Animal Ark.*

Mandy and her family join a village trip to London during the summer holidays. There's lots to see, but on a visit to Buckingham Palace on their first day, Mandy spots a cute labrador puppy, who poses for her camera, then runs off. Sightings of the puppy all over town confuse Mandy – until she reads about a missing *litter* of pups in the paper. Can Mandy help track them all down?

*Another Hodder Children's book*

## PANDA IN THE PARK
### Animal Ark in Danger, 38

*Lucy Daniels*

*Mandy Hope's mum is spending some time abroad with a wildlife conservation organisation – and Mandy and James have been offered the chance of a lifetime: to stay with Mrs Hope during the school holidays and help protect endangered animals!*

Soon after their arrival in China, Mandy and James spot a lone panda cub near the research park they are visiting. Mrs Hope warns them that the mother panda might reject her baby if they are apart for long. It's vital that the cub and his mother are quickly reunited if he is to be saved. And time is running out . . .

**TIGER ON THE TRACK**
**Animal Ark in Danger, 39**

*Lucy Daniels*

*Mandy Hope's mum is spending some time abroad with a wildlife conservation organisation – and Mandy and James have been offered the chance of a lifetime: to stay with Mrs Hope during the school holidays and help protect endangered animals!*

Mandy and James are visiting a tiger reserve in India, when the mother of young tigers, Bada and Chhota, goes missing. Other tigers have disappeared too, and poachers are suspected. Mandy and James are determined to help track down the real culprits. But is it too late to save the missing tigers?

**GORILLA IN THE GLADE**
**Animal Ark in Danger, 40**

*Lucy Daniels*

*Mandy Hope's mum is spending some time abroad with a wildlife conservation organisation – and Mandy and James have been offered the chance of a lifetime: to stay with Mrs Hope during the school holidays and help protect endangered animals!*

While visiting the Kahuzi National Park in Central Africa, Mandy and James help look after Jojo, an adorable baby gorilla who has been abandoned by his mother. Another female gorilla, with a newborn baby of her own, has been picked out as a potential surrogate mum. But will she be willing to take Jojo on?